D0825572

Also by Dawn Ryder

Dangerous to Know

Dare You to Run

Deep Into Trouble

Take to the Limit

Close to the Edge

DON'T LOOK BACK

DAWN RYDER

St. Martin's Paperbacks

This is a work of fiction. All of the characters, organizations, and events portrayed in this novel are either products of the author's imagination or are used fictitiously.

DON'T LOOK BACK

Copyright © 2018 by Dawn Ryder.

For information address St. Martin's Press, 175 Fifth Avenue, New York, NY 10010.

ISBN: 978-1-250-13274-1

Our books may be purchased in bulk for promotional, educational, or business use. Please contact your local bookseller or the Macmillan Corporate and Premium Sales Department at 1-800-221-7945, ext. 5442, or by e-mail at MacmillanSpecialMarkets@macmillan.com.

Printed in the United States of America

St. Martin's Paperbacks edition / September 2018

St. Martin's Paperbacks are published by St. Martin's Press, 175 Fifth Avenue, New York, NY 10010.

10 9 8 7 6 5 4 3 2 1

CHAPTER ONE

"You're doing it wrong, brother," Saxon Hale said as he slapped Vitus Hale on the shoulder.

Vitus sent Saxon a hard look. "Fuck off."

Saxon only grinned at Vitus's response, but there was a snort from Damascus Hale. She sent her husband a stern look designed to reprimand him. "Don't teach our daughter profanity."

"She's a little young to pick up words, princess," Vitus replied as he tried to adjust the way he was cradling his newborn daughter. The infant let out a little sound, earning a frown from Vitus. The assembled family members laughed at his expense.

"Babies absorb far more language than you realize," Damascus informed Vitus.

Miranda Delacroix cooed to the baby as she lifted her from Vitus's arms. "She's perfect . . . ," the new grandmother gushed.

It was a private gathering.

Pullman looked through the scope of his rifle,

lining up the crosshairs on Miranda Delacroix Ryland.

It would be easy to drop the Congress hopeful right there among her kin. Which was fortuitous, considering he'd been paid a lot of money to put a bullet through her head, and there was even a bonus if he got the job done quickly.

He lifted his head though and relaxed his hand, removing his finger from the trigger. It wasn't that he had any remorse about hitting his target while she was attending a christening for her grandchild.

He was a hitman; it was what he did.

A lack of concern went with the job. It was sort of a requirement.

But in this case, he settled for lifting up a camera and snapping pictures of the location. Saxon Hale and his team of Shadow Ops agents had been off the grid for over a year now. The top-secret location was referred to as the "nest."

The intel might have value on the black market.

It wasn't the job he was on, but a wise man never lets an opportunity go untried. Pullman indulged in a grin as he watched the family group. Sure, they looked pretty normal, until the high-powered lens on his camera started catching sight of chest harnesses and rifles stored on the sides of the buildings. There was a cute little vintage house, surrounded by a graveyard of cars and trucks rusting away. The twisted mass of metal was a smokescreen for the Cold War–era missile silo being refurbished two hundred yards behind the house.

Patience was key to success. The right time and the right place, essential to performance. At least the sort of performance Pullman was interested in being known for. A clean kill, no evidence for law enforcement to find and follow back to the person who had paid for the hit.

Pullman lowered his camera, watching as the christening ceremony got started. Vitus and Damascus Hale handed their infant daughter over to the selected godparents. Saxon Hale and Ginger Hale stood in their places as Colonel Bryan Magnus officiated.

Miranda stood off to one side, smiling like the proud grandmother she was.

Carl Davis would want Pullman to put a slug in Miranda right there.

But Carl Davis was an idiot. A vindictive one, too. Pullman avoided adding the word "evil" because he was working for the guy and couldn't get too picky about the way he made his income.

Pullman grunted and looked forward to finishing his job for the presidential hopeful Carl Davis because when the job was done, he would be free to have a beer. Pullman never drank while on a job. Being a hitman was becoming more challenging as the modern age made staying faceless far harder than it had ever been before.

There was no way Pullman would be stupid enough to drop Miranda Ryland while she was standing on a Shadow Ops location. Sure, it looked like a mess. A construction site just underway. Only a fool would buy that story.

Saxon and Vitus Hale were ex-SEALs. And they weren't the only seasoned operators attending the christening.

Colonel Bryan Magnus had an impressive service record, too, and there were other Shadow Ops agents as well.

Nope. No way was Pullman going to drop her there, even if he suspected Carl Davis just might want him to compromise the nest location as a nice added bonus.

Carl wasn't paying for that service, and Pullman never worked for free. If Carl wanted the Shadow Ops teams uprooted because they felt they were compromised, he'd have to shell out the cash.

So far, Carl had only paid for Miranda Delacroix to be dropped.

He'd do the job. But when the timing was right. He couldn't spend the money if he were in prison or dead. And Carl wouldn't mind a bit if he were killed trying to escape. Not that Pullman held it against Carl—the guy was paying a hitman to take out a rival, so expecting morality would be foolish.

Pullman shouldered his rifle and began trekking his way back through the forest that surrounded the area. He pulled a hat down on his head, looking like any of a dozen locals who were out hunting.

He'd get Miranda a little later. When she was away from the secret location. It would preserve his ability to sell the pictures of the site. If the Congress hopeful went down too close to it, the Shadow Ops team would abandon it and set up another location.

Planning was always key.

Vitus Hale had two places he called home.

He grinned for a moment as he watched the people on the sidewalk in Washington, D.C.

Only two—boy, marriage had domesticated him.

His wife, Damascus, would give him a look if she heard his sarcasm, but then again, she'd known what he was when they fell in love.

You mean you made the ultimate mistake of falling in love with your package . . .

He had, and he still wasn't sorry, either. Sure, there had been a year when he'd thought Damascus had chosen her rich father's lifestyle over him, but that was history now.

Yup.

Not that falling in love meant he was going to start reporting to a cubical every day.

Vitus caught sight of his section leader. Kagan didn't make it too easy. Vitus caught a glimpse of him in his peripheral vision. He held himself steady for a moment, making sure no one was watching him, before he moved off to where Kagan was settling down on a park bench.

Vitus moved slowly, stopping a few other places before sitting beside Kagan.

"It's too quiet," Kagan began.

Vitus gave his section leader a single nod but held silent. Kagan wasn't just his superior because someone had promoted him. No, Kagan was a man Vitus followed because he'd earned it. Kagan didn't talk often, and he didn't give away his motive, either. In short, Kagan was worth listening to, especially when he'd called Vitus for a meeting.

"Carl should have put his people on dealing with us threatening him," Kagan continued.

"My bet is, he has," Vitus responded. "This aide of his, Eric Geyer, seems to know how to keep a lid on what he's doing."

"That's what I'm concerned about," Kagan said with a hard look toward Vitus. "Tyler Martin might have been one of us, but his failing was his need to be recognized for his work."

Vitus's lips twitched. "Tyler liked to wear his I-was-there ribbons, sure enough."

Kagan's expression cracked for a second at Vitus's description of military medals. In the world of Shadow Ops teams, Vitus fit right in because he didn't care what people thought of him. He didn't need a medal to prove his worth, and he didn't flash the ones he'd earned around. No, he found his confidence deep inside himself, where he damn well knew the value of the service he'd done for his country and mankind.

Tyler Martin had been weak enough to need confirmation from the people around him.

"I assigned Dare Servant to a new location in case we need a plan B," Kagan continued. "My guess is, Carl won't be wise enough to take our warning."

Vitus enjoyed a flashback. They'd replaced Carl Davis's personal security and faced him down inside one of his plush presidential hotel suites. He'd been scared. In fact, Vitus doubted Carl had ever tasted fear quite that intense before. They could have killed him; they'd had plenty of reason to. Carl had charged Tyler Martin with killing Vitus and his brother, Saxon, as well as members of their teams.

More than once they'd overcome the odds.

Vitus savored the knowledge. But he wasn't foolish enough to overlook the fact that his victories were salt in Carl Davis's wounds.

"Miranda took a chance in giving us that tape she made," Kagan added. "Carl will want his pound of flesh. This campaign is the perfect cover for him to have a hitman take her out."

"I've been watching her," Vitus said.

"I know," Kagan offered dryly. "Officially, I don't have a reason to assign a team to her."

"Unless you want to confess that we threatened Carl Davis," Vitus said, offering his section leader a smirk.

"A warning," Kagan corrected him. "One none of us expects him to take . . ."

"But we made the effort," Vitus said. Yeah, they'd made the effort because they were men of honor. People used the word lightly too often for his peace of mind, but he'd found the sort of men and women who understood the true meaning in it among the SEALs and Shadow Ops. Kagan was a hard man who'd made tough choices, but Vitus followed his command because he knew without a shred of doubt that his section leader was motivated by integrity.

That was why they hadn't killed Carl Davis when they'd had the chance.

"Stay sharp," Kagan advised him with a knowing look. "It's going to hit the fan. Soon. Leave your family underground."

Vitus nodded, acknowledging the warning. "They're back under Colonel Magnus's command."

Kagan drew in a deep breath. "Bryan Magnus knows what to do if Carl takes us out."

Vitus felt his body shift. It was a slight tensing of the muscles with a tingle rippling along his spine. He was no stranger to the sensation, the only thing new to the situation was the fact that now he had a wife and daughter. On over a hundred missions with the SEALs, he'd taken the ultimate risk with his life. It had been his drug of choice, the need to put boot to ass for justice. Damascus might accept who he was, but there was still a little hollow feeling settling into the pit of his stomach as he saw the look on Kagan's face.

They were going to war. Only this time, it was on home soil.

At least his section leader thought so, and Vitus couldn't fault his logic.

"Shadow Miranda," Kagan said. "I've got Sinclair off grid in case we need her as a resource."

"Am I officially on a case?"

"At the moment there is no case," Kagan said, giving him a tilt of his head. "Officially, you're waiting for assignment." Kagan shot him a hard look. "Be ready for the call."

"Yes, sir."

They parted ways. Vitus moved through the crowded streets of the capital before ducking into a doorway and disappearing into an underground network of tunnels few civilians knew about. Hell, there were plenty of FBI and CIA agents who didn't know what lay beneath the pavement. Deep below the traffic-clogged streets, Vitus pressed his palm and let his retina be scanned before entering a facility that contained some of the most dangerous viruses on the planet. His wife worked daily in an effort to make sure they were prepared to deal with bio-attacks. It meant working with the viruses, and that was done where an accident could never leak out into the population.

Damascus had signed on in an effort to escape her father's plans to have her marry Carl Davis. Underground, Vitus was free to allow his lips to curve up. He'd enjoyed stealing his princess away by winning her heart. Her father hadn't made it easy, but, hell, Vitus had never been a fan of taking the easy path in life.

He made his way to the small center where his daughter was being cared for. She had her fist in her mouth, sucking on it, as he nodded to the day care personnel before gently scooping the infant up.

Life was a precious thing.

And a magical one.

He'd never realized how amazing it might be to hold his child.

Carl Davis had better heed their warning, because the next time Carl made a play against them, Vitus was going to kill him. The stakes were too high now.

Which meant he was going to have to step outside the lines of protocol.

"Be ready for the call."

There was a mountain of meaning in Kagan's words. Vitus held on to his daughter for a few more precious seconds before he forced himself into action. Being ready meant making sure he had every assist he could manage.

It also meant doing right by family.

He made his way into the small suite he shared with his wife and pulled a prepaid phone out of his pocket. Miranda Delacroix was his mother-in-law.

She was also Dunn Bateson's natural mother.

Vitus didn't know the man well. Of course, no one really did from what Vitus could tell. Dunn was a recluse who seemed to enjoy casting his aura of mystery. He certainly invested a lot of cash in keeping the paparazzi guessing on just where he was.

But Vitus had a number to reach him.

Vitus hesitated for a long moment. In the end, though, it was the lingering feeling of having his daughter in his hands that made him push the dial button on the phone.

Family was worth everything a man had in him to give. Not every man lived by that code, but Vitus knew Dunn did.

Miranda was his mother.

"Vitus Hale," Dunn answered on the third ring. "How can I bail your Shadow Ops team out today?"

There was a hint of a smirk coming through the line. Vitus enjoyed the brassy humor the Scotsman seemed to have an endless supply of.

"It's payback time," Vitus began. "I'm calling to give you a heads-up. Unofficially."

There was silence for a moment. "I'm listening," Dunn replied, all hints of teasing gone.

Dunn didn't disappoint him by drawing out the conversation. Vitus was left looking at his phone after Dunn ended the call just three minutes later.

No, Dunn wasn't going to waste time chatting. Miranda might have been forced to give birth to him in secret by her powerful political family because they wouldn't have the scandal of her having a child with a man they didn't approve of, but Dunn wasn't going to stand by idly while his mother might be on a hitman's list.

Was that what Kagan had meant by making sure Vitus had his resources in line?

Actually, Vitus did think Kagan had wanted him to call Dunn. His section leader couldn't do it. No, there were too many eyes on him.

But what Vitus did when he wasn't on a case, well, that was no one's business. It was the unspoken element that kept their Shadow Ops teams as effective as they were. It was also the thing so many hopeful recruits tried to get a grasp on but failed.

You either understood or you didn't, and that comprehension was a must for the men and women Kagan put Shadow Ops badges into the hands of. They took the cases no one wanted. Dealt with the criminals who won too damn often.

Dunn wasn't one of them.

And yet, he was by way of stepping up when he'd been needed. The guy liked his privacy though, living as a recluse, and he had enough money to help him pull it off well enough to have Vitus admiring him.

Dunn was the sort of ace in the hole they needed. The asset Carl Davis wouldn't see in play on the board. He'd been involved in operations before, but he was also a master of the art of being a recluse. He'd never left a trail, which meant Carl and his people wouldn't be looking for him.

Dunn Bateson stood gazing out of his office windows. Vitus Hale wasn't a man given to hype.

Dunn heard Vitus's words ringing in his ears. There was also a strange tingle going down his spine. Edinburgh was a place known for spirits and supernatural happenings. Tonight, Dunn found himself caught in a moment of contemplation that just might have been crafted by the hands of fate.

Miranda was his mother. Vitus had pegged him perfectly. Something Dunn would give the American full credit for achieving. Not many men could read him so well.

Maybe it was the connection of Vitus being married to his half sister, Damascus.

Dunn looked down at his phone and realized he

was hesitating. Miranda's number was illuminated
on the screen, waiting for him to push the dial function key.

He hated that he was still wondering if he should
reach out to her.

"Yer mother loved you, son . . . never doubt it . . ."

His father's words rose from his memory.

"She loved me . . ."

Duncan Bateson had insisted his son should know
the truth once he was old enough.

*"Miranda wanted to marry me, ran away with me,
but her family, they vowed to destroy everything I had
if she didn't return to them. I could have lived without
money, but what sort of son would I be to allow such a
thing to happen to my father?"*

His father's crusty face had twisted with a grief Dunn
hadn't imagined his sire could ever feel. Not Duncan
Miles Bateson, the icon of Bateson Industries.

And yet, Dunn recalled in vivid detail the way his
father's eyes had actually turned glassy with unshed
tears.

He'd loved her until the day he died.

And Miranda? She'd come to see Dunn the moment
her husband was dead.

Dunn pressed the button and held the phone up to
his ear.

"Dunn?" Miranda's voice came across the line, the
happiness undiminished by the miles between them.
"It's so . . . wonderful to have you calling me . . ."

The joy in her tone made him hesitate.

There was another first. Miranda seemed to have a
talent for giving the men in the Bateson family pause.

"Dunn?" Miranda asked softly.

"I'm here," he replied, battling a very unexpected reluctance to speak his mind. The empire he'd inherited from his father and grandfather was his to command. Yet Miranda was managing to tongue-tie him. It was a novel feeling, one he'd thought himself immune to. "I know you feel the need to do the right thing. But there are some men you should avoid crossing."

"You've had a call from my son-in-law, it would seem." Miranda's voice gained intensity. There was now a core of strength in her tone that made Dunn's lips twitch. It would seem his father hadn't been the only parent to pass a solid spine on to him.

"Miranda—" Dunn began.

"I am not a coward," Miranda informed him sternly. But her tone softened as she explained. "I realize you have good reason to doubt me on the matter. Believe me, Dunn, I would have stood up to my father if I was the only one he could lash out at. But he would have destroyed your father and grandfather. I couldn't allow it to happen to your grandfather. I simply couldn't stand by and see him become what he considered a failure. My family had the power to strangle your grandfather's business."

"That was a long time ago," Dunn answered her, enjoying the confidence of knowing he'd built up his business to something Miranda's family wasn't big enough to impact. "And I called to talk about you taking your safety lightly."

"There was nothing light about it," Miranda replied. "Carl Davis had your sister kidnapped . . . even had part of her ear cut off. I will not look the other way when I have the opportunity to show his true colors to the world."

"And here I thought my stubbornness came from my Scottish blood," Dunn grumbled.

Miranda offered him a peal of laughter that made him smile. Until two years ago, when Miranda's husband had died, Dunn had had no contact with her. Their relationship was something only spoken of in hushed whispers behind the very tightly closed door of his father's study.

Now? He could call her. See her. And honestly, Dunn found himself uncertain how to proceed with their relationship. The only thing he seemed sure of was the fact that Vitus's call had unsettled him, and there was no way he wasn't getting involved in the matter.

"I understand your feelings, Miranda, but Carl Davis is a dangerous man."

He heard Miranda draw in a deep breath on the other side of their connection.

"I can't tell you how much it means to me to have you call, Dunn," Miranda said.

Dunn felt his jaw tighten. Oh, yes, his mother had passed on a fair amount of stubbornness to him.

"You mustn't worry," Miranda told him firmly. "I am running for Congress, and one advantage of that is, I have wonderful security."

"Carl can cut through it and you know it," Dunn countered, trying to kill her argument.

His mother surprised him by replying in a steady and sure tone.

"Yes, well, I am not nineteen anymore. Carl appears to keep forgetting that. In fact, I am running for Congress to ensure he knows he will have to contend with me. I will not allow that villain to claim victory, not while I have breath left in my body."

"That's what I'm worried about," Dunn cut back. "Vitus isn't a man who gets rattled over little things. He called me. You need to stop making a target of yourself."

"What I did," Miranda responded, "was to refuse to look the other way. It's what more people should do in order to make this world a better place. Carl was so very foolish to have that conversation at an event I was hosting."

Dunn grunted. "No argument there. I don't see how he can be leading in the polls."

"Well, that lead is waning now that he doesn't have Kirkland Grog using his media empire to push Carl's ads in the faces of the plugged-in generation. If I hadn't turned that recording over to Kagan and his teams, Tom Hilliard wouldn't be closing in on Carl. This election isn't over yet."

And she wasn't going to back down. Dunn admitted to admiring her grit. "Promise me you will stay with your security escort."

"I shall," Miranda assured him.

Dunn ended the call and stood for a long moment with the phone in his hand. He wasn't a man who lingered on calls, but there was an unmistakable twinge of reluctance in him to sever the connection. Beyond the windows of his office, he could see the restaurants and lounges lit up. It was late in the evening, the nightlife flourishing as the nip of fall was in the air.

It wasn't the first time he'd stayed and worked while the rest of the world loosened their ties and unwound. He had the success to prove it, too. But money wasn't everything.

No, he'd never called his mother "Mom."

He hid inside his empire, where the control rested firmly in his hands. He ended up letting out a little scoff as he turned and pulled his jacket off the coatrack.

He hadn't been in control of the conversation with Miranda.

No, she'd gently deflected his warnings and left him admiring her for her integrity.

Carl Davis had better leave her alone, because Dunn wasn't planning on letting anyone touch his family.

Secret family or not.

Her son had called her.

Miranda wanted to twirl around in pure joy.

She settled for laughing until tears eased from the corners of her eyes and her security men cast her questioning looks.

Well, Dunn would enjoy knowing she was surrounded, even if she found it a bit oppressive from time to time.

Of course, she knew he was speaking the truth. Carl Davis had sold his soul in his bid for power. It wasn't her first encounter with his sort though. Her grandfather could have given Carl lessons on dirty dealing and getting ahead by underhanded tactics.

She was going to show her family there were other ways to get votes. In the era of connectivity, it was her firm belief there was a market for someone who spoke the truth and refused to make deals behind closed doors.

Her father would have laughed.

Her late husband, too.

But she was more concerned with how her granddaughter would look at her. Carl Davis had played the

Washington game, played it hard and without a shred of remorse for those he trampled on his way to the top.

Was it dangerous to give evidence against him? She wasn't a fool; Miranda knew the stakes. She'd lived too long beneath the thumb of her husband, Jeb Ryland. Kept her mouth shut for the sake of her daughter. Jeb hadn't shown his true colors until after she'd conceived. It had been a different time, when a powerful man like Jeb could make it impossible for Miranda to see her daughter. So she'd played the loving wife, learned her role, performed as expertly as any Oscar-winning actress.

Jeb was gone now. Miranda leaned forward to check her lipstick as her assistant signaled it was time to go out and make an appearance.

No, she wasn't a coward, and she'd take what fate handed to her.

There was a challenge in making a clean hit.

One Pullman enjoyed the rush of.

He spent a lot of time studying his targets, learning their habits so he'd be able to hit them like a ghost reaching up from the grave. No one would see it coming until it was far too late to stop him from claiming his victim.

Political figures were hard though.

Of course, that was why it paid so well.

Miranda Ryland was actually a little easier than most. She had a soft heart and an affection for charity projects. Pullman watched her as she got out of her black-windowed town car and walked straight into the mass of people waiting for her to join them at an outdoor festival. Her security escort was doing their best, but Miranda was too naive to realize she'd set them an impossible task by stepping so far out into the open.

Pullman had a camera on his shoulder. The press pass swinging from a lanyard around his neck was stolen from a guy no one would find in the trunk of his car until it was too late. Pullman put his eye to the lens of the camera, seeing the crosshairs of a scope inside the very cleverly disguised camera. The gun didn't have the range his rifle did, but in the crowd, he'd have plenty of opportunity to escape when the blood hit the pavement and everyone panicked.

Miranda was going full speed into the crowd, her security men turning to look both ways as they tried to maintain position. The excited crowd was pressing in, reaching for their candidate as Miranda smiled and tried to shake every hand extended.

He lined up the shot and pulled the trigger.

The noise was soft, the bullet flying toward the target. The seconds between pulling a trigger and impact were always the longest. Pullman was still exhaling when Miranda jerked, her body drawing tight and then falling out of sight.

The screaming started.

A wall of people came at the press. Pullman turned and ran because that was the only thing to do in a stampede.

Run or be trampled.

Of course, he wanted to run and didn't stop until he was around the corner. He ducked into an alley to rip off the press pass and tuck it into a pocket. He'd dispose of it later, somewhere far away from where the investigation would be happening. Pulling a hat from another pocket, he put it on and stuffed the camera into a backpack he'd had in the other pocket.

When he emerged onto the street, the security camera wouldn't connect him with the man who had gone into the alley. People were running past him, coming down the alley from the festival. He looked around, doing his part to appear flustered by the alarm.

In truth, he was perfectly at ease. Moving across a few city blocks before disappearing into traffic.

Power struggles were always bloody. From the Vikings to the White House. Pullman didn't feel sorry for any of those who made a grab for control, and the reason was simple. No matter how brightly they smiled, their hands were dirty, because there was only one path to the top.

Over the bodies of your competition.

Her husband wasn't always with her.

Damascus had known who Vitus Hale was when she married him, and he'd understood that she was attached to a classified underground lab complex where she studied infectious diseases. As a result, they were often separated by their work.

Damascus enjoyed the time she had with Vitus in her bed. He moved back and forth between their home and the nest where his brother, Saxon, was transforming a Cold War–era missile silo into a state-of-the-art communications hub. Somehow, they carved out enough time for one another, and she was grateful for the life they'd built in spite of the odds.

He shifted beside her, making her open her eyes and squint at the bedside clock. "Is Cassy fussing? It's not time to feed her yet."

Not that her breasts seemed to care. Just thinking about her baby was enough to start the milk moving. Damascus let out a sound of frustration because even if her baby wasn't hungry, she was getting up.

Vitus was taking a phone call. Damascus didn't give it too much of her attention because he worked with Shadow Ops. Which loosely translated into a cloak-and-dagger sort of life she was used to.

"Your mother is alive," Vitus muttered in his low tone.

Damascus froze, turning around from where she was looking at their sleeping daughter while trying to decide if the baby was hungry or not.

"Told you that up front, princess, so you know the important stuff first," he continued. "Miranda was shot a little more than an hour ago during an arts festival on the West Coast. She's in surgery."

Damascus felt the blood draining from her face. Vitus caught her by the bicep, taking her weight as she dragged in a ragged breath. "How . . . how badly was she hurt?"

Vitus didn't want to tell her. Damascus could see the way his expression tensed up. She knew him too well, had seen him when he was working a mission and understood the way he distanced himself from the harsh realities of the world he worked in.

She drew in a hard breath and turned toward her baby. "I have to go . . . to California and be there . . ."

Vitus caught her, clamping her against his hard body. She struggled, trying to push free. "Don't tell me I can't, Vitus. She's my mother!"

"The gunman is still at large," he said, his tone hard.

"But—" Damascus argued.

"She'd never forgive me if I allowed you to go near her with Cassy while whoever shot her is still out there. Miranda would want you and Cassy safe more than she'd want you with her."

Tears were escaping from her eyes, wetting the thin T-shirt her husband wore. He was right, and she hated it so very much at that moment.

But she didn't hate him. Vitus held her tightly as she broke down.

Special agent Thais Sinclair didn't take time off.

She pressed her lips into a firm line as she contemplated her phone, but left it on the table next to the lounge chair she was lying in.

She didn't surf social media, either, which left her peering through her sunglasses at the sparkling surface of the pool at the resort where she was staying.

Her section leader, Kagan, had ordered her to take some time off.

Thais let out a little sound of frustration, but that was going to be the extent of her argument because Kagan was her boss. Oh, she wasn't taking time off because he'd told her to . . . no, it was far more about the fact that Kagan had earned her respect. He'd told her to let her thoughts settle. She could either do it his way or balk and end up having him order her to stand down.

So she was lying in the sun, doing absolutely nothing important. She really didn't have much of a choice, but keeping her dignity had value.

Still . . . she worked with Shadow Ops because she didn't want to be alone with her thoughts.

You mean your ghosts . . .

"Please tell me your lips are pressed like that because your boyfriend is now an ex-boyfriend."

Thais knew who was talking to her. The guy had been watching her for the better part of a half hour and seemed to think he'd found the right time to make his play.

She stood, with all the grace and poise her mother had reared her with and which she learned to perform because of how much she'd feared her father.

No . . . "sire" was a better word than "father." He'd preferred "master of the family," but she wouldn't think of him in any fashion that might please him.

Thais offered the guy waiting for her response a few words. "I don't do boyfriends," she said. She liked men with balls, and he at least had more than the other men watching her from around the sitting area.

He wasn't her type though.

Too tame.

The guy grimaced. "Don't tell me you're a taco girl . . ."

Thais plucked her meager belongings off the side table and dumped them into her bag. She offered the guy a shake of her head, restoring his hopeful grin.

"I just don't do domesticated men," she muttered.

"I can be alpha, baby," he said, stepping up to her challenge. "Just give me a chance."

Thais only gave him a glance before she moved away.

An alpha didn't wait for a chance to be handed to him.

You're just in a bad mood . . .

That much was very true. Thais contemplated herself as she took the stairs up to the floor her room was on. She enjoyed the slight burn in her thighs from the climb. She was stripping down as she closed the door behind her and headed for the Jacuzzi-style tub the suite offered.

At least Kagan had put her in a nice place for her required cleansing time off.

She turned on the water and took a moment to consider the offering of spa body washes sitting on the countertop. Thais selected one and popped the little plastic top off so she could smell it.

Slipping into the tub she enjoyed the way the cold water sent goosebumps up her legs. In the midday light, the bathroom lacked something, a mood she discovered herself longing for.

Don't . . .

The warning was swift and cutting. Thais didn't temper her inner voice, either. What she shied away from was a memory of a night when she'd indulged in a bath, when she really shouldn't have allowed her secret fetish to be witnessed.

You knew he was watching you . . .

It was the truth. She'd known Dunn Bateson was likely watching her. In fact, she'd enjoyed thinking she had the Scot's complete attention.

Such a dangerous game she'd been playing. One that had come back around to extract a toll from her when she'd encountered him again.

She knew better.

Much, much better.

Emotions were best left far away from her life. It was a lesson she'd forced herself to memorize in order to survive.

As if on cue, her phone started to chime. She reached for it, swiping her finger across the screen as she used her foot to turn off the water so she could hear.

"Your vacation is being cut short." Her section leader's voice came across the line. Kagan was a cut-to-the-chase sort of man. He was all business, and Thais like that facet best about his personality.

"Suits me," she muttered. "I'm ready for assignment."

"Even one involving Dunn Bateson?" Kagan asked bluntly.

There was another facet of her section leader's personality, only this was one Thais wasn't nearly as fond of. Kagan knew too much. In his job of heading up Shadow Ops teams, Kagan noticed things she went to a great deal of effort to conceal. Even if she did enjoy knowing Kagan didn't miss details. That was exactly the sort of section leader every agent needed watching out for them.

On a personal note though, she didn't particularly care for the way he knew Dunn Bateson might be a soft spot for her.

And it was definitely only a "maybe."

"I can't think of any problem with a case connected to Dunn; we don't have a personal connection." She was lying. But that also went along with Shadow Ops teams. They worked the cases with the worst scum on the face of the planet, which translated into doing what had to be done in order to get results.

Lying wasn't the worst she'd done in order to gather evidence.

Kagan made a soft sound on the other end of the line. "Miranda Delacroix Ryland was shot. She's looking like she's going to pull through. I need eyes on Dunn.

Close proximity. I want to make certain he doesn't do anything rash while I run down the leads on who hired the hitman."

Thais felt the edges of the phone digging into her hand because she'd tightened her grip on it.

"Any problem with the assignment, Sinclair?" Kagan pressed her when she didn't answer him quickly.

"None." She killed the call. Kagan wouldn't necessarily be fooled into thinking she was at ease with her orders, but at least she wouldn't have to talk about it.

Kagan knew she couldn't shield herself completely from Dunn. Thais sat still for a moment, making certain she thought the assignment through. Dunn had helped them in the past. He wasn't a loose cannon. But the truth was, her team didn't know all that much about the reclusive Scotsman. There was one important thing about working under Kagan's command. It was vitally important to question everything. Rarely were things straightforward on the cases they worked, and the moment she relaxed too much was just about when things would turn ugly.

So she'd shadow Dunn and keep her eyes open. Kagan might not always clue her in to all the details of his decision-making process, but her section leader never wasted his time, either.

Thais stood and went to shower. Her phone chimed with an incoming file. It would include her assignment and details on how to find Dunn. He was a recluse and had tons of money, but the part Thais focused on was that Miranda was his birth mother, a fact Dunn seemed to hold in high esteem. He had few soft spots, Miranda being the only one Thais really knew about.

Finished with her shower, Thais stepped out and

grabbed one of the luxury towels set out for her use. She didn't care for how eager she was to look over the details of her mission.

When it came to Dunn, she needed to cultivate more control. Failure to do so would be devastating because Dunn was the alpha she'd compared the man by the poolside to. Dunn was ruthless and untamed and he embraced those traits. In short, he was exactly the sort of man she needed to remain poised around.

If she failed, he'd make a feast of her before moving on to his next kill.

"You really . . . shouldn't be here . . ." Miranda was weak. Her voice was thin and her face as white as the sheet pulled up to her shoulders.

Dunn focused on the way her eyes sparkled though. The glitter gave her away because she only looked at her daughter, her grandchild, and him like that. Her family had forced her to give him up, but the happiness in her eyes told him she'd been sincere when she said she loved him.

"You're my mother," he said softly. "Family is more important than anything. I wouldn't be anywhere else."

"But . . . what if someone realizes . . . ," she muttered, the pain medication starting to take her back into slumber. "It might hurt your interests."

"It wasn't my family who decided you weren't good enough to be their daughter-in-law."

Dunn regretted his words instantly. Miranda drew in a harsh breath, stiffening and then winching as pain went through her from her wound.

He felt like shit.

"I didn't mean that, the way it sounded," he said, his

brogue surfacing as he battled a surge of regret. "I know ye gave me to me father for my good. Ye made the right choice."

Miranda clasped his hand, her grip tight as she fought the pull of the drugs. "My father would have ruined your grandfather. It was a different world back then. Your family was so deeply involved in exporting goods into the US. My father . . . he would have . . . crushed . . ."

"Don't fret." Dunn rubbed his hand over the back of hers. "I do understand. Wouldn't be here if I didn't."

Miranda relaxed, tears escaping from her eyes as she blinked. "I was so young and it wasn't your fault . . . all I could give you was the protection of obeying my family . . ."

"And my life." Dunn spoke softly but Miranda was floating off, her eyelids closing as she sunk down into sleep. "I know they wanted you to have an abortion. I know you ran away, hiding long enough to keep them from pressuring you into breaking."

Miranda lifted her eyelids and sent him a look full of determination. "You were conceived in love . . . the only love of my life . . . It would have killed your father if I'd failed to safeguard you . . ."

Miranda drifted off into slumber, a happy grin on her lips. She had strength. A solid core of it that her soft manners hid so very effectively. The thing was, he didn't get the feeling she meant to dull her edges, and that fact just made him love her all the more.

His mother was a lady. A genuine, genteel woman of class and distinction. Her father hadn't realized that morality was the most important part of being a lady and that the manners weren't just for show.

Too many people didn't realize what a gift it was to be drawing breath.

Dunn did.

Was it due to his father calling his attention to it for as long as he could remember? Dunn didn't know, and frankly he fucking didn't care. Let the masses of the world spend their time in angry railing against what they didn't have as far as worldly possessions went. And let them say he was a rich man's son who didn't understand what it was like to struggle.

He'd turn on them and let them know how foolish he thought they were for not valuing being able to hug their mothers or present them with a grade-school holiday present made of macaroni and food coloring.

Nobody had it all, and money didn't make a man rich.

It was the one solid truth in his life.

He placed Miranda's hand down on the side of her bed before leaving the room. The security men outside the door watched him, pissing him off because it had taken a call to a friend to get his name on the entrance list of approved visitors.

Sure, he was happy to know his mother's safety was being seen to, and yet he needed permission to visit.

Special agent Vitus Hale was leaning against the wall. The ex-SEAL gave every appearance of looking relaxed.

Dunn knew it was only camouflage.

Vitus was positioned to see both sides of the hallway and Miranda's door. Leaning on the wall was a ruse, one employed to make it seem like he was at ease. Dunn knew differently. A man like Vitus never completely let his guard down. He was a warrior, plain and simple, even if there were plenty of people who felt that word was outdated.

"Where are you headed?" Vitus asked, straightening away from the wall.

Dunn offered him a raised eyebrow. "If you have to ask, you've misjudged me."

Vitus fell into step beside him. "We have a team on this case, Dunn."

Dunn turned his head for a split second, long enough to shoot Vitus a hard look.

"You really need to let us find the shooter," Vitus continued in spite of the warning.

An elevator opened and Dunn stepped into it, turning around to face Vitus. "I like you, Hale. Don't screw that up by telling me to leave a family matter in the hands of strangers."

Vitus had stopped outside the elevator, clearly unwilling to leave his post. Dunn watched him as the elevator doors slid shut.

Dunn did like Vitus. Liked him even more because the man wasn't in the elevator trying to talk Dunn out of his choices.

No, Vitus was wise enough to understand there would be no changing Dunn's mind.

Blood was blood.

And whoever had put a hit out on his mother was going to learn exactly how big a mistake they'd made.

No, he didn't have a badge. What he did have was connections in the global community. Carl Davis had better hope his hands were clean because Dunn would call on every single one of his resources to bring the man down if Carl had put the hit on Miranda.

Team? Dunn strode out of the elevator, his personal

security man, Kent, falling into step beside him. He had his own team, and Kent headed it up.

"Who did you get?"

Kent offered Dunn a small tablet as they cleared the hospital doors and Kent opened a door of a waiting SUV that was illegally stopped in front of the entrance.

The driver was pulling away before the private security guard managed to make it across the expanse of the parking lot to take issue with them. Dunn swept his fingertip across the screen of the tablet, taking note of each man Kent had assembled into a team.

Vitus Hale would approve, Dunn decided as he finished. The Shadow Ops teams had the best resources but not always the best funding. In the private sector, Dunn held the advantage of being able to contract above the going rate.

Another thing to thank his mother for.

The empire his grandfather had built was thriving after three generations of Batesons working toward the goal of making the company a global force. A fact Miranda had traded her happiness for.

"You were conceived in love . . . the only love of my life . . ."

The fruit of her sacrifice was in his bank accounts and at his disposal. The team Vitus talked about being on the case only had one true concern.

They'd better stay the hell out of Dunn's way.

Carl Davis was pacing.

The carpet in his penthouse suite showed the tracks he was wearing into it. Eric Geyer, his head of security, took in the signs of his boss's agitation before opening his mouth.

"Pullman says the hospital is a no go. Miranda's personal security has it locked down, and her son-in-law, Vitus Hale, is on site as well. Which likely means—"

"The fucking Shadow Ops are there, too," Carl hissed as he stopped and pointed at Eric. "I told you to get a man who could do the job! If Miranda were dead, that bastard Kagan would know not to fuck with me. Now? Every man with a Shadow Ops badge thinks he can get away with messing with my business."

"Don't panic, keep your head down, and there is no way for anyone to trace this back to you. Tyler made the mistake of getting too personal with the Shadow Ops teams," Eric advised his boss. "It was a stroke of luck that Miranda survived. Any man with Kagan's teams knows it was a windfall. Everyone runs short on luck at some point."

Carl let out a dry chuckle as he lifted one hand into the air. "Are you saying I should be happy to know Kagan and his teams are now crawling all over this event, looking for evidence that might just lead them back to me?"

"My job is to make sure there is no trail," Eric said, defending himself. "I'm advising you not to engage them. There is nothing to be gained and a lot to lose if they decide to take a personal interest in you."

Carl grunted and moved over to the bar. He wrapped his fingers around a whiskey glass but didn't lift it to his lips. Instead he turned and looked at Eric. "Better hope not. I go down, you go down."

"The only place you're going to is the White House," Eric replied with complete confidence. "You wanted Kagan to feel vulnerable and he does. Miranda might have survived, but it was a stroke of luck. And the people in Washington now know you'll do what needs doing, and they might not be so lucky if they cross you. All in all, you've accomplished a great deal even if she did survive."

Carl nodded, taking a sip from his whiskey as he mulled over what Eric had said. "Fair enough. Senator McFarlan was minding his tone a whole hell of a lot better yesterday."

"You're leading and we're in the home stretch," Eric said. "Just keep your smile in place and leave the enforcement to me."

"At least until after the election," Carl replied. "It's going to be a pleasure to shut down the Shadow Ops teams the moment I have the power to do so. I'm going to toss Kagan and his agents out and enjoy knowing the wolves are eating them and everyone they love."

Eric didn't blink an eye over the cold-bloodedness coming out of his boss's mouth. Life was a competition sport and politics had always been a bloody one. Eric knew what he'd signed up for and now was no time to grow a conscience. He'd chosen his side, so now he was all in because Kagan and his Shadow Ops agents wouldn't think twice about cutting him down.

Miranda Delacroix was no innocent, either. Or at least she was trying to get into the power game, so she needed to learn the rules of the game. She'd turned evidence in on Carl to Kagan and it had been Eric's job to make sure she understood the price for that action.

Eric made his way into a room he knew was secure so he could pull a burner phone from his pocket. He punched in the redial and waited.

Pullman picked it up, but true to the hitman's nature, Pullman didn't say anything.

"When possible, we want you to complete the assignment," Eric said. "Your fee will be paid."

"It will be tricky," Pullman responded. "And it's gonna take time to set it up. I expect double pay for the risk."

"Understood."

Eric killed the call. A burner phone might be a better option for keeping conversations private, but cell towers could be hacked. Keeping things short was the key. Not that there was anything much else to talk about. Pullman would do his job and Eric would enjoy delivering the news to Carl when the task his boss had given him was completed.

It was an assignment.

Thais Sinclair refused to allow herself to ponder the subject of her case. No, Dunn Bateson was just another package she was keeping tabs on. The hotel was everything she expected a man with the sort of money Dunn was rumored to have would stay at. Polished marble floors and an ultra-high ceiling that seemed to suck up the noise from conversations, giving the illusion of privacy.

The elevator bank had a desk man making sure no one went past him unless they had a key. Thais flashed hers, moving past the guy without a single acknowledgment for the grin he sent her.

She had a job to do.

No, you just prefer Dunn . . .

She wouldn't allow herself to think about him beyond the terms of her job.

"I pride myself on not losing my temper very often."

Thais stiffened. Just a small response to the way

Dunn Bateson appeared from behind a pillar. She turned and hated the way a tingle went down her nape.

Dunn had black hair and a pair of green eyes that tended to draw her attention. Beneath his Royal Mile suit, he was toned and fit in a way the civilian male so often wasn't. Thais saw that type of muscle among the ranks of the agents she worked among and often in the criminal element she was investigating.

"Today though," Dunn continued as he moved closer, "I might just make an exception and forget to control myself."

She liked the sound of that far too much.

Dunn wore his hair longer than most businessmen, and there was a definite way he moved that made it plain he was less than civilized. In short, he was ruthless and hands-on. Two traits she had a very hard time resisting.

He stopped just a pace from her, looking down into her eyes. The urge to retreat was strong, and she quelled it through sheer determination. He let out a soft grunt.

"Not even going to try and tell me some story about you being here for a reason other than me?" he demanded softly.

She shifted, a riot of responses running though her system. "I didn't judge you to be the sort of man who enjoyed having his ass kissed."

She gained a sort of male half-amused response from him.

"In your case, I might make an exception," he said.

An elevator chimed behind them, and the gleaming doors slid open. Dunn reached down and closed his fingers around her wrist.

The touch caught her off guard, sending far too much

awareness through her. Thais lifted her arm and dropped it on the other side of his wrist to break the hold. He turned and contemplated her. Another tingle went down her spine because the gleam in his eyes told her he was considering reaching for her again.

And looking forward to what sort of fight she'd give him.

She should have taken up the offer from the guy at the pool. Sexual tension was distracting her.

"Since you're following me, Thais, I thought we'd just cut to the business," Dunn suggested.

There was a strong edge of distaste in his voice. Thais felt her eyes narrowing. Dunn caught her wrist again while she was deciding what to say. He tugged her toward the open doors of the elevator and she followed because he was her target.

At least that was as far as she managed to get along the lines of logical thinking.

Dunn pushed his room keycard into the elevator slot for the penthouse floor and the doors slid shut immediately.

Time tended to slow down in moments when she was focused. Frustration nipped at her as she felt her senses sharpening. Thais didn't need to be more aware of Dunn. Arousal was a finicky bitch, one she didn't need any interaction with when she was working an assignment.

Not that her body was interested in logical reasoning.

What she was interested in, well, it wouldn't be happening with Dunn. She'd made that choice just after her first encounter with the reclusive Scot. He might be something she had interest in, but the very same qualities she was drawn to made her realize she could never allow him to be too close or she'd risk losing herself to his persona.

Self-preservation . . . something Thais took very seriously.

The doors chimed again as they reached the floor. Dunn strode out into the hallway without a glance back at her. At last it was her turn to enjoy knowing he was making assumptions about her. He slid his key into a door and pushed it in while she inserted her own key into the door of the suite next to his. She slipped inside, just taking enough time to watch the surprise flicker in his eyes.

Her door closed with a whisper, but she would have sworn she still felt Dunn.

He was only a few feet away.

Alone, she could take a moment to really contemplate her feelings. What she discovered didn't please her at all.

She was restless.

A state she didn't allow herself to reach very often. A seasoned agent never took the chance of having sexual energy undermine their thinking.

She should have taken up the offer from the guy at the pool, she thought again.

An ugly idea?

Not really. More of a necessary one in her world. It would have dampened her urges at least, even if she'd found the experience less than completely satisfying. Dunn was too captivating a target when she'd allowed herself to go so long without any sexual contact.

At least she had her own suite.

There was a soft click and beep. Thais turned in a

flash as the door came open. She leveled her gun at Dunn as he strode inside without a hint of remorse and tossed a keycard down on the dining room table while the door closed behind him.

"Shoot me or put the gun down, Agent Sinclair," he informed her bluntly. "Just don't think I'm going to put up with your little stunt of following me and hiding behind the door of this suite."

Thais was slipping the gun into her waist band. "Using your influence with the owner of this hotel to gain a keycard to my suite?"

Dunn shrugged. "Why not? Won't it make it a lot easier for you to perform your job of keeping tabs on me?"

Disgust edged his tone. Something very unexpected went through her in response. A sense of misgiving that Thais hadn't felt in a very long time.

Almost as though she'd disappointed him and it mattered to her.

She couldn't go there . . .

Being a bitch while working protected her sanity. Even if there was a large part of her that desperately wanted to be free of the need to be a bitch. As an operative, she used it as an enticement. Bored, rich men liked to think they'd succeeded in breaking through a hard shell. And then there was her husband, who'd seen her as a toy, something to amuse him, even if part of the entertainment was fighting with her.

All of it was such a waste. All the while she was screaming, hoping someone would see past her shell and notice she didn't want to be any sort of hardened creature.

But in the real world, life was hard, so she had to be as well.

"My job is more than slipping between the sheets of my targets." It was an impulse to defend herself. "And I love my job, even when the expectations are high. Shadow Ops isn't for those without barriers between their personal choices and the ones they make in the line of duty."

Dunn's eyes narrowed. She caught the signs of his expression tightening until his jaw was clenched and his chin tucked.

"Your superiors use your gender a little too freely for my taste," he said.

He was digging in.

And she really shouldn't have found it heartwarming. He was chipping away at her shell, the one she'd built herself to shelter her from the disillusionment that had shattered her world.

"I don't need you to approve of me, Dunn Bateson." It was another impulsive retort. A comment she would have normally felt 100 percent confident in, and yet, there was something about the way Dunn was watching her that undermined her peace of mind. "Or to protect me."

Made her feel soft and feminine . . .

Thais stiffened. "Leave."

Dunn shook his head. The corners of his mouth twitched up into an arrogant little grin that she should have hated, and she did, in one corner of her mind, but there was a whole other part of her brain focused on the fact that he was every inch the alpha.

He wouldn't leave her unsatisfied . . .

"Won't Kagan insist on you keeping an eye on me?" Dunn asked slowly. He was closing the distance between them. "Since you claim to be so devoted to your badge, my being here is just what you should want."

He was challenging her. It wasn't that she was surprised by his head-on approach; she expected boldness from Dunn. What had her hesitating was the rush of approval moving through her.

It was far too personal an effect. He was a target. She needed to get her thinking straight.

"My assignment was to make sure you knew you were being watched," she retorted. "You know. Consider yourself forewarned about taking any action against your mother's attacker. We're finished now."

She really hated the way she felt about telling him this. Like she was hiding behind her badge.

Using the law to deny him justice for a wrong done to his own blood.

It was the way it had to be . . .

Dunn was close now. It was a calculated risk, allowing him to get within touching distance. She'd used the tactic before, to lure in a subject and allow them to think she trusted them.

Thais realized she hadn't employed any thought process this time to allow Dunn to close the distance between them. No, she'd flatly been mesmerized by him. Stuck in place by the impulse to have him come to her.

"We've only just begun, Thais," Dunn promised her, his tone sending a ripple of anticipation down her spine.

"Don't flatter yourself, Mr. Bateson," she answered, relieved to have her poise respond even if her wits were scattering. "I'm only here because I was sent."

It was a cutting remark, one she'd practiced. Today

though, she was less than pleased with the way his eyes narrowed in response.

"Oh, aye, I believe you." He tilted his head to one side, his lips parting to flash his teeth at her. "You've done a good job of making sure our paths don't cross. Still, I can't help but notice that you're blushing. Again."

There was a flash of promise in his eyes before he reached out and stroked the surface of her cheek. She gasped, jerking back out of his reach, and all the while insanely aware of the sensation of his skin against hers.

How long had it been since she'd felt such a connection?

"You're having trouble separating mission goals from personal ones when it comes to me," he muttered, stepping toward her.

"In that case, shouldn't you be running for the door? I know your style, Dunn: women on your terms, no negotiation. No personal involvement." She needed to stand in place. Wanted to make it clear she wouldn't back down from him.

But her poise joined her wits, deserting her as Dunn's all-too-impressive form closed in on her.

"True," he answered, following her as they started weaving a slow trail through the dining area of the suite and toward the plush sofa that overlooked the city. "You have the same set of rules though . . . Sounds like it could be an interesting match-up between us. An even playing field."

Thais narrowed her eyes at him. "I thought you just said you didn't like the way my gender came into play as often as it does on cases. Are you planning to play the hypocrite by wanting to enjoy me since I'm here?"

He drew in a stiff breath.

"I'm sure there are a couple of candidates in the bar who can deal with your restlessness. You and I might see each other again, and I know how much you enjoy a clean getaway," Thais added.

There was a flash of something in his eyes that hinted at an unspoken agreement. His complexion darkened, almost as if he wasn't too pleased with the blunt truth.

Well, there was something they had in common.

Thais allowed herself to savor the moment; it was a rare one after all. She wasn't immune to the desire for love and deeper emotions, just wise to the realities of what could happen to those who made a try at grabbing a life full of those wonderful feelings.

After all, she'd been one. For a moment she felt the sting of having her young heart smashed to bits by her husband a few months after their wedding when she'd discovered him in her best friend's bed. He'd enjoyed knowing she'd thought him in love with her, laughed at the love in her eyes.

Thais jerked her attention back to the moment.

It was far safer to seal her heart against letting loose her inner longings.

"I'm not asking you to change, Dunn," Thais muttered as she walked past him and opened the door of her suite. "Consider me kicking you out as a little gift. I'm sure you'll appreciate it in the morning, when you're all finished feeling protective."

And she would, too. Or at least she'd spare herself another round of misgivings over giving in to her impulses.

No matter how tempting they were.

He contemplated her for a long moment with those

emerald eyes of his. There was a battle raging between them, one that fascinated her just as much as it frustrated her.

The intensity was off the scale.

Or at least the scale she was used to living within the confines of.

"You might be right," Dunn said in a low tone. "But I'm not quite in the mood to thank you for your gift."

He turned and offered her a look at his wide back as he left.

Just what you asked him to do . . .

Yes, well, wisdom and logic might be traits prized throughout the world, but no one said they came without a high cost.

A very high one indeed.

Dunn caught sight of his security man the moment he crossed into the hallway.

Kent was watching for him, every bit as attentive as Dunn expected the man to be for the sum he paid him.

Dunn checked himself. Kent wasn't the right target for his temper. His security team didn't have a life because they had to travel with him, which meant Kent was entitled to every cent he was paid. Because the man earned it with dedication.

"I'm in for the night, Kent," Dunn muttered. "Thank you."

"Mr. Bateson."

Dunn normally found Kent's formal address a reason for a grin. Tonight, Dunn ducked into the penthouse before his man noticed the way he was drawn tight.

But Dunn ended up chuckling.

Thais pushed his buttons.

Alone in the penthouse suite, Dunn loosened his tie before pulling the length of silk free and leaving it draped over a chair at the dining table. With no one else around, he indulged in a moment of blunt honesty.

Thais Sinclair fascinated him.

It was a strange little anomaly in his very organized life. She'd called it right on the nose when she'd said he liked his women in the place he'd defined for them. But there was part of him that almost wanted to defend himself to her.

She was right, he was thankful she'd kicked him out before he'd exposed himself by telling her he only kept women out of his personal life as a defense. It was a shame, really, he wasn't actually ice-cold at his core. He'd love to meet an honest woman who wasn't just playing a very well-rehearsed game to get attached to his money. He just wasn't willing to stick his neck out at the moment. He had plenty of scars.

She'd call you a coward.

Well, he'd be able to use her pot-calling-the-kettle-black remark on her.

He chuckled softly. They were a pair alright. Both drawn to each other, both jaded and too damned chicken to step up and give whatever was between them a chance.

And neither of them would like knowing they were being cowards.

He'd rather be in her bed at that precise moment.

He drew in a deep breath and poured a measure of whiskey into a glass at the bar. Then, carrying the neat and well-aged drink, he walked toward the floor-to-ceiling glass windows and contemplated the city view.

She wasn't as right as she thought, however, because there was part of him feeling a very strong sense of regret for the fact that she'd kicked him out.

But his father's face surfaced from his memory.

Love was more trouble than it was worth. Thais was right about how he dealt with women. Dunn wasn't planning on making the same mistakes his parents did.

He lifted his glass in the direction of the wall between him and Thais. "Thank you, Thais."

Scrubs were wonderful camouflage.

Thais grabbed a set of light green surgery ones and pulled them on. Dunn would be back to see Miranda and she would be in position to make sure she kept an eye on him. She twisted her hair up into a knot and used a few pins to secure it before pulling a disposable cap over her hair and tucking every last strand beneath the elastic edge. Vitus Hale was somewhere nearby and it would be good practice to slip beneath his notice.

A harmless enough game while on an assignment that wasn't as tense as most.

She clipped a security badge to her chest and completed her disguise with a face mask. Her assignment was to keep tabs on Dunn, so she tucked her gun into her drawstring waist pants and ducked out into the hallway to get in position.

She didn't go unnoticed. The security was high and more than one man checked her badge. But she made it through because hospitals had to be staffed. Even when there was an aspiring congresswoman in the ward. It was quieter in the hallway where Miranda was resting because the other rooms were empty as a security precaution. Thais listened to her footsteps, light as they were, as she heard the elevator behind her arrive with a soft ding.

Thais caught sight of Dunn as she turned and went into Miranda's room. The man at her door started down the hallway toward Dunn, intent on checking his identification. And then she was moving into the room where Miranda was in the bed near the window.

The curtain was drawn between the bed and the door. Thais felt her muscles tighten.

It shouldn't be drawn.

The man on protection detail at the door would have checked the small window and investigated if his sight had been blocked to his target.

Thais reached for the gun she had clipped to the back of her waistband but the curtain moved as someone shoved the empty bed into her. She rolled up and across it, unwilling to go down so easily but ended up in the fabric, fighting to be free of it.

She emerged but whoever was in the room caught her in a choke. It was a brutal one, applied perfectly and with all the skill of a practiced killer. Thais turned and tried to rotate enough to jab her elbow into the belly of her attacker but he dragged her back, using his greater height to keep her from using her feet.

He was squeezing the blood flow off from her brain. Three minutes was all it would take, her vision already starting to blur.

She dug in and shoved her feet against the floor, running the man into the wall. The impact was enough to shake his hold. Thais turned and jabbed with her elbow, feeling the impact with the soft spot under the man's ribs. He released her, her knees buckling from the lack of oxygen.

"Fuck this," he growled, before moving back toward Miranda. He yanked a plastic cap off a syringe, exposing the sharp needle, and started to push it into the port on the side of Miranda's IV.

He'd underestimated her. Thais intended to make sure it was the last mistake he made. She surged off the floor, lunging at him. The IV stand went skidding across the floor, falling with a clatter as Thais yanked the syringe free.

"Bitch," the man said as he watched Thais pull her gun and level it at him.

Thais watched panic move through his eyes. She laid the syringe down on the foot of Miranda's bed, widening her stance in case the guy made a grab for her weapon.

Instead, he bolted for the door.

"Help!" he yelled outside the door. "There's a woman . . . with a gun . . ."

Thais grunted, moving after the guy. She didn't make it two paces past the door before she was tackled. Dressed as a nurse, the real attacker was ignored by Miranda's security and believed.

"I'm a federal agent." She raised her voice but the security detail wasn't listening.

They were hyped on adrenaline, flipping her over so they could handcuff her. She fought to lift her face and look after her suspect.

She met Dunn's furious green eyes. "He was in with your mother."

Dunn didn't disappoint her. He spun around and

went tearing around the same corner the man had. At least Dunn could beat the truth out of the guy before any of the security team realized she wasn't the threat.

Carl Davis looked at his head of security, Eric Geyer, and cussed.

"So your hitman made it even worse?" Carl demanded.

Eric shook his head. "Maybe he did even better than we might ever have hoped."

Carl bit back another round of temper-infused profanity and made a get-going motion with his hand.

"The agent was Thais Sinclair, one of Saxon Hale's team. She's also hand-picked by Kagan out of the prison population. She's a convicted killer, given a badge by Shadow Ops. Homeland has her, and we have some great footage from the hospital of her coming out of the room while a nurse screams for help."

Carl was thinking. Eric watched the information filter through his brain as he started nodding. "If we leak that footage, the facts won't matter . . . People believe anything they see on social media."

"Not everyone does, but the damage will be enough to discredit the Shadow Ops teams," Eric confirmed. "With the way Miranda has been showing up at your events, all you need to do is visit her and make a good show of doing everything in your power to bring this rogue agent to justice."

Eric watched the way Carl started pacing. His boss had made a lot of noise about ending the Shadow Ops teams and Kagan had made it clear to Carl how unwise such a move would be. It was a power struggle at the highest levels. Carl was against the wall now:

either he had to take his shot at Kagan or bow down to the section leader.

Eric could see the merit of both actions. But Carl would make his choice.

Carl suddenly stopped and pegged Eric with a determined look. "Release the footage and tell the press downstairs that I'm going to make an announcement."

Eric didn't let Carl's choice rattle him. Unlike his predecessor, Tyler Martin, Eric had a plan for escaping if Carl went down in flames. In the meantime, Eric planned to ride it out with Carl and hopefully land next to the man in the White House. Eric wasn't a fool though; he expected to get his hands dirty along the way. Kagan and his Shadow Ops wouldn't be the first network to fall to a new regime and they wouldn't be the last.

"Who in the hell leaked the footage?" Vitus Hale demanded.

"You know the answer," Kagan replied to his man. The section lead was his normal controlled self, and yet, there was a look in his eyes Vitus and Saxon recognized. Both agents snapped their mouths shut, waiting for Kagan to take the lead in the conversation.

"I knew who Sinclair was when I recruited her," Kagan began. "She was a killer but not a murderer. You two understand the difference. She took out a monster. One no one else could get close to."

Vitus was standing with his arms crossed over his chest. He cocked his head to one side in agreement while his brother, Saxon, nodded.

"Carl is going for our throats, gentlemen," Kagan said, laying down the facts. "The way I see it, he's just waiting for us to protect our own, so he can whip the media up into backing his decision to end our teams."

"It will be a shitstorm," Saxon said, nailing it in six words. "Abuse of federal powers, trying to keep Miranda out of office . . ."

Kagan nodded.

"So what's the plan to stop Carl in his tracks?" Vitus cut to the point. "We know that bastard has been trying to destroy us for over two years. Personally, I'm ready to get down to the final battle."

"Carl isn't going to fight that honorably," Kagan told Vitus. "You know it, have tasted it. That's why he had that footage leaked. It's also why Agent Sinclair is being held by inexperienced agents over at Homeland instead of ones who know bullshit when they see it."

"We'll start by finding the other nurse," Saxon said.

"I can't free Sinclair," Kagan said, stating aloud what all three of them knew. "Carl is just waiting for me to make a move to prove I sanctioned the hit on Miranda."

None of them liked the facts. Shadow Ops teams were tighter than most families. Kagan could see his two agents bristling at the concept of leaving one of their own without resources.

"Carl had a target killed in interrogation a few months ago, one of Dare Servant's cases," Vitus said. "You leave Sinclair in lockup and she'll end up dead."

"I'm betting Sinclair will put up a little better fight than anyone anticipates," Kagan answered. "And before you argue, let me clarify that I'm wagering all our futures on her being able to survive an attack and live to provide some evidence in our favor. I don't like it any more than you two do. But the fact is, if someone makes a try for her, it will be the evidence we need to prove she is innocent and needs to be silenced. It's the only move we have to make."

It was taking Kagan a long time to free her.

Thais twisted against the handcuffs still locking her wrists behind her back and had to force herself to relax. Her wrists were already bruised because she was slowly going insane sitting in the interrogation room, just listening to the air-conditioning coming through the vent.

She needed her wits. Composure was key to survival. A fact she'd learned long before Kagan had shown up and offered her a Shadow Ops badge. The other prisoners had called it a lucky break. Thais knew it for what it was, her due. Fate had finally delivered a measure of fairness to her.

Was she a killer?

Yes.

Her husband and brother-in-law were scum. The sort that made street criminals look like Boy Scouts. She'd killed them because she just couldn't stomach knowing what they'd planned to do and she'd been the only one who could get close enough to pull it off. Oh, it had never been her intention. No, she'd been swept off her feet, romanced and trusting when she'd taken her wedding vows. Her husband had enjoyed plucking her while she was so tender and innocent.

But she'd just been another conquest. He'd married her because of who her father was, for the business connection, and she had been expected to stay in the place she'd been put. The virgin bride, installed in the hilltop mansion, where she'd keep house and produce children and never, ever step outside her role. Or do anything such as question her husband's word.

They'd both misjudged her. The innocence her husband had been drawn to was something rooted so deeply inside her, even long after her virginity was gone, and her dreams of happy ever after smashed. Thais still believed in justice and honor. Being labeled a possession hadn't pushed her over the edge . . . no, that had happened when she'd discovered how cheaply her husband held the lives of those who worked for him. How he'd kill to increase profits and that her father had known it. She simply hadn't been able to lie in her huge bed and enjoy her mansion while knowing blood was being spilled to keep the money flowing.

Her husband had never thought she'd pose any threat to him. Oh, no. He'd planned murder in the place he expected her to make into a home and told her to go to bed when he'd caught her listening.

Business was between men . . .

She'd hear his final words to her forever but not in the way he'd intended. Thais heard victory in them. Her personal achievement in not bending in front of greed as her husband expected. He'd told her it was just the way the world was. But she hadn't been willing to turn a blind eye to it.

So she'd killed him and her brother-in-law right there in that mansion.

She didn't see it as murder. More of a service to humanity, or maybe it was a little more precise to say she'd been desperately trying to make sure she hung on to her soul.

Kagan had agreed.

Unbeknown to her, her husband had been under surveillance by a Shadow Ops team. They'd been waiting for enough evidence. She'd prevented them from getting it but had done the world a favor.

So Kagan had done her a favor in return. Offered her something other than a double murder with special circumstance charge. Offered her an opportunity to become something more than a victim of fate.

She loved her badge.

Enough to make it her identity.

Even her fascination with Dunn wasn't enough to make her change her direction in life.

She did feel a little twinge of lament for it though. Dunn Bateson was the sort of man she'd often longed for her husband to be. Dunn might be arrogant, but it could also be argued that it was confidence. Something earned versus something produced by pride. Before becoming a Shadow Ops agent, she might have let the feeling grow.

Now, relationships and her badge were two conflicting forces. A fork in the road and she knew without a doubt which one she was choosing. It was a kindness, really, because she was taking risks, large ones, and didn't have the right to inflict the consequences on a romantic partner.

"I'm not sitting this one out."

Saxon Hale didn't like being surprised, and it didn't happen very often. He jerked his head around, catching Dunn sitting in the far corner of the room.

"I own this hotel chain," Dunn began. "Made a deal years ago with your acquisitions team."

"A deal that included no names," Saxon responded, turning so he was facing Dunn all the way. "Where did you get mine?"

His tone was deadly, but Dunn didn't take it personally. He stood, now that Saxon knew he was there, and faced off with him.

"A back door no one else can find, much less activate," Dunn said in answer to Saxon's question. "Miranda is my mother. The only blood I have left. There is no line I won't cross to find the name of the man who hired that hitman. Where's Thais?"

Saxon stiffened. It was just a fraction of a reaction, but coming from someone Dunn knew to be a seasoned operator, it was beyond telling.

"I've been there . . . for you and your brother, when family was on the line," Dunn said, pressing.

"You're a civilian," Saxon offered in a tone that made it clear he was less than happy with having to deny Dunn the information. "And you're not an American."

"You've got that right," Dunn said, letting his Scottish accent out just a bit. "But then again, Thais is an American and it looks like you're letting her risk her neck."

Saxon drew up tighter, crossing his arms over his chest as Dunn perched himself on the edge of the wet bar in the suite.

"I've done my homework on her," Dunn growled. "What bothers me is how much the press is able to dig up on her. Are your superiors really going to let her take the blame?"

"You seem sure she's not guilty."

Dunn took a moment to think. His eyes narrowed

and his jaw tightened. "You're dangling her like bait." He shook his head and pointed at Saxon. "Fuck you and your section leader."

Dunn headed for the door, his stride long and powerful.

"Wait." Saxon raised his voice as Dunn closed his fingers around the door handle.

Dunn turned to look at Saxon.

"When you helped my brother and me get Damascus off the grid, the man we were running from was Tyler Martin," Saxon said softly.

"Chief security head to Carl Davis?" Dunn asked as he released the handle.

Saxon tilted his head to one side. "He was working for Jeb Ryland at the time and made the jump to Carl after Ryland was killed. Tyler was my former team lead. He sold out and sold us out to secure a place for himself."

"Miranda . . ." Saxon let out a grunt, making it clear he was fighting back the urge to refuse to give Dunn the classified information. "She recorded a conversation between Carl and Kirkland Grog. She turned it over to Vitus."

Dunn held still. His temper was raging but he'd learned a long time ago to funnel his energy into action. Particularly, action that could meet with success.

"So my mother got a hit put out on her." Dunn put his thoughts into words. "And it would be a double victory for Carl if he could let a Shadow Ops agent go down for the hit since your brother, Vitus, stole Miranda's daughter, Damascus, from him."

Saxon nodded. "My section leader tried to make it clear to Carl Davis that we're more useful to him alive than dead . . ."

Dunn let out a chuckle. "Davis is too much of a power junkie to listen to reason. He thinks of the men surrounding him as disposable."

Saxon nodded again. "We know Thais isn't guilty, but right now, we need something to go on."

"So your plan is to leave her out as bait?" Dunn asked, as he closed the distance between them. "Is that really the best you can come up with?"

"Thais is a proven agent," Saxon insisted.

Dunn maintained his position for a long moment, one foot from Saxon, both men unwilling to bend.

"Like I said . . . fuck you." Dunn was moving back toward the door.

"Thais would agree with the plan," Saxon called after him.

"I imagine she would, not that it changes my opinion," Dunn said before pulling the door open and leaving.

Thais Sinclair would agree to let her life be at risk. It was one of the things he was going to have to have a very long conversation with her about once he got his hands on her.

The woman took too many foolish risks.

Dunn didn't check himself as he took the stairs instead of the elevator and crossed through the lobby too fast for his staff to realize he was there before he was gone.

That suited him perfectly. He didn't like being anticipated. A ghost of a grin lifted the corners of his lips as Kent emerged from behind one of the pillars at the main entrance.

Kent was an exception.

And Dunn liked the guy's style. A four-wheel-drive vehicle slid up the moment Dunn came through the double-wide entry doors of the hotel. The man driving it was a stranger, but Kent climbed right in, making it clear he was performing his duties as seamlessly as he always did.

"Are we going ahead with becoming federal criminals?" Kent asked as they pulled away.

"I'm not leaving her in there, just waiting on an assassin," Dunn assured his men.

Kent's lips twitched, rising up into a grin. Dunn enjoyed the sight as he nodded.

"You realize Kagan could have your badge for all the information you just spilled." Vitus Hale emerged from the bedroom of the suite where he'd taken up a position hours earlier.

Saxon took a moment to pull his gun from his chest harness and check it while they were still in the suite. "I wish the only concern we had was losing our badges."

Vitus offered his brother a nod. They'd always been good at sharing each other's thoughts, a trait that made them good operators in the field. Today, however, it meant Saxon knew his brother was thinking about his family and just how much danger their Shadow Ops involvement placed the ones they loved in.

"Dunn's a good choice," Vitus offered. "As far as civilians go, he's got more resources than most and actually has a head on his shoulders I find myself respecting."

"He's emotionally invested." Saxon replaced the gun and shrugged on his jacket before heading toward the door.

"The only thing I'm worried about is that he actually thought you were going to sleep here," Vitus confessed as they made it into the hallway.

"I'm not so sure about that," Saxon answered as he jabbed a call button for the elevator. "Dunn hasn't earned a reputation as a recluse by making the mistake of being out in the open."

"Let's hope for Thais's sake your instincts are on the mark."

It wasn't a new experience for either of them.

Having someone's life hanging in the balance of an operation.

More than one person would argue the point about Thais knowing the risks of the badge she carried.

That didn't mean shit to either of them.

She was one of them, a member of the family. There was no way they were going to let her go down without a fight.

Even if the odds seemed stacked against them.

CHAPTER TWO

Solitary confinement messed with a person's internal clock.

Thais wasn't a stranger to the way a prisoner was broken down. She smiled ruefully though, as she admitted she'd sampled the experience from both sides.

Maybe that made her more effective. At the moment, however, she was trying to keep her brain from undermining her composure with a flood of facts.

The tiny room she was in was hot. A thin film of perspiration coated her skin as she crouched in the corner where she could see the door. Just about the time the air felt like it was too thick to breathe, the vent would suddenly deliver a cooling reprieve that kept up until she was shivering.

Stress.

Applied ever so precisely as the constant level of light kept her unaware of the passing of time, or maybe it was more correct to say, kept her aware of every moment as it crawled by. Her belly was groaning, making her glance at the sandwich sitting on the floor just inside the door. Without water, the food would only make her more miserable. It was a battle to not eat it for the quick relief she'd gain but there was at least a satisfaction in seeing it there after so long.

She'd claimed victory in tougher situations.

Although, looking over to the wall where the door was, Thais admitted this was going to be a hard one.

Assignment . . .

She repeated the word a few times, allowing her brain to shift into work mode. It downgraded the immediate level of threat.

She heard someone on the other side of the door. Just the first little hints of a palm print scanner being used. There was a soft chirp and then the door was opening.

"Stand and face the wall."

The guy was clothed in black. All black from his recently shined boots to the mask covering his face and hair. There was a slit for his eyes, which gave away the fact that he had dark brown ones. She watched those narrow as she took longer than he liked in complying.

"Sure thing," she muttered as his hands were clenching into fists. Thais pushed up from her seat on the floor, enjoying the way the guy tensed up.

He'd read her file . . .

She'd earned every bit of respect and his tensing up was a sign of it. She heard him step toward her the moment she crossed her wrists in back of her.

Thais felt her muscles drawing tight as he slipped a pair of handcuffs onto her wrists.

There was another little fact of solitary confinement. The entire body became hypersensitive, making something as impersonal as having her wrists touched feel ultra extreme.

Thais focused on this fact. Letting her brain process took the edge off the hold on her bicep as the guy turned her toward the door and guided her out. The hallway was nondescript, unless she counted the rather dismal sight of small doors just like the one she'd been locked behind.

Thais didn't dwell on it though, since hopelessness lurked in places like the hallway. In order to escape depression, she had to keep her thoughts on a tight leash.

The elevator doors had the Homeland Security seal on them. Thais enjoyed the sight before they slid open and her escort took her inside. He released her for a moment as he pressed his hand to the surface of a scanner and the red light of a laser flashed over it. The control panel turned green and he punched a button. There was a jerk and hum as the elevator went into motion.

Maybe now he'd try to kill her.

The thought didn't alarm Thais. No, she was expecting an attack because it was the only reason she was still in the holding facility.

As bait.

She knew the game, had witnessed it being played out before, and truthfully, it wasn't her first time playing the part of the prize.

Carl Davis had been working hard to kill them off for the better part of two years. The Shadow Ops had uncovered too many of his links to organized crime. Of course, there had also been Carl's determination to marry Damascus Ryland, at her father's bidding. A plan Carl had hatched to unite himself with Miranda's very established and old political family. She was a Delacroix by birth, a fact Carl had deemed important enough to give Jeb Ryland a spot as his running mate in ex-change for his daughter.

Thais felt her lips twitch. Vitus Hale had spoiled that plan. Love was finicky and unpredictable and fate had very different plans for Damascus. Of course, it helped a great deal that Damascus wasn't like her father. No, she might have been born into the Washington elite, but she was Miranda's daughter at heart.

Carl hadn't forgiven Saxon Hale and his team for making sure Damascus ended up with the man she loved. Nor had the presidential hopeful forgotten that Miranda had pulled the trigger inside her late husband's sealed office to protect her daughter.

Yes, someone was going to try and kill her. Carl wasn't wise enough to leave it alone. Thais knew his type too well.

The conflict was written in blood. Thais knew the side she was on and she didn't regret it. Her Shadow Ops badge was the most precious thing she owned.

Because it had restored her soul.

The elevator reached its destination, interrupting her thoughts. The guard renewed his grip on her bi-cep and pulled her out into another passageway. They traveled up to the ground floor. Even inside a climate-controlled facility, there was a chill that lingered when you were below the surface of the earth.

Thais felt the change in the air as the man pulled her through another doorway and into a back corridor. Pipes and large control boxes now ran along the walls. There was a marked path down the center of it where the infrequent foot travel had disturbed the dust.

"So . . . going to make it look like I was trying to escape?" she asked. "Is that the plan?"

The guy's eyes narrowed again, his fingers tightening on her upper arm. She might have made a fuss, tried to knock the handcuffs against one of the metal pipes that housed electrical wires. One good impact would vibrate along the length of the metal.

"No answer, huh?" She decided to continue on with trying to get her escort to start bragging. Her gender was mistaken for weakness, and more than one assassin had seen it as permission to voice their plans out loud because they assumed she wouldn't put up much of a fight.

She'd enjoyed schooling them on just how adept she was at defending herself.

The guard stopped at another panel, pressing his palm to its surface. The laser light crossed over his hand but there was no chirp. This time there was a warning sound, one that gained a grunt from her escort. He turned his palm up and looked at the surface of it. He licked the tip of his index finger on his left hand and eased it along the edge of his right palm.

"Just once more . . . ," he muttered under his breath before pressing his hand into position on the scanner. The red light flashed and then the chirp of approval gained a nod from him. He looked back at her, his eyes glittering with victory. "I shouldn't have grasped your arm. Almost screwed us both."

He went through the door, leaving her to follow. Thais crossed into the small space as her escort reached behind her to unlock the handcuffs. The door closed behind them and sealed.

"Don't step on him," her escort muttered. "He's already having a rough day."

They were in a small access closet, facing a ladder

that had dust clinging to its surface. Pushed off to one side was a guard in his undershirt and shorts. He was hunched over, his right hand on top of his folded legs, a slight shine left from the process of lifting his print.

"No, I'm not going to kill you." Her escort had ripped off his mask. "The job is to get you out of here."

He pointed up. Thais briefly thought about asking who was paying for her escape, but the answer wasn't as important as making it a reality. Her mental discipline broke down like an eggshell as she caught the hint of freedom.

She'd sort it out later. Besides, it would be easier to defend herself on the roof if the guy was there to kill her and make it look like a failed escape attempt.

Pick your battles . . .

A good Shadow Ops agent always prioritized. She gripped the ladder rung and started to climb. Below her, she heard her unexpected assistant locking the handcuffs around the wrist of the unconscious guard and securing him to the ladder.

She climbed two stories, popping out on the roof. Stashed behind one of the air-conditioning vents, another uniform was waiting for her. She didn't hesitate to strip and step into it as her companion joined her on the roof. The sun was setting, flashing across them as it sunk low on the horizon. It was the perfect time of day, when bright light messed with the cameras.

"Mask," her companion said, handing her the garment. "We're going to walk right out the front gate."

Sometimes bold was the way to go.

She followed to a set of stairs, descending with a quick pace. On the ground, they encountered foot traffic but their face masks didn't cause any alarm. Quite the opposite, really. People looked away from them the moment they realized they had the masks on. Proving it wasn't uncommon.

And that the masked were better unseen.

Thais understood that mind-set. Knowing the wrong things was deadly. Shadow Ops worked cases where they found the bodies of those who had been unfortunate enough to see things the darker elements didn't want witnessed.

Every now and then though, her team managed to cheat the scum of the earth out of what they were very willing to kill for.

She liked that feeling.

Loved it.

Lived on it.

Thais felt it welling up inside her as they neared the street. A dark car eased off the curb and headed toward them. It was in motion before she'd even closed the door all the way.

Not that she was quibbling.

It was smooth and executed perfectly. The driver pulled into traffic, moving into the flow without calling attention to himself.

Seamless execution.

That's what her section leader, Kagan, would call it.

She called it a relief, even if she wasn't going to voice her feelings out loud. Keeping her personal self separated from events was key. She was a Shadow Ops agent, and the men in the car were also putting their lives at risk for the same calling she had.

There was no reason to start babbling.

Instead, Thais enjoyed watching the blocks slip by as the driver took them through the evening flow of traffic.

Now, she could let the memories of the last two days slip into the back of her mind, knowing that she'd come out alive.

Saxon Hale picked up his cell phone the moment it rang. His section leader, Kagan, didn't waste any time in getting to the point of the call, either.

"Where is Sinclair?" Kagan's low, crusty tone came over the connection.

Saxon shot his brother a look. "I don't know."

There was a moment of silence. "Sure about that?" Kagan pressed. "Because someone broke her out of Homeland. A task not exactly suited to the average citizen."

Saxon experienced a surge of enjoyment that he was very careful to keep off his face.

"I've been on protection detail all day," Saxon answered.

Saxon knew he wasn't fooling Kagan. Not by a long shot. His section leader had never assigned him or Vitus to watching Miranda. But it was a damned good alibi because the rest of Miranda's security detail had been tripping over him and Vitus.

Kagan let out a barely audible grunt. "Let me know if she checks in with either of you."

The call ended, leaving Saxon sharing a long look with his brother. It wasn't the first time they'd engaged in choices that left them standing on thin ice. He'd be a liar if Saxon said he didn't foresee it not being the last time, either. Even if his wife would have something to say about him taking risks.

But Ginger knew who he was.

"Boss wants us to tag him in if Sinclair contacts us,"

Saxon muttered for the sake of the other agents lingering in the hallways of the private clinic they had Miranda moved to for her recovery.

"Copy that," Vitus replied without moving.

The security detail assigned to Miranda was watching. Those men might be on the level, but Saxon knew the way Carl Davis played. Even if none of the men working with Miranda sold out, they still might be worked over for information without realizing it.

So he and Vitus remained in place. Vitus's family connection was enough to make their story plausible.

Saxon just hoped Dunn really did know what the fuck he was doing. Because the shit was going to hit the fan.

And it was going to be a case of them or us. Saxon knew it, so did Vitus. Saxon sure as hell hoped Dunn did, too.

"We're cleared for lift-off as soon as you're on board."

The driver was the one who spoke. After so long in solitary, the sound of a human voice hit her hard. She felt his words as much as heard them, but at least her training kicked in, too, allowing her to keep her jaw tight as she looked out the window of the vehicle. The driver made a turn when the traffic light changed, driving onto a private entrance to a small airfield. He lowered his window and used a keycard to open the gate.

The plane was sitting in a hangar. The huge doors in front of it opened, lending validation to the driver's words about them being ready to take off. The stairs were down but the blocks used to brace the wheels were pulled out of the way.

"Right," Thais responded. She had her hand on the

door handle, opening it as the car slid to a smooth stop just a couple of paces from the lowered stairs. It was textbook perfect, as well as being street savvy. She'd cross to the plane inside the hangar, where satellites couldn't get a good shot of her face.

A seamless departure from the grid.

"Thanks," she muttered as she departed the vehicle and moved toward the stairs. The driver didn't respond, just pulled away. He parked the car at the back of the hangar, got out, and walked toward a manhole cover that was open. He slipped inside, along with the man who had helped her escape, both of them disappearing from sight as another man pushed the manhole cover into place.

The engines on the plane began to increase their speed. Thais gripped the handrails and focused on climbing the steep stairs. She ducked beneath the opening in the body as the copilot reached behind her to pull the steps up and secure the door. He was back through the cockpit door and buckling up without a single glance her way.

They were a good team.

Perhaps a Shadow Ops team, but Thais doubted it. Kagan was under a spotlight at the moment.

Thais sat down in one of the leather seats and buckled her seat belt. True to the driver's word, the plane was already pushing forward. The light changed as they came out of the hangar and headed toward the runway. The engines filled the air with noise as the pilot paused for a moment before pushing those engines into full thrust and heading down the runway. She felt the vibration as the plane started to lift away from the surface of the earth, the thrust from the engines making the wings support the weight of the aircraft. She felt the pressure pushing her into the seat as they gained altitude.

Fatigue was trying to sack her. Thais blinked a few times before giving into it. Kagan had a lot of resources. His connections made him a very good section leader. From the exterior of the plane, there had been nothing to hint at who was responsible for her extraction.

Honestly, it didn't matter.

She'd face whatever new threat came her way, even if the hardest part of the next few days was going to have to be doing nothing while her teammates found the real hitman and the evidence trail to clear her name.

She frowned but allowed her eyes to close. Whatever she would face, she'd do better with some sleep.

"You're not going to find anything that way." Dare Servant entered the room and looked at Saxon Hale's computer screen. "Dunn has his planes flying all the time, just to make it easier for him to disappear. Must cost him a stinking fortune."

Saxon grunted. The list of flight plans for Dunn's three private plans was up on his computer screen. Three planes, all departing out of airports in the area, all heading different directions.

"If he's smart," Vitus said, from where he was shifting through security camera footage from street cameras in the area of the prison Thais had been in, "Dunn will have gone underground with Thais, not put himself in a plane with her when she has no idea he's the one who broke her out."

Dare let out a low whistle. "Truth be told, I think our

reclusive Scotsman might just be looking forward to the fight."

"I might just tell Sinclair you said that," Saxon muttered.

"As long as we clear her name," Dare responded as his laptop flickered to life and started booting, "I don't care how pissed she is at me."

Vitus and Saxon nodded. They all turned toward their screens. Evidence was key to success. It was the foundation of what they did. The blinds were drawn tightly in the little town house they'd taken over as the owner of it was slipping deeper into a coma after the car accident from the day before.

It was a twist of fate Shadow Ops teams often took advantage of. Using the property to move around off the grid. In this case, Saxon and his team could take a few hours to prowl through the Internet for evidence before they needed to move on. No one would find them at the house, something they couldn't be certain of if they used a permanent address. Shadow Ops teams worked off the grid, which meant even the Internet they used had to be under someone else's name. They were always on the lookout for a property with an owner newly deceased or, as in this case, in a coma. Someone with no next of kin or at least no relative who had an interest in showing up at the house.

Thais had worked as hard for all of them in the past.

And today, they had her back.

Someone had covered her with a blanket.

Thais shifted, her neck aching from sleeping in the seat. Her feet were freezing from the change in air pressure and she knew she'd be even colder if the blanket wasn't there to keep her body warm.

Still, she didn't care to know someone felt they needed to pamper her. While there would be plenty of people who'd advise her to not sweat it, she knew from experience that respect only came when she refused to be seen as a female.

"There's a bedroom in back."

Thais opened her eyes wide.

"As well as two bunks you're welcome to make use of."

Dunn's voice was unmistakable. She turned her head and caught sight of him where he was sitting on the sofa that ran along one side of the plane.

He was more informal than she'd ever seen him. His suit jacket was missing, along with his tie. She had a view of his skin at his throat, where the first two buttons were open on his shirt.

Decadent . . .

She drew in a stiff breath and started out of the chair but the seat belt held her, making her clumsy as she snapped it open.

Dunn was grinning when she stood and faced him. "I enjoy surprising you, Thais."

Somehow, the deep timber of his voice hit her as being more personal. Maybe it was the setting or the fact that she had no avenue of escape. In short, she had a lack of control over the moment.

He knew that though.

Had planned it.

She bristled but there was something else: a sense of recognition for his skill.

"You shouldn't," she muttered, reaching deep for her professional persona. She never would have fallen asleep if she'd known he was there.

Never let her guard down . . .

"Have I misjudged this case?" she continued, taking a moment to look around the rest of the plane. "Is it really so desperate that Kagan brought in a civilian?"

Dunn's eyes narrowed. He didn't care for being classified as a civilian.

At least not in the tone she used to say the word. It was on purpose, however. She needed to cut through the surge of emotions flooding her. Detachment was her haven but Dunn seemed to have a knack of reaching her through the thick walls she'd surrounded herself with.

"I have more resources than you give me credit for," Dunn responded. "Kagan was set to leave you in Homeland custody until someone tried to kill you. Your position seemed to be the one of bait."

"It's a proven method." She'd never really struggled to push those words past her lips before. Logic had always helped her see the validity of the argument. There was something about the way Dunn looked at her though, that undermined her confidence.

In short, it shone a light on her ideas that made her see how foolish they were, even if logic was there in spades.

"It's also proven effective in getting the bait killed," Dunn said, pinpointing his opinion. "Something I wasn't willing to sit back and wait for."

"It wasn't your choice." Thais strove to find her disinterested tone. She'd found it to be a very useful tool in the field, being the icy bitch.

Dunn offered her a slight shrug. "I made my choice."

And she was there. An accomplishment there was no way to overlook.

Or dismiss how much you agree with him . . .

Dunn had an uncanny method of looking at her with his green eyes that made it seem like he was looking straight into her soul. It was a ridiculous idea and yet he seemed far too perceptive for her poise.

He shook her.

At her core.

"Is there a shower back there?" she asked, seeking an escape.

"Everything you need is there, Thais," he answered smoothly.

Everything you need . . .

God, she wanted to drink that in. From the tone of his voice to the way his expression settled into one of confidence. Maybe it was smug and she'd be a whole lot better off composure-wise if she could apply that word to Dunn.

She couldn't though.

Thais let herself into the bathroom and discovered a neat little marble-top vanity with a cosmetic case on its gleaming surface with all of her personal favorites waiting for her. A tingle went through her because she recognized sharp work when she saw it. Digging up personal information took someone with skill, and when it came to her personal information, Dunn should hand out a bonus to whichever of his men had managed to discover her preferred brand of eyeliner. Someone had been peering intently at shots of her face.

Maybe Saxon had spilled the information.

She picked up a travel-size bar of soap in sandalwood and knew without a doubt her team leader, Saxon Hale, wouldn't have known it was her favorite. Not in a million years.

Does it matter?

She reached in and turned on the water in the shower, tearing the paper off the little bar of soap and lifting it to her nose to indulge in the scent.

Maybe she should just enjoy the moment . . .

She was free, and the plane had to land sometime.

A memory surfaced. One of a bathtub that she'd indulged in on a case. She recalled stripping down and selecting a similar bar of soap from a box containing them in that cabin. Thais smiled as she realized how Dunn had known she liked sandalwood.

You knew he was watching you . . .

Well, she'd certainly suspected Dunn was monitoring his cabin. The soap confirmed it.

How long had it been since someone had noticed a personal detail?

Thais stiffened. She had to shut the doors on her emotions and quick. Otherwise, she had the feeling she was going to end up as another one of Dunn's castoffs. It wasn't just her need to remain untouched that had warnings ringing though her head.

Dunn had a reputation of avoiding entanglements.

His parents had been denied the love they'd had for each other. It made sense that he carried the scars of knowing what love had done to his father. She had her scars as well and wasn't foolish enough to believe they might heal each other.

No, once jaded, there was no reversing the process. Not for either of them.

"Find out." Carl Davis was already beaming with the anticipation of victory. "Find out who got her out of Homeland."

Eric nodded. Carl was pacing—something he'd taken to doing more and more often behind closed doors as the election neared and tension drew tight enough to snap.

"Kagan made his mistake at last," Carl continued. "A rogue Shadow Ops agent. It's perfect!" Carl chuckled for a moment before turning to look at Eric. "Have you found Miranda? I want to visit that bitch while she's in a hospital bed."

Carl didn't pull his punches. Eric kept his distaste hidden behind a stern expression, but the truth was, he was a tad sickened by the way Carl went after Miranda. A mother had the right to defend her child, and that's all Miranda had ever done. Entering the election for Congress, well, that was something Eric rather admired in the middle-aged woman. Miranda had shown them she had a solid backbone when push had turned to shove.

"I know where she is," Eric answered Carl when he turned and stared at him. "But if you show up, Kagan will know you had me dig up the information. She's locked down after the last attempt on her life."

Carl waved a finger in the air. "Right . . . right . . . Don't show them my hand. Well, she'll surface sooner rather than later. If she stays hidden, she'll lose the lead she has in the polls. She has to hit the campaign trail like the rest of us. I'll catch up with her soon enough."

* * *

Dunn's flight crew knew their stuff.

Of course, Thais expected it of the man, but the truth was, she didn't know too much about him. Thais rolled out of the bunk she'd found across from the bedroom in the back of the plane. The fasten-seat-belt light was on. She dropped into one of the backseats and secured herself for landing.

No, she'd avoided looking too deeply into who Dunn Bateson was.

It had been an act of self-preservation.

One she couldn't really regret or second-guess. Thais only had one feeling about Dunn and that was an unmistakable warning. He triggered something inside her she refused to name.

Or unleash.

She'd made her choice and invested a lot of effort in locking away the feelings her life didn't afford her.

Everyone made choices.

Sacrifices for what they wanted to achieve. From the professional ballerina who ate a salad when she wanted a burger to the businessman who watched his toddlers' first steps on his cell phone because he was away from home working.

The aircraft touched down smoothly, taking a short taxi ride across the airfield before driving into another open hangar.

"You'll want to meet the team," Dunn said.

Thais unlatched her seat belt and stood. Dunn was watching her. He waited to see what she made of his words before one side of his lips twitched up. "Hoping I'll clear out of here and try to have this conversation down on the ground, Agent Sinclair? Where you have escape routes available?"

"Do you somehow expect me to blush over you knowing what I'm thinking?" she asked.

His eyes narrowed. "I do enjoy knowing what you blush over."

He turned the topic so very neatly back to something personal. She watched a flash of satisfaction cross his eyes before he turned and ducked beneath the door opening and disappeared from sight.

She hadn't expected that.

Damn, he surprised her too often. It was frustrating because she enjoyed it, and there was no way to deny it to herself.

Thais shook off her musings and followed him. The best course of action was to bury herself in work.

"I appreciate the help, Mr. Bateson," she began.

"But I'm a civilian?" He turned and closed the distance between them. Somewhere behind them, a car was waiting. The driver sitting behind the wheel in a dark suit and sunglasses. Looking straight ahead to avoid infringing on his boss's privacy.

Dunn made full use of the moment. Stepping up close and filling her senses with his persona. He just blocked everything else out. Touching off something inside her that made her unable to break her attention away from him.

He was big, but she worked with plenty of muscle-bound men. That fact alone didn't account for the level of intensity.

"Try contacting your team and you'll end up back in handcuffs, Thais," Dunn informed her. "They're playing nice with the media, and Carl Davis likes it that way. A rogue Shadow Ops agent is exactly what Carl needs to support his desire to shut Kagan down. Your section leader will let you be collateral damage if it means the difference between his teams surviving and Carl signing an executive order to disband them."

Thais held her hand up. "I am not discussing this with you, Dunn. You're a civilian."

She caught a flash of his teeth as he leaned toward her.

"A very well-informed civilian," he muttered, clearly pleased with himself.

Thais felt her emotions battling one another. Sure, he was smug. But he was extremely well-informed and that wasn't an easy feat. He'd earned the smugness. Cutting men down was something she excelled at, but she only had a taste for slicing into falsely inflated egos. She knew how hard it was to earn things.

"The key word is 'civilian,'" she answered smoothly.

He crossed his arms over his chest and leveled a hard look at her. "How long do you expect that little word to stand between us?"

"It's more of a concept," she answered, feeling a little twinge of regret. "If I have to take the heat on a case, well, it goes with the badge."

"Ah," Dunn responded softly. "Is that your way of saying you'd rather I left you in that cell until an assassin showed up to silence you?"

She didn't.

But she couldn't tell him so. No, Dunn would home in on the weakness and press against it as he tried to get inside her personal space.

"Yes," she informed him firmly. "I know what I signed up for."

"Liar," he shot back at her. "You enjoy knowing

someone is very nervous right now because they can't explain how you slipped out of their maximum security facility."

He offered her a smug look that she admitted she richly deserved.

"And you want to know how I managed it," he finished.

"Okay, I do want to know," she admitted.

Dunn inclined his head toward the waiting car. Thais offered him a raised eyebrow. "Just get in the car with me, little girl, and I'll get you some candy?"

He flashed her a grin before he turned and went toward the car.

He was baiting her.

The problem was, he was using really premium bait.

And she wanted a taste pretty bad.

It wasn't that Thais didn't know how to find her way on her own. Maybe she didn't know where they'd landed but that little bit of information wouldn't stand in her way. She had only the clothing on her back, and yet again, she wouldn't allow that fact to prevent her from reconnecting with her team.

One call and she'd have resources.

You'll also have to deal with Kagan calling the shots.

Thais liked her section leader. The fact that she trusted him was more important, but trust was built on a solid history together. One in which she'd learned a few things about Kagan, and one of them was, he would use bait when he felt it had the best odds of success.

She'd bit her tongue while her teammates went undercover.

Her teammates would be expected to keep their jaws tight while she was laid out, too.

Dunn had resources as well.

She narrowed her eyes but felt the decision taking form in her thoughts. Turning her back on Dunn's offer was illogical. So unless she wanted to know she'd turned tail and run because she couldn't control her emotional responses, the only choice left was to get into the car.

The door closed right after she pulled her feet inside. A second man moved up to take a position next to the driver before the man pulled the car out of the hangar.

"Show me your resources," Thais said. "And we'll see if it's worth my time."

Dunn didn't answer her.

Instead he cast her a look full of confidence. But what tempted her to smile back at him was the flash of intent in his eyes. She'd seen glimpses of the part of him no sane person would ever want to mess with.

Today, she was getting a look at the man who wasn't going to be denied satisfaction. Dunn was going to hunt down the person behind his mother's attack.

And kill them.

Damned if she didn't want to be along for the ride.

"Vitus," Miranda Delacroix said, fixing him with a look meant to break him down. "What can I do to help?"

"Focus on getting your strength back," Vitus responded.

Saxon was hanging back. Vitus shifted his gaze toward his brother for a moment but Saxon shook his head.

Miranda let out a little huff. "I see there is only one way to put this matter to rest."

There was a creak from her bed as she swung her legs over the side.

"Miranda—" Vitus began.

His mother-in-law sent him a raised eyebrow before she pushed herself right off the bed and stood for a moment. Saxon was suddenly there, offering her a forearm to lean on.

Miranda shook her head and walked away from the bed. "I . . . am perfectly fine"—she sent them both a solid look—"due a great deal to Agent Sinclair. So . . . you will allow me to assist in clearing her name."

Miranda faltered, causing both of them to converge on her. She ended up lowering herself into a chair, her pallor white but her gaze still sharp and demanding.

Vitus caved in. "We need support, against Carl."

Miranda frowned. "Yes, I can see how that would be useful. But wouldn't it be better if he somehow thought I had buckled beneath his demands?"

Saxon grunted. "Useful, yes. I don't see him trusting you after you turned over that conversation between him and Kirkland."

Miranda fiddled her fingers for a moment, lost in contemplation. "We need to cause an uproar. Shift the voters away from Carl and onto Tom Hilliard."

"Miranda," Vitus began. "You have done enough. Leave this to us."

His mother-in-law fluttered her eyelashes, sending a chill down his spine. Because his wife, Damascus, had the exact same look when she was planning on digging in her heels and defying him.

His wife would never forgive him if something happened to her mother on his watch.

The fight coming was a firestorm. They'd either all be in the clear or all dead.

The cabin the car delivered her to was magnificent.

Thais paused as she climbed out of the car, sweeping the huge log-cabin-style home with a critical eye. It was set against the red and orange rocks of the Arizona desert. The dry heat didn't distract from the magnificence of the setting.

"Inside," Dunn muttered as he cupped her elbow and helped raise her up. "Kent went to great lengths to get you up here without anyone catching sight of you from above. Don't ruin his work now."

Thais felt a charge go through her from the contact. She lifted her elbow out of his hand and strode forward. The driver had parked beneath an awning that cut the direct sun, as well as offering shelter from satellites.

"Do I get to meet Kent?" she asked.

Dunn crooked his finger at her. "You get to meet the team. I promised you resources."

And satisfaction . . .

She drew in a deep breath, wishing her inner voice wasn't on such a mission to turn her into a wreck at Dunn's feet. Seriously, Dunn Bateman was super rich and that fact alone had women hunting him in droves.

The fact that he kept his body in shape only added to the allure.

That's not what attracts you . . .

Thais felt heat creeping into her cheeks. It was a solid truth. She'd had plenty of men in prime condition. Could get a bed partner in about two minutes from among her fellow agents or the military escort they so often brushed elbows with.

It had all become so very boring.

Dunn woke something inside her.

A sensation she'd dismissed as something produced by her youth and inexperience.

You mean a need . . .

She did, and there was no way she could allow him to know about it.

Except he already does . . .

"Allow me to introduce Kent," Dunn said, interrupting her thoughts as he reached a man.

Thais swept him up and down, noting the way he stood. Kent wasn't a shit talker. No, Thais knew a trained man from his stance. Kent had it. His eyes taking her in with all the same experience she'd swept him over with. They were taking each other's measure, the nod she earned from Kent was something she knew the true value of.

"Nice to meet you," Kent offered with a slight brogue. He looked at Dunn. "Team is ready to bring you up to speed."

Kent pushed a door open. The glass was mirrored, allowing for one-way sight only. Inside she found herself face-to-face with a control center Kagan would have been proud to call his own.

Monitors were mounted on the wall. Along with live shots from around the cabin itself, there was an unmistakable view from a satellite. There was also a white board with a very crisp timeline on it. Miranda's attack was there, the angle of the shooter circled along with details of the types of amination and rifles it fit into. Every possible escape route was mapped. In short, she didn't see anything missing.

"Ready to get to work?"

Thais turned around to discover Dunn watching her. He'd shrugged out of his suit jacket and rolled up the cuffs of his expensive shirt. He also had a chest harness on with a pistol in it.

"Want to see my permit?" he inquired when her attention remained on the gun.

"Guess it stands to reason you'd have one," she answered, while leaning over to peer at a laptop screen. Thais blinked. "You're wormed into the federal net . . ."

"As I said," Dunn answered her, "Kent laid down some serious work to get you out of Homeland."

"Damn it, Dunn!" She whirled around to face him. "This is my point. You're a civilian and that"—she pointed at the laptop behind her—"is a federal offense."

"Unless someone else did the worming and I'm checking the system installed by my company to ensure that it's functioning."

Dunn didn't miss a beat. He pushed off the table, daring her to try another attack on him.

Thais squared off with him, feeling the rise of anticipation inside herself.

"Arrogance won't save you from espionage charges," she said.

"And it won't save your life if you go running back to Kagan and the Hale brothers." Dunn took another step and looked down at her. "On your own, your chances aren't very high. Carl Davis has Kagan over a barrel and you know it, Thais. We're not going to solve this one by playing nice. I'd expect a Shadow Ops agent to realize that."

She drew in a stiff breath. Suddenly the need to argue

with him dissipated, leaving her on shaky ground as she realized how much she didn't like knowing he was willing to put himself in jeopardy for her sake.

He wasn't a teammate.

No, this was personal.

And it made her insides quiver.

"I know it," she offered in a low voice. "And there is no way I can allow you to place yourself at risk for me. I had full knowledge of what I signed up for when I accepted my badge."

Thais tried to step back. Wanting to leave him with a firm but not unkind rejection. Dunn caught her upper arm.

"They put a hit out on my mother, Thais." His eyes flashed with unsatisfied rage. "No one is going to stop me from being involved."

He released her. She ended up falling back a pace because she'd been pulling against his grip so hard.

"The only thing you need to decide, Thais," Dunn informed her sternly, "is whether or not you want in on the hunt."

Because he was going to go after his mother's attacker regardless of her or the legal walls he had to go through.

She admired his tenacity.

And dedication to his family.

Whatever else she might think, Thais didn't doubt that Dunn was someone the hitman had better be very worried about. The room was full of resources, ones her own Shadow Ops team would have enjoyed having on a case.

"I'm in." She wasn't too sure exactly when she decided on her answer, only that the words were past her lips before anything like logical reasoning managed to stop them.

Dunn's lips twitched. Just a tiny amount before his expression tightened with intent. "Let's get to work."

"Miranda," Mason Kingston said, "I have been very concerned for you."

Miranda was a credit to her years of training to be the perfect political family pawn. She glided over to a chair and sat down with only a slight pinching around her lips to betray the pain it caused her. Congressman Kingston didn't notice because she kept her eyelashes fluttering.

"I'm really quite well," Miranda informed her future colleague.

"I hope they've brought that rogue agent in," Kingston added.

Miranda widened her eyes. Vitus watched from his post, admiring the way Miranda made sure the neighboring tables at the benefit could overhear her.

"Really, Mason," she admonished him in a perfect mothering tone that landed softly enough to keep Mason from bristling. "You simply cannot put any faith in what the press is saying. Special Agent Sinclair saved me from being murdered."

Mason Kingston frowned, interlacing his hands over his plump belly. Miranda swooped in for the kill.

"Not that I am surprised," Miranda muttered as she cast a look around. "Carl Davis has been working with that Kirkland Grog. His father was a criminal mastermind! That family owns half the media sites in the country and they say the most incorrect things. Now you all know I am not one to dwell on gossip . . ."

The elite of Washington offered Miranda a soft round of laughter. They were clustered in the rose garden of a very expensive resort. Enjoying the expertly prepared food while presidential candidate Tom Hilliard conducted a meet-and-greet with the press. Tom was lagging in the polls but Vitus had to hand it to the man, he was going down swinging.

"If I believed what the press was saying"—Miranda looked at Mason—"I'd accept their charges against you about payoffs from the unions."

Vitus watched Saxon's eyes narrow. Mason Kingston was taking payoffs. The feds hadn't moved in yet because they needed more evidence to make sure his impressive list of legal representatives couldn't wiggle him out of a conviction.

"I saw that charge in the same publication as the one about Special Agent Sinclair being an assassin," Miranda said, finishing up with a bright smile. "Pure nonsense, as I'm certain you'll agree."

Mason received her message loud and clear. Saxon watched the way the man flipped his attitude. Miranda continued to move around the gathering, taking the opportunity to tar and feather the charges against Thais while linking those false accusations very neatly to Carl Davis.

And then there was the unmistakable suggestion from the older woman that more than just Mason realized was a warning. They either got on board with her in condemning the press or she'd take them all down with Thais.

She was drawing a line and it was a dangerous thing to do. The Washington elite might just decide to watch her crash and burn. But Miranda knew it, had been reared among the flesh-eating animals surrounding her. The demure poise and flutters of eyelashes were as practiced as any other form of fighting. In short, she was in her element. Twisting words and making subtle promises to play nice so long as everyone went along with the way she wanted things to be said.

Networking—the silent, and so very necessary skill of the elected leader.

By the end of the event, however, Saxon could see the signs of Miranda's strength diminishing. She held herself up though, only allowing Vitus to help her into the car.

"I hope that was a good effort for our cause," she said after they'd pulled away from the curb and privacy was ensured.

Saxon sent her an approving look. "Remind me to have you teach a session on intimidation tactics when this is all over."

Miranda's expression lit with pleasure. "I learned everything my father wanted me to know about twisting people into line with a very precisely worded warning." She relaxed back into the seat now that no one was around to see her lack of bearing. "To be truthful, I never enjoyed the skill so much until today. Carl really is overdue for a reckoning. It was a pleasure working toward that goal."

The three occupants in the car shared a moment of agreement. But Vitus sent Miranda a stern look.

Miranda lifted her hand to silence him before he started in on warning her. "I know the risks, Vitus. It isn't my intention to lecture you but I have been doing this a lot longer than you have. Mason Kingston used to pinch my bottom when he thought my father wasn't

looking. The truth is, my father knew and didn't want
to risk offending Mason's father over it."

Vitus's expression tightened with disapproval.

"Carl started this," Miranda said firmly. "And by
Christ, I am going to finish it now. I've been silent far
too long."

Miranda had spent the better part of thirty years
playing the loving wife of Jeb Ryland. She'd been
groomed for the role by her father and a family of what
many labeled Washington elite. The Delacroix family
had been in office for over a hundred years. She had
been reared to be the dutiful wife and mother, expected
to transform her daughter into a copy of herself.

Instead she had fooled them all. Hiding a solid spine
while quietly encouraging her daughter, Damascus, to
be her own woman and marry the man of her choice.
Jeb Ryland had forbidden Damascus to marry Vitus,
and had instead arranged a match with Carl Davis.

Now, it was done, the lines firmly drawn between
Carl and the Shadow Ops teams.

Thais remembered the bubble bath.

She felt a blush staining her cheeks but at least she
was alone.

At last.

Working a case meant skimming through data. Tons
of it. Looking for that one odd fact, which might lead
to another and one more to form an evidence chain.
They had the bullet and a short list of people who would
put a hit out on Miranda. Finding the money, well, Thais
stretched her neck and heard it pop. She'd been looking
for the money all day.

She rubbed her eyes on the way toward the bedroom Dunn pointed out as hers for the night. Working data had never been as hard as it was with Dunn in the room. The guy was a distraction but he wasn't lazy, she'd give him that. He'd been working as hard as the rest of the team.

The bubble bath . . .

With the doors of the suite closed behind her, Thais looked at the large slipper tub. It had gold feet and sat in front of floor-to-ceiling windows that overlooked a section of red rock. The spa town of Sedona was just over the ridge, the private residence nestled into a section of private estates that came with enough land to ensure privacy.

The tub sat in a hexagon section of glass so it could overlook the rocks.

You baited him . . .

She had. Thais couldn't stop the memory from rising up to play across her mind. She might have called Dunn a civilian justly but he'd been involved in cases from time to time over the last two years. Shadow Ops teams needed to operate off grid, an action that was becoming harder and harder to pull off in a world of cell phones and social media junkies.

Dunn's reputation as a recluse was the perfect resource. He invested a small fortune in keeping his planes flying so no one really knew his location.

There was a rap on the door a moment before it opened to reveal Dunn. She felt his arrival as much as she witnessed it. All of her senses rippling with awareness. He was better than a double espresso when it came to waking her up.

And she couldn't allow it to keep growing. She dug deep, looking for the professional persona she'd perfected over the years of working with Shadow Ops.

"I agreed to work a case with you, Dunn." She sent him a hard look. "You don't like me calling you a civilian but coming in here tells me you aren't getting what it means to be teammates. This isn't playtime. I'm working and you should be, too."

He came forward, stopping for a moment near the tub. "We've finished the day's work."

"A case is finished when it's closed," she replied. "A good agent doesn't take time off when lives hang in the balance."

Her retort earned her a half grin. He was devastating enough without his lips in that cocky grin. "And yet"—he trailed a finger along the edge of the tub—"you've made use of downtime on cases in the past."

Her cheeks warmed. "I shouldn't have."

"Why not?" he asked in a husky tone. "There is only so much we can do on this end. It's a waiting game now."

"One which would have been better served if you'd left me where my section leader did." Thais latched onto the topic to avoid the issue of the tub.

And the fact that you knew Dunn was watching when you took that bath . . . teased him . . .

She had. Switched in as bait while Saxon Hale took their real witness off grid, Thais had indulged in a bubble bath in Dunn's cabin. She'd only suspected he'd been watching.

Now, she knew for certain he had.

"I won't apologize for getting you out of Homeland." His tone had sharpened. "Ever."

She felt their gazes lock, felt a reaction inside herself that was uncontrollable. She'd gone to a great deal of effort to make certain she wasn't the weak link of her team. She protected others but Dunn was making it clear he'd decided to cover her when she needed it. She shouldn't like the feeling, but denying it was impossible, and he knew it.

He was closer than she realized, making it necessary to tip her head up to maintain eye contact. He reached out and brushed her lips.

Straight across them, the connection sending a ripple of awareness through her.

"You can't deny the attraction between us, Thais," he whispered.

She turned, facing him head-on. "I'm not. Just doing the logical thing and walking away. Neither of us is looking for more than release."

Professional and cold.

Her delivery lacked none of the sharp edges she was known for in the field. She should have felt a sense of mild satisfaction. Instead, Thais realized she felt hollow.

Like she was denying herself something she needed.

She drew in a sharp breath, pushing back a step.

She couldn't need.

"It's for the best, Bateson," she added.

The gauntlet was down now. Dunn's eyes narrowed, confirming her assessment of the situation a moment before he was coming toward her. She retreated, reacting to his approach, moving back until she was against the wall, his hands flattened on either side of her head.

He was going to kiss her.

The certainty of it crashed down on her like a wave.

Stunning her with the force of the connection and wiping out everything except the feeling of the force of the water.

Only, he didn't kiss her.

Thais opened her eyes and found Dunn's emerald ones fixed on her.

"I want to," he informed her, his fingers flexing on the wall beside her head. "I want to smother you in a kiss hard enough to drown out your ideas of what should be between us in favor of what we both want."

Thais reached up and pressed her own hand over her lips.

She mustn't.

"You," he rasped out, "are something I've tried very hard not to think about."

The common ground between them was strangely alluring. Like a haven she might enter if she was willing to take the risk.

Don't kid yourself . . . he's not the sort of man a girl domesticates . . . he will always roam . . .

"Ye're hiding behind your badge, Thais," he muttered, his voice dipping down into a timbre that touched off a shiver inside her. "Label me as ye will but I'm more honest than ye are."

Dunn pushed back, moving several paces away from her. "I want more from this relationship than professional interaction." His eyes flashed with hunger. "Much, much more. But I'm not going to overwhelm ye. We're either partners with full knowledge of what we're getting into or nothing."

He meant it.

And loathed it as much as she did.

Thais watched his jaw clamp tight with frustration

before he turned and gave her a view of his back while he left the suite. She stayed against the wall for a long moment, needing the support as she ordered herself to stay where she was.

It was the last thing she truly wanted.

"Has that contract man checked back in?"

Carl Davis launched into what was on his mind the moment Eric Geyer closed the door of his office. It was a tiny space because they were on Carl's campaign plane. But it was very private.

"No," Eric answered as he sat down. "I advise against moving forward with your plans for Miranda."

Carl slapped the desk top. "Why? Thais Sinclair is on the run, giving us a perfect scapegoat. I want that bitch Miranda dead. I want her friends to know what I do to people who cross me. This is how the game is played, Eric. The man on the top is the one who made all the others fall into line and took out the ones who got in his way."

"If you want to be president, I suggest you leave it alone this time. Miranda has too many eyes on her now."

Carl didn't care for Eric arguing. His eyes widened in outrage, his cheeks darkening. He worked his mouth a few times before getting words out.

"Do it! Or I'll find a man with the balls to spill the blood that needs spilling. Don't kid yourself, Geyer, we're no different than bucks fighting in a herd of stags. Miranda chose a side. If I let her live, the others will just think they can step out of line, too. I'm going to be the master, Eric, and the rest of them are my slaves." Carl leaned back in his chair. "If you want to have a pampered position, get busy earning it. The only thing being a nice guy earns you is a lot of people standing at your graveside."

She understood arousal.

It was a topic Thais had spent time acquainting herself with. Some would argue that it was her induction into the world of espionage that had given birth to her extremely blunt approach to sex and how it affected her body.

They would be wrong.

Her mother had reared her to use sex and the allure of pleasure as a means of gaining everything she desired. Every detail of her body was for pleasing and enticing. The only factor she applied her personal choice to was her targets.

Dunn was something else though.

A source of stimuli that defied her grasp on the entire concept of sex. He would have overwhelmed her. It was a harsh little reality she'd be unwise to ignore.

Maybe you're a fool for pushing him away . . .

The word "coward" was a harsh one, and yet she found herself contemplating it and discovering it fit all too well under the circumstances.

She had good reasons, of course. Experience was a harsh master. An effective one, however. She'd stopped believing in joy and was too jaded to change her mind, even in the face of the storm Dunn seemed able to brew inside her.

The wiser choice.

The bitterness in her mouth confirmed it was so.

Pullman disconnected the call. He contemplated the little burner phone in his hand.

Smashing it felt like a solid plan.

His jobs were always dangerous and often financed by people with anger control issues. His lips twisted into a grin. He was a hitman. It was only a very rare case that offered him some sort of enjoyment in the spilling of blood.

Like a father avenging the death of his son's murder. Pullman turned and pulled his hood up so he could walk down the sidewalk. The sun had set, which meant it was time to move again.

Yeah, dropping a street thug who had killed a kid who'd been in the wrong part of town was a contract Pullman had enjoyed taking.

Working with Carl Davis? It was wearing on Pullman's patience.

Not that Pullman had any real choice. Carl Davis was too big of a dog. Stupid, maybe. But there was one universal rule in life. Everywhere you went, there was one top dog no one crossed. Learn who that was fast, because the alternative was to step on its tail and get your throat ripped out.

So Miranda Delacroix needed to die.

Pullman made his way toward what had once been a gas station. People had taken to using the empty lot as a place to display used cars for sale. He walked between them, selecting one and dialing the number on the sign in the window. When the call went to voice mail, he moved on to another vehicle and dialed.

"I'm calling about the car, can you meet me now? I have cash."

Pullman killed the call a second after the excited owner said he'd be there in ten minutes. Half an hour later, Pullman was driving away, the owner slightly befuddled to be holding ten grand in cash. The guy would never realize how easy he made it for Pullman to move across the country without traffic cameras picking up on his whereabouts. In the digital age, where license plates could be flagged by a central agency and patrol cars scanned ten license plates a minute, Pullman needed a car registered to someone no one was looking for and someone who wasn't smart enough to insist on doing the transfer of ownership together. By the time the guy realized Pullman was never going to show up at the DMV, it wouldn't matter if the cops were looking for the car.

"Miranda's handled."

Eric watched Carl Davis absorb the news. The presidential hopeful was arrogant, something not unfamiliar to Eric. Yet it was still a bit unnerving to witness the way Carl's eyes began to glow with anticipation over Miranda's impending murder.

Eric took solace in the sensation, however. Using it as confirmation of the fact that he still had some part of a soul left.

Carl was tapping his desktop, his mood clearly improving.

"Kagan is going to regret his little stunt now," Carl declared jovially.

Eric wasn't so certain. At least, he wouldn't bet on Kagan scaring so easily. Miranda Delacroix was a prime candidate when it came to possibly hitting the Shadow Ops section leader in something that might be called a soft spot.

She was motherly, kissed babies, and wanted to clean up the environment.

But Kagan was an experienced operator in the field. No one got to the position Kagan was in if they didn't grow some very thick skin. Kagan would be a fool to think Miranda wouldn't be in danger after she turned over a voice recording of Carl and Kirkland Grog.

The action had paid off though. Kirkland was sitting in federal prison, his media empire being torn to bits by his siblings. The lack of a strong leader emerging from among the Raven's offspring meant Carl lost a great deal of his free media coverage.

Kagan had to know Carl would seek retaliation.

Well, Eric would bet Kagan expected it, but what Carl really should have been worried about was whether or not Kagan was planning the entire thing.

Carl Davis believed himself too far removed from it though. He was an arrogant pile of shit but Eric stood with him because life was about winners and losers. Carl was a winner and Eric wanted his seat at the victory feast.

Was he a sellout?

Maybe.

But so was everyone else. Some of them were just too full of shit to admit it. So there was no way Eric would allow guilt to land on his shoulders. He was just doing what any other man in the same position would have done. There were twenty Secret Service men traveling with them and Eric didn't doubt they'd all fall into line with whatever Carl demanded if he was offering them the position of head of his security.

The only thing left to do was syphon off some of the cash from the offshore accounts Carl gave him access to for dealing with hitmen.

An insurance policy.

Retirement fund.

Escape plan.

Whatever anyone wanted to call it, Eric moved money between the slush funds, placing 10 percent into his own accounts before paying Pullman his fee.

CHAPTER THREE

Carl Davis was a good public speaker.

He knew it and utilized the skill to stoke up the passion of his followers. He might be leading in the polls, but there were ten weeks until the election, and he wasn't going to take a chance on a last-minute upset.

"It is a travesty of justice . . . to see the federal agent Thais Sinclair being sheltered by her own kind to avoid facing the penalty of the law."

The crowd roared with approval.

"I promise you . . ."—Carl had to wait for the screaming to die down—"I will bring this rogue agent to justice, along with anyone who helps her."

His followers cheered. He scanned the crowd, taking delight in the number of posters made up picturing Thais in handcuffs.

"Miranda Delacroix is a beacon of hope for our planet and children . . . I will not stand to see her silenced by corrupt businessmen who value only their profits . . . who would see our oceans polluted and our air unfit to breathe!"

* * *

"He's laying it on thick." Saxon Hale muttered out loud what they were all thinking. Inside the small town house, the Shadow Ops teams were clustered around a monitor to watch Carl Davis.

"He's declaring war on us," Dare Servant answered. "I'd hoped busting Kirkland would cut enough of his funds off to slow the bastard down."

"It did," Vitus remarked. "That . . ."—he pointed at the monitor—"that's a desperate man. He's trying to push Kagan into a corner."

"I wouldn't trust Carl to honor any option he offered," Dare Servant said. "We all know too much about him."

"So we'd better get busy finding out who paid for the hit on Miranda," Saxon declared grimly. "Kagan will have to order us after Thais soon."

"I'm surprised the order hasn't already come down," Dare Servant answered. "We're on borrowed time."

It wasn't a first for any man in the room. They worked high-risk cases, ones where the consequences were often their own lives. Thais knew it as well.

Thais was restless.

She shifted in her sleep, not really deep enough into slumber to completely shut out the world around her.

She heard the door open to her suite.

Her body responded with every bit of the sharpness she expected from herself. Her mind cleared instantly, allowing her to listen for the footfalls of the person approaching her bed.

"Thais . . ." Dunn's voice came across the room. "We've got company."

He was as collected as she expected her teammates to be. She rolled over, landing on her feet as she took in the way he'd braced himself between her and the door.

"There's a bunker inside the back wall," Dunn informed her. "Scent sealed."

He moved past her as she stepped into the boots she'd placed beside her bed. Dunn reached the back wall of the room as she heard heavy steps on the floor beyond the suite door.

"Federal agents! Search warrant!"

"Thais . . . here . . ." Dunn had pulled part of the wall open. What looked like a privacy wall between the bathroom and the bedroom opened to show a dark space between. "Inside . . . now."

She was in motion before he finished. Slipping inside and moving back to make room for him.

Only Dunn didn't join her.

"You'll be safe here," he informed her before he closed the door.

She surged forward but it was too late. There was a click and then a whoosh of air as the pressure stabilized. She dug at the place where the door was but it was smooth, only offering her a thin line of disruption between where the door panel was and the wall met it.

"Dunn!"

She shouldn't have cried out.

But she just couldn't stop herself.

Her poise was crumbling as she thought about Dunn stepping between her and danger. She couldn't allow him to do it.

Which is why he locked you inside here . . .

It was infuriating.

And touching . . .

She ended up hitting the door with frustration. Damn him for making her feel.

And damn her for liking it.

"Clear!"

Dunn fought the urge to try to flip over. "I'm not resisting," he growled at the agent who was pressing his knee into Dunn's shoulder. "So get off me."

The suite was lit up now, agents scouring the place, the frowns on their faces making it clear they didn't like coming up empty-handed.

Two of them hooked Dunn by his handcuffed arms and hauled him off the floor. They strong-armed him toward a chair near the fireplace in the suite and dropped him into it.

"Where is she?" one demanded.

"My partners don't spend the night," Dunn remarked.

Thais's bra was hanging over the back of a chair, so there was no point in claiming there hadn't been a woman present.

"Where is she?" the agent persisted. "I'll haul you in if you don't tell me what I want to know."

Dunn sent the guy a hard look. "A gentleman doesn't kiss and tell. So unless that search warrant says I have to divulge the name of my dinner date, you're never going to hear it. My man will already have my lawyer on the line."

"You know we're looking for Thais Sinclair."

"How the fuck would I know that?" Dunn demanded. "Maybe you should start by showing me that damned warrant and it had better be good because I've never dated Thais Sinclair."

The best lies were the ones that didn't deviate from the truth very far. An old espionage trick. Play as close to yourself as you could because it would limit the number of possible times you could be taken by surprise.

"And while you're at it," Dunn continued. "Better get a list together of evidence supporting your appearance here tonight."

"We wouldn't have a warrant if we didn't have evidence," one of the agents said as he flashed a badge and identification card. "Agent Bradford and I'll get you the list. But your plane took off right after she was broken out of Homeland. You have the resources to accomplish that sort of an operation."

Dunn raised an eyebrow. "So I'm being detained because I'm rich?"

Agent Bradford shook his head. "You were on the plane that left the area at the same time Agent Sinclair would have."

Dunn grunted. "As you can see . . . she's not here and I have never dated her. So my leaving town at the same time is a little thin."

"You forgot the resources."

Dunn leveled a hard look at Agent Bradford. "Miranda Delacroix is my mother."

The agents searching through the closets went still, turning to look his way.

"You heard me." Dunn didn't raise his voice, but he didn't need to, because the search had come to a standstill. "Check the records. I visited her in the hospital, flew in the moment I heard about her being shot. There is no way in hell I'd help whoever hurt her. So I don't give a damn what sort of evidence you think you have. I wouldn't be alive if she hadn't risked her reputation and future against having me instead of the very quiet abortion her image-loving family preferred."

Dunn enjoyed the looks on the faces of the men in his home.

Hell, he just plain loved being able to say what so many people had told him never to talk about.

The truth had been burning a hole in him since he was old enough to understand that his mother wasn't in his life because of her parents. When you were five years old, all you wanted was a mommy and grandparents. A five-year-old didn't grasp the ugliness of the power-hungry world.

At least, he shouldn't have had to come face-to-face with the fact that his grandparents didn't want him to be alive.

Now? He was going to enjoy letting the information out. He was going to enjoy every last second of knowing that those who had kept Miranda from the man she loved were inconvenienced by his revelation.

And he was going to love knowing Thais was safer for it all.

Time was crawling by.

Sealed behind the door, Thais flattened her head against the seam, straining to hear what was happening on the other side.

Nothing.

She was truly sealed in tight. It made sense. In the era of heat-sensing scopes, Dunn had ensured his bunker was a true haven. Scent sealed, so even a dog wasn't going to sniff her out.

And he'd put her in it.

Protected her . . .

She paced down the length of the narrow hallway, agitated by the fact that she wasn't facing down the situation.

They'll only haul you back to a cell . . .

It made more sense to stay hidden. But Thais wasn't thinking at the moment. No, she was reacting. Emotion was rising up and over the walls she'd built to keep them back. Hitting her like a tsunami.

She moved faster, trying to escape, and ended up looking at a set of stairs. Lights flickered on as she came close, showing her that they descended below the level of the house. At the bottom, a living space opened up. Spacious and furnished well, Thais roamed around it, impressed by the details. Against one wall, there was even an electric fireplace to give the space a homey feel.

A kitchen was against one wall. A peek inside the cabinets showed her enough stock for someone to live there for weeks on end without worry. Dunn's reputation as a recluse was suddenly a lot easier to understand.

She sensed Dunn more than she heard him. Turning around and hesitating for a second because she wasn't sure if she'd just conjured him up or if he was really emerging from the stairwell.

"They're gone," Dunn offered, a hint of disgust in his tone. "Or so they say. Personally, I don't think they've tossed in the towel just yet."

"Unlikely," she agreed, coming around the breakfast bar. "You should have let me deal with them."

One of Dunn's dark eyebrows rose. Thais felt her eyes narrow in response and he didn't miss it.

Dunn scoffed at her annoyance. "I would think you'd have a little more flexibility when it came to working on a team, Thais."

"You're not my team," she retorted. Her heart was accelerating, the wave of emotions she'd walked down the stairs to escape reforming.

Dunn met her head-on. "Yes I am."

"You're a civilian—" And her control was slipping. She knew how to deal with men like him—never take a straight, frontal approach.

But she marched up to him and hit him straight in the center of his chest. "Don't *ever* . . . cut me out of the action . . ."

Her heart was racing and her respiration, too. Her rapid breathing drew in his scent, setting off a whole new awareness of him.

"I will not let you be bait, Thais," he growled.

"You don't have a choice," she insisted with another sock to his chest. He was just as hard-bodied as she'd determined he was.

And she liked knowing it.

Heat was flaring up inside her, melting the walls she'd learned to live inside of for the sake of her choices. Her entire world was coming down as the part of her she'd kept contained broke free.

"Yes, I do," he informed her before wrapping his hand around the back of her head. He threaded his fingers through her hair, pulling the strands just tight enough to send a ripple of awareness through her core.

She craved that strength.

And Dunn didn't deny her.

He caught her against his body, wrapping his opposite arm around her waist and pulling her close. She was reeling for a moment, intoxicated by the sensation overload of being pressed up against him.

And then he kissed her.

Thinking . . . control . . . even reason . . . they all went up in a wisp of smoke as the flames inside her flared up.

And she liked it.

There was no denying it or even a pretense of seeking out enough self-discipline to rein herself back in.

She wanted him and she rose up onto her toes to kiss him back.

His chest rumbled with a growl. Thais felt an answering sound coming from herself as she flattened her hands on his chest, smoothing over the ridges she'd only suspected lay beneath his shirt.

She shivered.

And let out a little moan that gained an instant response from Dunn. His arms tightened around her, his lips parting hers to deepen the kiss. His tongue swept along her lower lip, awakening a throbbing in her clit.

She liked sex.

But Dunn made her crave it.

Crave him . . .

His clothing irritated her. Presenting a barrier she wasn't willing to suffer. Thais dug her fingers into the knot of his tie, loosening it before pulling it away from his neck. She gained her freedom for a moment as she drew the length of silk away from his throat. She caught the flash of hunger in his eyes a moment before he caught the edge of her shirt and pulled the garment up and over her head.

The rush of cool air against her overheated skin was welcome. Her bra was somewhere in the suite above. Dunn enjoyed the sight of her breasts, his lips thinning as his green eyes lowered to them.

She knew what lust looked like.

Knew how a man looked at her when she was nothing but an amusement.

Dunn's expression was different. The intensity of it sent a chill through her. He was going to be intimate with her and what frightened her had nothing to do with the physical realities of sex.

She stepped back.

His eyes narrowed as he unbuttoned the cuffs of his shirt. "I know I scare you, Thais."

He worked the buttons on his shirtfront, baring his chest before he shrugged out of it.

"You don't," she muttered, the need to shield her weakness too strong to resist. But her tone betrayed her. Husky and full of uncertainty. "I'm just wondering how wise . . . this is . . ."

His lips twitched. "Wise? Maybe not, but it feels like a necessity from where I'm standing . . ."

She knew the feeling. He reached out and cupped her breast. The touch so simple, and yet, there was a gleam in his eyes that made it seem so very tender. He was caressing her.

She couldn't recall the last time she'd seen someone look at her like that.

It shook her to her core, drawing her back toward him, back into the feeling of intimacy. Having a taste of it made her realize how truly starved she was for more than the physical act of intercourse.

And how long it had been since she'd let anyone strip her walls down.

She reached out for him, fumbling with his belt as she worked the buckle loose and pulled it open.

"It's not going to be that simple, Thais."

His tone was husky and full of intent. He scooped

her off her feet, lifting her up and onto the island in the kitchen. She sucked in her breath at the coolness of the marble against her bare skin. But it just made her more conscious of how hot his skin was when he cupped her breasts in both hands.

"I've thought too much about you . . . about having you . . ." His tone was almost too low to hear, or maybe she was just too focused on the way he was kneading her breasts.

"We're going to do more than fuck."

It was a promise.

A very male, dominant sort of thing to say.

Her eyes had been slipping closed, as he drew his hands down her body, slowly rubbing her abdomen. But she lifted her eyelids as he caught the waistband of her soft pajama bottoms. There was a flash of determination in his eyes, one he waited for her to see before he pulled her clothing from her body, laying her bare.

He swept her up and down, his lips curving up with male satisfaction. She might have felt exposed, maybe she should have felt that way, but she didn't. Instead, she was caught up once more in the sensation of seeing the way he looked at her.

And noticing just how different it was from the countless targets she'd engaged with over the years.

But what exactly was it?

Dunn didn't give her time to think her feelings through.

And the truth was, she didn't want to think.

No, she let out a breathy sound as he leaned over her body, his bare skin connecting with hers. It was mind-blowing.

And exactly what she craved.

There were a million points of contact between them. He framed the sides of her face, stroking her skin before turning his head and fitting his mouth against hers. He took the kiss slow, savoring the interaction of their lips. It was a sweet torment, one that kept her suspended between intimacy and lust. She wanted to move faster, trying to lift her head up and kiss him harder.

"No," he growled, keeping her head in place before he trailed kisses down her neck and onto her chest.

Her nipples drew tight as she felt like she was twisting on the end of a thread while waiting for him to draw her nipple into his mouth. Seconds swelled up until they felt as long as minutes. She felt his breath brush the tender skin on her breast first. Goosebumps went racing across her skin, her senses heightened to an almost unbearable level.

"You're driving me insane . . . ," she muttered. Her admission drew a grunt from him.

"I know the feeling well," he offered, cupping her breast in his hand so he could lock gazes with her before she let her eyelids slide shut in favor of just immersing herself in the sensation of the moment.

She wanted to keep her eyes closed.

But it was cowardly of her.

The sting of that knowledge was too much to bear, or maybe it was the way his hand went still that she just couldn't tolerate. Either way, Thais opened her eyes.

"Should I let it be that easy for you, Thais?" His hand moved once more on her breast.

Somehow, she'd forgotten just how intense it felt to have her breasts kneaded.

Her clit was throbbing now. The little bundle of nerve endings eager for the next step.

"Let you close your eyes . . . ," Dunn continued as he stroked her, drawing his hand down from her breast. Across her abdomen. "And steal the moment of surrender from me?"

"I'm not surrendering," she argued. Her pride flared up, burning enough of her lust away for her to contemplate rolling across the surface of the marble to make an escape.

"You will," he promised her.

A moment later he was giving her the hard kiss she'd tried to take. His mouth claiming hers as he pressed her down onto the marble. His strength was what she craved. Thais met him in the middle, kissing him back just as hard. She reached for him, drawing her fingernails down his back.

His chest rumbled with a growl, and she answered with a sound that was something between a purr and a howl. Communication between them was transforming into emotions and reactions. Words fell away as Dunn lost control over his instincts.

He pushed himself up, reaching down to free his cock. Thais watched with eager anticipation, opening her thighs because nothing else mattered at that moment except having him satisfy the need clawing at her insides.

The first thrust was hard.

But that was exactly how she wanted him.

She clasped him between her thighs, raising her hips for the next thrust, opening her eyes when he pressed her thighs open so he controlled their pace.

His eyes were full of the need to dominate. She might have said she'd seen it before but there was a stark difference. Dunn was intent on making sure she climaxed.

He slowed down, thrusting deeply into her and pausing before withdrawing. The muscles along his neck
were corded with the effort.

She might have watched him longer but her body
was too insistent. She needed to be pushed over the
edge into climax. He knew it and she might have taken
issue with it, if she'd been able to form any real thoughts.

But she couldn't. There was only the building tempo
of the moment. Her eyes slid shut as he drew a hand
down the inside of her thigh so he could rub her clit.

She gasped, letting out a harsh cry. Control vanished
in a second as she began to twist and clench with or-
gasm. Dunn thrust deep, filling her as her body tightened around his length. She surged upward, straining
toward him as she clawed at the marble beneath her
back.

"Christ . . . ," he growled, thrusting into her with
short, hard motions. His tone was hoarse as he lost control, his cock spurting inside her while he growled.

When it was done, she was too spent to think.

Okay, she just didn't want to deal with things like
logic or rational thinking. Not when she felt so relaxed,
so very satisfied. So safe.

How fucking long had it been?

She didn't know.

And later would be soon enough to think the matter
through.

She shouldn't have let him kiss her.

*Ha! You mean you shouldn't have kissed him back
like you did . . .*

Thais hadn't even opened her eyes yet when her brain

snapped on. There were plenty of times she enjoyed the way her brain engaged in a lightning-fast flash.

There had been times when being clear-witted the moment she awoke meant the difference between life and death.

Today, though, she admitted to longing for just a little brain fog.

It was a weak, emotional need.

She knew it and, still, there was a hint of hesitation in her as she enjoyed the feeling of the clean sheets around her bare body. They were high-quality ones, bamboo if she didn't miss her guess, and there wasn't even a hint of mustiness.

Dunn's staff performed their duties well.

Thais took in the room but she'd already guessed she was alone.

Are you disappointed?

She let out a little hiss on her way into the bathroom. Normally a shower helped her clear her head and get her emotions straightened out.

No such luck today.

Dunn was firmly rooted in her thoughts as she rubbed a towel through her hair and went looking for some clothing. Her clothes were lying across the foot of the bed when she emerged from the bathroom, proving Dunn was awake and aware of what she was doing.

He was anticipating her and making sure she knew he understood her.

So tempting . . .

The idea of letting him close was mesmerizing, teasing her with the idea of not being alone.

The scent of fresh coffee drifted in while she was

dressing. As an enticement to wake up next to him more often, it was hard to resist.

But like anything, there was a price. Today it would be dealing with Dunn. Or perhaps more precisely, facing her impulsive actions.

What's the big deal? It wasn't her first one-night stand.

You know it was a lapse in self-control . . .

One she wasn't entirely repentant over. Thais let out a little huff of defeat and went looking for the coffee. It wasn't the first time she'd been disappointed in herself. The important thing would be to learn from her mistake.

The problem was, Dunn was waiting for her. She felt his gaze touch on her as she emerged from the bedroom. His emerald eyes were glittering with anticipation and she realized she felt the same emotion rippling through her system.

He was such a live wire.

And you like grabbing it with both hands too much . . .

That was the sort of thing that could kill her.

"You should have woken me," she muttered after her first sip of coffee.

One of his dark eyebrows lifted. There was a distinctly suggestive look on his face as his lips rose into a cocky grin.

"Don't go there," she warned him. "You want to be considered a teammate? Keep your mind on business."

"I want a hell of a lot more," Dunn said, stepping up to the challenge she was laying down. "You do, too."

She took too big a sip of coffee and felt it burn her tongue. "Let's get back on topic. The FBI isn't going to drop their interest in you until I'm back in custody." She started to draw off another sip of coffee but stopped. "How did you convince them to not arrest you last night?"

Dunn ventured closer, invading her space. He knew exactly what he was doing, too. She witnessed the awareness in his eyes. It was over the top the way she seemed to know what he was thinking. Or maybe she was just stressed out and imagining things.

He picked up the coffeepot and refilled his mug. "They had no clear evidence." He shot her a look she'd seen before. It was full of confidence and sent a tingle down her spine because a lot of men put up a good show of making it appear they knew what they were doing.

Dunn was a genuine badass.

It wasn't something a guy could convince you of, it was just a truth or not. Dunn didn't give a rat's ass for what the FBI thought they knew. The previous night's raid wasn't stressing him out. If anything, he was buzzed on the event and hungry to finish the fight they'd started. Not because he wanted to prove himself innocent.

No, Dunn just loved a good rumble.

"They will be back," Thais stated.

Dunn grunted and settled back against the marble-topped island. "Not until they get more than circumstantial evidence linking me to the city you escaped from. You and I have never dated. My lawyer is having a field day with their warrant."

"They must have seen the work room upstairs," Thais countered. "They know you're working on this case. As far as the rest of the world knows, I'm the only reason you'd do something like that."

Dunn's lips curved up, splitting to flash his teeth at

her. "Which is why I told them Miranda is my mother. My departure point became irrelevant the moment I divulged that information."

Thais froze. "You did . . . what?"

"Told them the truth." Dunn set his coffee down. "Isn't that what a good little civilian should do when a federal agent asks him questions?"

Thais was stunned. She realized she agreed with him, silently applauding the way he'd told the world to go fuck off with the truth after years of hiding.

"You get it, Thais," he whispered softly. "The fledgling business Miranda's parents might have crushed back when I was born is now full-grown and thriving." He shot her a look full of intent. "I won't be intimidated and I won't let anyone hurt my mother."

"I don't enjoy arguing with you, Dunn."

He tilted his head to one side and raised one eyebrow. Thais ended up losing the battle to flash a smile at him.

Damn . . . why was it so easy to respond to him? She'd been fine. Just fine in her life. There hadn't been a glaring deficiency. At least, she hadn't felt one until Dunn was close enough for her to realize how much she wanted more.

"We need a plan." She was grasping at straws. Looking to hide inside her work. Dunn's eyes narrowed, proving he knew exactly what she was doing, but he nodded.

"We have two options for exit from this bunker," he set his coffee down and turned to look at a tablet that was lying on the breakfast bar.

Thais joined him, feeling a jolt of awareness shake

her as she drew in the scent of his skin. She focused on the screen and the display of the cabin blueprints.

"There's no point in going anywhere unless we have a plan," he muttered. "We'll have less resources once we leave."

"The FBI will crack your Internet at some point," she answered. "They'll find this bunker. I need to be gone before it happens."

She pushed away from the breakfast bar.

"Kent is arranging transportation," Dunn answered.

"You're not going with me, Dunn," she informed him softly.

He turned to face her. "The hell I'm not."

He wasn't going to budge. Thais saw the determination etched into his expression. Her options weren't many when it came to making him do things her way, either. On the wrong side of the law, she didn't have her badge or team to help her make him comply.

The only way to separate from him was to solve the case.

"Ricky Sullivan," she said.

Dunn's brows lowered. "The contract killer? I thought he was dead after that shoot-out at Bram's wedding."

Thais shook her head. "Kagan kept him on ice. Pulled him in on a case a few months ago in exchange for a valid passport."

She was crossing lines. Spilling information that was classified.

"So why are you sharing this with me?" Dunn demanded. "I'm a civilian . . . right?"

"I understand wanting to protect your blood." Maybe she could never have admitted it out loud if they weren't in a sealed bunker. Thais didn't dwell on the circumstance. An effective agent was also one who used the resources at hand.

"Ricky Sullivan was a hitman," Thais continued. "One who was first brought in by Tyler Martin, when he was working for Carl Davis."

Dunn's lips thinned. "So it would stand to reason he might know who Carl hired to kill my mother."

"If Kagan gave him a valid passport, he might tell me where to find him," Thais said.

"Your section leader might also inform the FBI where you are if you contact him," Dunn insisted.

"I can be long gone from here," she said.

Dunn's expression became unreadable. A moment later he was closing the distance between them. She might have fallen back and maybe she did actually recoil from the sheer force of his approach. Honestly, she wasn't sure because he caught her in the midst of a riot of reactions to his presence.

"I think you need to remember why we should stay together, Thais."

Dunn didn't give her time to argue. He lowered his head, tilting it so he could fit his mouth against hers. His fingers were threaded through her hair once more but the hold on her head wasn't what bound her to him.

No, it was her craving for him.

She was twisting up against him. Gasping as his mouth took hers in a hard kiss that stripped aside all her reasoning. His shirt irritated her because it was a barrier between them. She wanted skin.

His skin.

Against her own.

It was blunt and sexual and yet, there was a deeper

need combining with the hunger urging her to kiss him back. A desperation to get just another taste of the thing she was planning on denying herself.

He lifted his head, giving her a view of the way his eyes glittered with need. She tried to lift up onto her toes and kiss him again, just shut out the rest of the world and take refuge in impulses.

Dunn held her head, refusing to allow her to move toward him.

"Tell me you want me to be your lover," he ordered her in a raspy tone.

"Lover?" She wasn't a stranger to making sure she sounded breathless, but today, she realized it was genuine. "Do you even know what that means? Because I'm not sure I do."

Something crossed his eyes. A ripple of acceptance she realized she shared with him. They were both masters of hiding their true identities from the world.

The hold on her hair eased before he was rubbing her scalp and slipping his hand along the side of her face.

"I think I'd like to learn," he admitted.

"Maybe," she agreed. "But your mother needs our attention now."

She felt his body tense. It was a feeling she shared, a plea from her flesh to reject anything that meant they wouldn't be returning to the bedroom to satisfy their hunger for each other.

He let out a harsh breath before leaning down and kissing her again. This time, it was in farewell. Which made it sweeter somehow. She reached for him, twisting her hands into his hair as she lifted up onto her toes so she could kiss him in return. For a moment, the world dissipated beyond where their mouths met. There was only the taste of him and her need for more of it.

But he set her back, pulling away from her as she dug deep for the strength to release him.

It was by far one of the hardest things she'd ever demanded of herself.

"I'm going to make an appearance above," Dunn informed her. "Eat. I'll be back to join you."

There was no point in trying to talk him out of it.

You'd have been disappointed if he let you . . .

Still, it was her duty to protect and serve. She'd made her badge the foundation of her life. So many other personal desires had fallen aside in her dedication.

Dunn would only be the newest one.

At least, that was what she told herself as she watched him disappear behind the door he'd closed her behind the night before.

To protect her . . .

Thais felt her resolve strengthen. She turned and headed for one of the passageways. It was time to repay the favor and protect Dunn. From himself, yes, but they were both guilty of being willing to stand firm in the face of adversity.

She was a Shadow Ops agent and it was her duty to protect Miranda. Even if it meant her life.

Ricky Sullivan was a hard man.

His life hadn't been close to a fairy tale, and he'd learned to give as good as he got in the struggle to survive.

But now?

He stepped outside and took the time to fill his lungs

with a deep breath, one he savored, allowing his eyes
to close as he just took in the way the air smelled.

Ireland.

He'd left it with anger on his lips for the injustice
done to his father and the hardships his mother had en-
dured as she raised Ricky alone.

But somewhere along the path he'd taken, between
extortion, murder, and double crosses, he'd found himself longing for the home country.

By a twist of fate, he was back in Ireland and dan-
gerously close to calling it home. In the distance, a
church bell was ringing. He watched as people made
their way toward the stone church that was linked to a
different era and yet somehow still managed to be a
draw to the modern-day man.

At least some of them anyway.

"Come on, Cat . . ."

Three girls were hurrying down the side of the path.
The older one catching his eye as her younger sister ver-
balized her impatience.

"We're going to be late . . ."

Cat offered him a shy grin before she picked up her
pace. Just a little flirting with a stranger, and yet Ricky
felt himself transfixed by the girl.

She had a nice backside.

Ricky grinned and moved a little further across his
yard so he could see her. Cat turned her head and caught
him coming closer to take a better look at her. There
was a glitter of amusement in her eyes as she tilted her
head to one side and contemplated him. He reached up
and offered her a mocking two-finger salute. Her sister
finally turned to see what was holding up Cat. Her sibling

sent Ricky a narrow-eyed look before grabbing her sister by the hand and pulling her toward the church.

His mother would have liked him to settle down with a good girl. Maybe he would and just maybe he'd remember to be thankful to Kagan for giving Ricky the opportunity to earn back his passport.

Money. Well, money Ricky knew how to earn on his own. Not always legally though, and that little fact had landed him in a bit of red tape over in America.

Not that it mattered now.

Nope.

Ricky turned around and went to log in to his computer system. The money he'd salted away over the years of working on the black market was there and he was going to grow it. Maybe open himself a little fight club. He scanned the notices up on a site where hitmen sometimes found their jobs and felt his eyes narrow as he found one for him. An old code name only a few of his closest fellow hitmen would know.

He wasn't in the business any longer.

No one would know if he just ignored it.

Ricky fingered his mouse, debating the wisdom of just deleting the address from his system and never looking for it again. He had what he wanted and yet he just couldn't seem to tap the button and kill the link.

He knew Pullman and he knew what the nest was.

What surprised Ricky the most was how he was thinking about Kagan instead of his buddy Pullman. His fellow hitman should have been the one Ricky was worried about pissing off. A year ago, Ricky would have tried to rip the heart out of any man who said Ricky was too much of a pussy for worrying about pissing off some badge-holding federal agents.

The problem was, Ricky wasn't thinking about pissing off Kagan. No, Ricky was weighing the fact that if Kagan went down, someone might just look into Kagan's files and find where Ricky was.

Ricky couldn't marry little Cat if he had to worry about Pullman doing something to uncover where he was.

Ricky sent back a response. If Pullman had pictures of the nest where the Hale brothers were dug in, Kagan would want to know.

It wasn't that Ricky was getting back into the business.

No. Ricky was just making sure no one would be left around who knew how to contact him. For a moment, Ricky was tempted to feel guilty, because he'd been a "loose end" once. Tyler Martin had left him to rot in a Mexican jail, double-crossing him because Ricky was nothing more than a loose end.

He would fucking make sure no one ever tied him off.

The tunnel led her out into the desert morning.

Sedona boasted rock formations that rose into the blue skyline with majestic poise. Thais didn't have time to enjoy it. She took a moment to consider the opening of the tunnel. Nothing stirred, giving her hope that Dunn's man wasn't there yet.

She emerged and headed toward a road. It was a climb up an embankment but she popped up on the side of a winding road. A truck was headed her way. She waved at the driver, smiling as he slowed down and stopped.

"Can I help you, ma'am?"

The driver was wearing a polo shirt with the name of one of the local resorts embroidered on it.

"Yeah . . . I thought I knew which way the trail went but . . . I seem to be lost."

She heard the door unlock. The guy leaned over and picked up a backpack that was lying in the passenger seat. He dropped it into the back as she opened the door and sat down.

"Happens all the time," the guy said. "Be happy to give you a lift into town. Where are you staying?"

"The Sands," she answered. "But you don't need to take me up there. Just into town would be great."

"No problem," the driver said. "Sedona is proud of our hospitality. Just be more careful when you venture out, the desert can be unforgiving."

"I will," Thais answered as they pulled into the small town where privately owned gift shops were open for the day. People were milling around, looking at handmade pottery and handblown glass. She hopped out as the driver stopped for a crosswalk. "Thanks a million!"

The driver likely thought her strange, but she moved away from the road too quickly for him to question her over it. The scent of breakfast was floating in the air, making her lament her quick departure from Dunn's residence.

She ignored her empty belly and headed toward the shops. They were mostly privately owned by artists. Sedona catered to those seeking serenity and escape from the metropolitan craze. That sentiment applied to the owners of the studios as well. A woman was sitting at a pottery wheel, her hands coated in wet mud as she worked the pedals of the wheel and used her hands to shape the mound of clay in front of her. A cat was lying across a shelf above her head, flicking its tail back and forth as the woman hummed.

Her shop assistant was off to one side, answering questions. Thais slipped into the back room and found the phone. Pressing in a memorized number, she waited for an answer.

Kagan didn't disappoint her. "Report." That was the single-word greeting she received from her section leader.

"It's Sinclair."

"About time," Kagan replied.

"Orders?" Thais asked. There was no point in putting it off. Chit-chat wasn't Kagan's style.

"Return to Bateson."

Thais hesitated for a long moment. "Did I hear you correctly?"

Her section leader made a low sound on the other end of the line. "Utilize the resource at hand. Contact again in three days."

The line cut off. For all that she was used to her section leader's blunt, often unexplained orders, today she was mystified. She replaced the phone and slipped out of the shop, fairly certain only the cat noted her coming and going.

At least until Dunn pulled up along the curb in front of her driving a Jeep that blended in really well. The side of it was painted with a sign advertising desert tours. Dunn turned his head toward her, watching her through sunglasses without a care for the fact that he was on the wrong side of the road and in a red zone.

The lazy pace of the area made it so people looked up, curious as to what was happening. Thais let out a little huff as she went around the front of the vehicle and opened the passenger side door and climbed in.

"Nice to know Kagan agrees with me." Dunn only waited for the door to close before he spoke.

Thais grabbed the seat belt and pulled it across her body. "Sure he agrees with you?"

Dunn offered her a nod as he pulled away from the curb. "You'd be gone otherwise."

There was a grim certainty in his tone. It produced a surge of guilt that took her by surprise. Working cases as a Shadow Ops agent meant she did a lot of things people didn't like. More than one witness had dealt with losing their freedom for the good of the case. She'd remained silent as personal boundaries were crossed and decency was expected to make way for safety.

"It would be better for you if I was gone," Thais said. "I'm a fugitive. Your money won't save you if you get caught with me. The FBI will haul you in and lock you up, too."

"Good." Dunn took a curve in the road and flashed her a grin. "Glad to hear your section leader has told you to stay with me."

And he didn't care how much personal risk he was taking.

Which made her feel that surge of caring once again. She wanted to argue against it but facts were facts. Her emotions weren't going to fall into line.

Not when it came to Dunn Bateson, it would appear.

She let out a little sound of frustration as she climbed through the center of the Jeep and lay down across the backseat.

Thais woke with a start.

Her body tensed, her muscles tightening as she tried

to get a grasp on her surroundings. Something had woken her.

Shit! Agents didn't fall asleep . . .

Dunn was slowing down. She realized the decrease in speed must have pulled her out of slumber. The sun was starting to set as he turned the Jeep around a corner and gave the engine enough gas to shoot them up a long private entrance.

She didn't expect to see a rotting shell of a mansion.

"Disappointed?" Dunn asked.

She looked into the rearview mirror to catch him watching her.

"I'm a recluse . . . remember?"

The bunker under the mansion came to mind. Ahead of them, what had once been a magnificent home was nothing but a burned out shell. A few of the walls had jagged pieces, blackened by a long-ago fire. The setting sun shone through them while Dunn drove around one side of the ruin and pressed a remote. A section of the wall made way, allowing them to drive smoothly inside an underground garage.

Dunn stretched as he stepped out of the Jeep.

"Why?" she asked after he'd rolled his shoulders and popped his neck. He turned to look at her. "Why are you a recluse, Dunn?"

He'd been asked the question before.

She witnessed the flash in his eyes and watched the way he tightened his jaw. He started to turn away but she reached out to catch his upper arm.

"Lovers . . . that was your request . . . so tell me why, you do . . . this . . ." She opened her hand to indicate the garage they stood in. Motion-activated lights had flickered on, illuminating a rather well-maintained parking area. There was a small sedan parked off to one side and a workbench with a small selection of household tools.

He reached out and cupped her chin. "Why do you do what you do, Thais? Why deny the passion between us in favor of being alone? Are you really sorry you indulged your passions with me instead of that stranger by the poolside?"

It wasn't her first encounter with his ruthless side. Dunn knew how to ensure he had enough information to undermine his opponents with. But there was something in his eyes that hinted at the situation being much more personal than even he was sure he was comfortable with. "Maybe the real question you should ask me is why I turned the guy down."

She shouldn't have told him something so personal. It was a fatal slip, one of those impulses she knew so very well needed to be controlled.

Of course, with Dunn, her poise had enough holes in it to qualify as a net.

"I know why you turned him down," Dunn said, sliding his hand up the side of her face. The touch awakened a thousand different points of connection between them, awakening the need they'd walked away from that morning. He was turning toward her, his body heat touching her as her lips tingled with anticipation.

"Lovers talk, Dunn." She was stepping away, ripping herself from the source of her obsession.

"You don't know a thing about lovers, Thais."

There was a bitterness in his tone that betrayed an understanding she'd assumed he didn't have. A look into his emerald eyes confirmed it. She felt her breath catch, and then there was a surge of anger toward whoever had broken his trust.

Broken his heart.

She never would have guessed it, and that shamed her because he didn't deserve to be thought of as shallow. Jaded maybe, but she knew that path so very well herself.

"Let's get some food," he muttered.

It was an excuse.

Oh, she didn't doubt he was hungry. Her body was clamoring for a few necessities as well after the long drive. But Dunn punched in a security code and opened a door for her as a means of escaping the topic.

Jaded.

Heartbroken.

Which left her with one firm idea.

He truly was the sort of man she wished she might reach out to. It was just too bad that she was so broken herself.

But they were a pair after all. The best partner was the one who understood you.

"Let's find a way to contact Ricky Sullivan," she muttered on her way inside. "He'll likely be interested in selling us the information we want."

He should have expected someone who held a badge with the elite Shadow Ops to pick apart his facades.

"Why are you a recluse, Dunn?"

Thais Sinclair knew how to ask questions. She'd mastered the art of interrogation. What Dunn heard ringing in his ears wasn't the professional tone of a Shadow Ops agent.

It was the sound of the woman beneath her shell asking him to expose his feelings.

Maybe he should have never pursued her.

He stripped down and stepped in the shower. It was the one place he couldn't hide from himself. Beneath the spray of hot water, he was alone with his ghosts.

Or maybe it was more correct to say, he was left facing the opportunity Thais had presented him with.

He grabbed a soap bar and ripped the paper off it before applying it to his skin. His lips curved up as he contemplated just what would happen if he spilled his guts. She'd picked up his offer of being lovers, he knew she had her own scars to contend with when it came to opening up.

Maybe that was the reason he'd been unable to shake her from his thoughts.

Dunn turned and rinsed off. Steam was curling along the ceiling of the bathroom as he stepped out of the shower and grabbed a towel.

Should he call her on it? Drop the information in her lap and see what she offered up?

And then what?

It wasn't that he'd stopped believing in happy ever afters, it was more that he'd never learned to believe in them in the first place. He was the kid without a mother, the kid the rest of the family didn't want dumped on them because he was a male and therefore the heir. He was the reason his father lost the love of his life and he'd been stupid enough to challenge Thais Sinclair.

Or maybe what was killing him was the fact that he'd been desperate enough to let her close enough to see how thin his skin was if she looked in the right spot.

Peace was something he'd found in making damn sure he didn't care about what others thought. He controlled his world and everything, absolutely everything that touched him.

He strode through the bathroom and into the bedroom. Flipping open a laptop, he typed in a line of encrypted passcode that would have impressed even Kagan. Dunn dressed while the system went through several cycles of connections that bounced the signal around the globe before allowing him access to the web. It wasn't foolproof, nothing was. But it would take days to decipher his signal from the ghost ones.

Ricky Sullivan.

He'd find him.

And just maybe, it would be best if it happened quickly, so Thais could run back to her life. She wanted to go but there was something inside him warning him to dig in and hold on. Take the chance on her.

Hell, she was quickly becoming an addiction.

One he needed to cut himself off from before he ended up losing all control over his world for another taste of.

The problem was, he was too damned hungry for another taste of her.

CHAPTER FOUR

Vitus Hale had stopped plenty of people from doing things in his life. As an active duty SEAL, it had been his job to be the last line of defense against bad guys who would cheerfully destroy life without remorse. He'd trained hard and performed under stressful conditions.

Today, though, he felt his belly quiver just a bit as he stepped into his mother-in-law's path. "Miranda," he began. "We don't have the hitman or a clear evidence trail leading to who paid him to kill you. It would be best if you stayed out of sight."

Miranda Delacroix wasn't intimidated. If anything, Vitus felt like his collar was shrinking as she looked up and locked gazes with him.

He was suddenly about seven years old.

"Carl Davis will not make me cower," Miranda declared firmly. "He's behind this, we all know it."

"But we haven't proven it yet," Vitus stressed.

Miranda only smiled at him. "There are several sorts

of deaths in this life. I've lived a few of them, and one thing I've learned is that half a life is far more of a torment than you think it will be."

Vitus drew in a stiff breath. The rest of his team shifted, feeling the impact of Miranda's words.

"If I don't go out there," Miranda said firmly, "I will lose the election. Unlike my late husband or Carl, I honestly want to keep my campaign promises and do my best to make this a better place to live for everyone. So . . ." She swept the other agents in the room. "Just as all of you will face danger when it is for the greater good . . . I am going out there and Carl Davis will see me doing it with a smile on my lips."

"I'd like to be a fly on the wall of his office when he sees you," Saxon Hale offered.

Vitus shot his brother a narrow-eyed look. "You're not helping."

"Yes, he is," Miranda insisted. "We need to light a fire under Carl's tail. Force him to make another move. If I stay hidden, Carl just might consider the entire thing done because I lost the election. He wants to send a message to anyone willing to cross him. Keeping me out of office will be a powerful message, trust me on that."

Miranda fluttered her eyelashes once more, making it plain she considered the topic closed. Vitus didn't want to let her go, but there was part of him that just admired her spunk too much to stand in her way.

"What can I say?" He stepped aside, clearing her path toward the door. "I love a good fight."

Miranda surprised him by winking at him before she moved forward. It put a grin on his lips as he fell into step with her. Time might have left her looking fragile, but inside, she had all the spark and vigor her daughter had inherited from her.

Outside the doors, the press was waiting. They'd been camped out for days, hoping to get a look at her. Miranda lifted her hand in a wave, smiling brightly as cameras began to snap pictures. Questions came at her from all sides. She moved through the crowd, making sure to answer a lot of them before she was ducking into the backseat of a sedan car.

Saxon held Vitus back when he started to follow Miranda. "Kagan's orders," Saxon informed his brother softly.

"And you're planning on . . . doing exactly what?" Vitus demanded as Miranda's car pulled smoothly away from the curb. The press settled back down as the doors of the private hospital closed, sealing Saxon and Vitus inside the now empty lobby.

"Dare and Bram will be keeping tabs on Miranda," Saxon informed his brother. "We need to find Thais before someone kills her to cover up this whole mess and pin it neatly on her."

"Thais knows a lot about staying off grid." Vitus fell into step with his brother as they went toward the roof.

"She also knows Carl Davis won't drop trying to do away with us. Kagan's hands are tied."

"So it's up to us to blow the lid off this case," Vitus finished.

A helicopter was sitting on the landing pad, the pilot waiting for them. They flashed their badges before climbing aboard and strapping in. Carl Davis had declared war on them. It wasn't the first time they'd faced a bloody fight, but there was a bitterness in both their mouths as they realized they were facing off against their own countryman. Still, it was the thing they'd both dedicated their lives to. The idea that justice wasn't for sale, no matter who you were.

The Shadow Ops teams held the line against corruption at the highest levels of government. They were the underdog, with the exception of one major point. Truth was on their side, and they were men who measured themselves against the idea of honor.

It was go time.

"Looks like Miranda is a tough old bird after all," Mason Kingston muttered toward Carl Davis.

Inside a private lobby, both men were waiting for another political event. Mason was watching the coverage of Miranda standing at a podium in another state, one that had the name of Carl's rival, Tom Hilliard, on it.

"Too stupid to learn when to get out of the way of the rest of the herd," Carl shot back at Mason.

Mason offered Carl a nod and a smile. "Still, you've got to hand it to her, she's really pulling in the numbers when it comes to the polls. The voters love her grandma-save-the-planet shit. Tom is going to feel the effects of her showing up to support him."

Carl looked past Mason to where Eric was standing. Mason made a show of appearing to be interested in the live coverage of the campaign. In truth, he was far more interested in why Carl was sweating. It wasn't that Mason was all too fond of Carl but they were on the same team. Washington was a place where might made right. Miranda Delacroix was an anomaly in their world. Like an albino deer. Sure, it was pretty to look at.

And pretty damn easy for the wolves to spot, too.

She wouldn't last. Couldn't last if Mason was going to keep his spot. Mason stretched out his hand and picked up an expertly decorated miniature cupcake. He popped it into his mouth and reached for another before he'd swallowed.

Miranda knew better than to rock the boat. She was a Delacroix after all. He wouldn't spare a tear over her demise. If you shook the tree, you might get some apples, but one of them might just kill you when it hit you on the head, too.

He enjoyed the second cupcake with a grin as Carl walked toward a private office in the back of the room and Eric disappeared inside with him.

Mason was left licking the frosting off his thumb and chuckling. He wasn't going to have to lift a finger. Just keep on supporting Carl. It was turning out to be a very lucrative arrangement.

Especially the part where all he had to do was watch Carl deal with the dirty work.

Eric held up his finger. Carl's eyes narrowed but he remained silent as his chief of security reached into his suit jacket to withdraw what looked like a double-thick tablet. Eric pressed down on a button, causing a small flashing on the end of the jamming unit. Video and audio would be rendered useless for thirty feet around them.

"Any word from Pullman?" Carl demanded in a hushed tone.

"There is no reason to expect any," Eric replied. "He was waiting for her to emerge."

Carl was rubbing his hands together. "Just wait . . . is that it?"

Eric nodded.

Carl started pacing. Something he'd taken to doing more often as the stress of the election mounted.

"Just . . . wait while she helps Tom close the gap between us," Carl exclaimed under his breath. He turned and looked at Eric. "I go down . . . you go down."

"The only way you're going down is if you lose your shit," Eric replied.

Carl's eyes bulged. "I made you into what you are, Geyer."

"I'm pulling my weight in this arrangement," Eric said. "And I'm going to lose everything if you can't keep it together. Mason isn't an idiot."

Carl fell back a pace. He stood for a long moment before nodding. "You're . . . right." The two words took a lot of effort. Carl's complexion had darkened but he resumed walking while still nodding. "Mason has his share of dirt on his hands. He won't talk."

"Good to know," Eric stated.

Carl snapped around and pointed at Eric. "You just remember I'm the master here. Get the job done or I'll find someone who will."

Carl wasn't planning on listening to any response Eric might have made. He turned and went toward the door, opening it and striding out.

"Mason . . . let's talk about that program of yours . . . the urban renewal project . . ."

The door closed, sealing Eric in the room.

Master.

It was an outdated word and yet what stuck in Eric's throat was the way Carl said it. He believed in the idea 100 percent. Eric moved toward the door and opened it. Carl and Mason were intent on each other as they plotted the best way to entice voters with their ideas. Neither man cared that there were six security men in the private lounge or that those men could hear every word.

Master.

Eric felt the word weighing on him like a yoke. He'd willingly signed on with Carl, willing to traded a piece of his soul for the position of head of Carl's security during his years in the White House. It was a position that glimmered with a life full of opportunities he wouldn't get near without shackling himself to someone like Carl Davis.

Well, after Carl departed from the presidency, there would be book deals and interviews and training seminars for Eric. The sort of name recognition celebrities enjoyed.

But it wasn't free.

Eric had known that. Nothing in life was free. A man had only two choices in life. He could keep his soul and struggle as one of the members of the lower middle class or he could sell his integrity and strap a rocket to his back, one that would raise him up and out of worrying about making his next mortgage payment and watching his retirement funds for miniscule growth.

So, Eric had made his choice. It was a contract signed in blood. Miranda's would only be the most recent blood to be spilled. There would be more. It was the price of his success.

Dunn knew her weakness.

Thais circled the tub sitting in the bathroom of the suite she'd wandered into. It wasn't a copy of the other one. No, Dunn was too creative to be second-guessed.

This tub was copper. It was sealed to keep the color bright and the faucet was constructed to look like pipes. There was a steam-punk feeling to the decoration or maybe an old mining one. She walked around it, trailing her fingers along the rim as she debated allowing herself to think about why he had his different residences furnished with tubs.

Maybe she was being far too presumptuous in assuming they were for her. Any good designer would have listed a tub as a necessity for the lavish decor the suite came with.

She loved it.

But she turned and used the shower instead. It wasn't a matter of being perverse.

No, it was more about self-preservation. They were circling one another, each giving just a little at a time. If she wasn't careful, she could lose control and give him access to everything she was. No promises; just open, bare trust.

The idea of it tantalized her.

And it also terrified her.

She stepped out of the shower, almost restless beyond endurance. Wrapping her body in a towel was as far as she got when it came to dressing.

The truth was, she wanted to be naked.

And she wanted Dunn to know it.

Sure about that?

No, she wasn't but she sat down on a padded bench as she pulled a brush through her hair and avoided making any real decisions while enjoying the sight of the tub.

Was he trying to entice her?

Impress her?

She set the brush aside and realized none of it mattered unless she was willing to toss caution to the wind and act on her impulses. She'd always been the one rejecting him. Her reasons were sound but based on past pain. For the first time, she contemplated just letting it all go in favor of living in the moment.

Standing up, Thais moved toward the tub. She fingered the rim of it as she chewed on her lower lip in indecision.

"I hope you like it." Dunn's voice came from the hallway.

She felt awareness of him washing over her. Coming around the tub she caught sight of his form.

"You've been hiding from me," Thais muttered.

Dunn was still in the doorway, hanging back in that spot where the light didn't quite cut through the darkness of the hallway.

"And you're denying yourself an indulgence," he answered.

She was . . .

He knew it was her weakness. The real question was, did she really want to take shelter behind her walls?

"Disappointed?" She didn't really care for the way the word escaped her lips. Any other time, she would have used a tone that made her question sound sultry or suggestive. Tonight, she just sounded needy.

"Yes," he answered as he crossed into the bathroom. "And then again, no." He stopped a few paces from her, bracing his feet wide as he crossed his arms over his wide chest and leveled his chin down so he could contemplate her. "If you were in the tub, I think I might not have disturbed you. You don't indulge yourself very often."

She'd indulged herself with him . . .

Heat teased her cheeks. It was flickering all along her skin actually but what drew her attention the most was the blush. Honestly, she'd thought herself far too jaded to do something so simple. There was a sense of excitement that came with it, a simple sensation of awareness of him she'd thought long destroyed by her life's path.

He noticed the stain on her face. His eyes narrowing as he moved closer and reached out to stroke the surface of her cheek with one hand.

Just a brush of fingertips.

Yet she shuddered.

And let out a frustrated sound as she stepped out of his reach.

"Don't run."

Thais froze, realizing he'd called it on the money.

"Sure you won't thank me for it tomorrow?" It was likely the most honest question she'd ever voiced toward him.

Dunn shrugged. "Maybe. The problem is, that course of action leaves us both facing just how cowardly we both are. It's not sitting too well with me. How about you?"

Thais felt the impact of his words. Harsh and without mercy, they sliced neatly into her shell.

You're not alone . . .

He moved closer, reaching out to stroke her cheek again. "This fascinates me . . . ," he whispered, his voice rough and husky. "So simple . . . what the hell am I supposed to do now?"

"Beats me," she answered truthfully. "We're both well past simplicity."

His gaze locked with hers. "Maybe the problem is, we've forgotten that simple is often best."

Thais found herself smiling. "Just . . . turn back the clock? I don't think it works that way."

She felt her heart accelerating. The tile floor was cool against her feet and yet her skin was warm, heating up as anticipation grew inside her. There was no fight left in her, and she realized it was because he'd come to her. She just couldn't seem to bear the idea of putting up a wall.

"Maybe I'm suggesting we reboot and see if the system recovers."

It was a tantalizing idea. He knew she liked it, read it off her face as they stood there, so close and yet so very distanced from one another by the realities of life.

Of course, it left her feeling exposed. So very, very bare. His gaze just stripped her down to the person she'd been . . . once . . . a very long time ago.

On impulse, she reached up and tugged the edge of the towel that she'd tucked in to hold the terry cloth around her body. It dropped down her body with a little slump. "So let's hit the power button and kill the system."

She watched the corners of his mouth twitch up. There was a raw look of lust in his eyes but it was tempered with something else. A hard look of appreciation was there as well, and she realized it was the first time she'd seen it aimed at her.

He pushed her back, enveloping her with his larger form and crowding her back until she felt the wall behind her. He threaded his fingers through the strands of her hair, pulling just tight enough to make her his captive and tilt her head up so he could loom over her.

"I want to take you . . . ," he muttered, his eyes flashing with intent. "Take what you just offered . . ."

"Good," she said with a hiss. Her tone was half challenge and she enjoyed watching the way his eyes narrowed in response.

A moment later he was kissing her. It was hard and demanding, stripping aside her thoughts until all that remained was the need he seemed able to kindle inside her.

She kissed him back but he held her tight, controlling her motions and earning a frustrated sound from her.

His chest rumbled with a chuckle in response. "Easy, baby . . ."

He framed her head with his hands, trapping her against the wall with his body. Thais wanted to twist against his embrace, wanted to just let the cravings inside her run free.

"I . . . don't . . . want . . . easy . . . ," she hissed.

Reaching out, she dug her fingers into the tie he wore. The silk gave easily, and a moment later she smiled as she watched the tie flutter to the floor.

Forgotten.

That was what she wanted, complete and total immersion in the moment. Everything about the rest of the world banished while she indulged, reverted to something she sensed was locked inside her.

Dunn grunted. "Neither do I . . ."

He pressed her back against the wall, his hand slipping into her hair again and tipping her face up so their gazes locked.

"I want to do things to you . . . watch you enjoy my touch . . ." His eyes glittered with hard purpose.

A shiver went down her back. She might have thought to shake her head, deny him so much control but any form of thinking was long gone. Now, she was caught in the grip of impulse and her cravings only cared about one thing.

Being in contact with him.

"I want to make you cum, Thais . . ." His tone was raspy and thick with promise. "I want it to be just . . . about you . . ."

He slid his hand down her body, awakening a thousand little points of pleasure along the way.

Somehow, she'd forgotten just how good it felt to be touched.

"Purr for me, Thais." He'd leaned close, pressing a kiss against her neck as he stroked her again. "Make those little sounds . . . for me . . ."

She couldn't have silenced herself if she'd wanted to. No, there was just too much pleasure coming from the connection of their skin. She arched, her eyes slipping shut because she wanted to be totally immersed in the feeling of his hand on her.

She couldn't remember the last time she'd let go so very completely.

Dunn made a sound against her neck, a dark, low rumble that set off a shudder inside her. He seemed to know how to rock her very foundation.

And she wanted more.

She shifted but he held her tight, his hand venturing across her belly to her mons. Her eyes opened wide as he plunged his fingers into her slit.

"You don't want it soft . . . do you, baby?"

"No." Her lips were dry as her breath came in short gasps. He was pressing her hard, plunging his thick fingers in and out of her. Her slit was wet, making it simple for him to work her, rubbing her clit until she felt climax rushing toward her.

She didn't want it so quickly but that was just a weak protest from her mind. Her body was famished for satisfaction, her hips straining up toward his hand as he rubbed her faster, penetrating deeper until she let out a hoarse cry that bounced around the bathroom while she contorted in the moment of pleasure.

It was over too soon. Dropping her back into the cold grasp of reality. She lifted her eyelids to find Dunn watching her. His emerald eyes glittering with satisfaction. They lacked arrogance, though. Leaving her breathless as she tried to decide how to define what they were doing.

Sex?

Intercourse?

Making love?

"Now I'm going to take you to bed, Thais," he informed her softly before he pressed a kiss against her open mouth.

It was the sweetest kiss she'd ever experienced. A soft meeting of their lips, for once it wasn't hurried. Dunn explored her mouth, teasing her tongue with his as he stroked the back of her head. When he lifted his head, she was basking in the glow of the satisfaction he'd given her.

"I've thought too many times about carrying you off to my bed." It was an admission. One that gave her a strange little sensation of intimacy. As though he was trying to share that part of himself that she'd sensed he was hiding.

Dunn didn't give her time to ponder it though. He

scooped her off her feet, cradling her against his chest as he walked through the doorway and on into a hallway. Soft lighting illuminated the floor as he moved.

The bedroom was his.

She realized that when he laid her down and she caught the darker tones of the decor. Mahogany wood, navy, and maroon. She sat up as he stripped.

"Don't," he warned her as he dropped his pants. "Don't move."

He wanted to control the moment. But there was something different about the need she witnessed glittering in his eyes. She knew only too well what it was like to be viewed as a conquest.

This was something different.

Something she'd shied away from for years, and now, Thais honestly questioned if it was just a trick of her imagination. Something left from her childhood, when Santa was real and people really lived happily ever after.

She knew better.

But so did he.

Just reboot the system and see what they both had when they weren't trying to be modern humans. What did they have at their cores, deep down inside where feelings were genuine and impossible to design? You just had to take them as they came.

"What are we doing, Dunn?" The question came across her lips as she stood. Sex wasn't something she broke a sweat over anymore, but just then, her heart was hammering inside her chest. She reached out on impulse and flattened her hand on his chest just over his heart.

"What we both can't resist any longer." He held her

hand against his chest, watching the way her eyes widened because his heart was beating at the same frantic pace.

"Call it fate," he said, stepping closer. "Or the universe . . ." He cupped her shoulders and smoothed his hands along her arms until he closed them around her and drew her tight against him. "Something keeps throwing us together, so let's discover what there is between us."

She kissed him first. Rising up to press her mouth against him. It was more than the feeling of his hard body against hers that drew her up to claim that kiss. In his words, she glimpsed a look at the thing she'd been disillusioned about. That elusive element so lacking in every relationship she'd had. Raw, hard sex she'd encountered in the world.

What she craved was intimacy.

There was a hint of it in Dunn's eyes. Did he know it was there? She wasn't sure but it drew her to him, making her reach for him as he pushed her back onto the bed. They fell in a tangle of limbs, frantic to touch and be touched. The moment of total immersion finally arrived as Thais let her legs tangle with his and threaded her fingers through the crisp hair on his chest.

He rolled her over, but she kept going, ending on top of him. His cock was hard and pulsing against her slit. She stretched her back, arching as she let the sensation ripple through her, drawing her nipples tight with anticipation.

"Christ in heaven . . . ," he muttered, reaching up to cup her breasts. He kneaded them and rolled her nipples through his fingers.

"It's my turn, Dunn," she informed him. Her tone

was husky and she realized for once, it wasn't a practiced application of her skills. "I'm going to watch you this time . . ."

She lifted up and his cock sprang away from his belly. The head glided into her wet slit, making it so simple to lower herself onto. He caught her hips as she sheathed him, his lips drawing thin to expose his teeth.

It was raw . . .

She'd known the element of lust would be there. Part of her enjoyed watching him as she rose up and plunged down onto his cock, answering the same need inside herself.

The hard edge of pleasure glittered in his eyes. It spurred her up again and brought her down with enough strength to see the bed rocking beneath them. She wanted to push him as far over the edge as he'd done to her.

But there was something else, too. Another need clawing its way up from deep inside her where she'd banished all of her personal emotions.

She wanted to be with him . . .

Not merely experiencing the physical connection between their flesh. There was something else beyond the climax, a thing she'd never truly stopped believing in, no matter how hard she'd tried to.

He tried to turn them again.

"No," she said, through her teeth. "I'm going to . . . push you over the edge . . ."

Thais didn't think she'd ever meant anything quite so much. Dunn bared his teeth at her.

"You're coming, too, baby . . . ," he rasped out.

His cock was rock hard. Letting her know he was close to climax. Her thighs were burning from the repetitive motion. Perspiration coated her as she listened to her own raspy breath and heard the headboard begin hitting the wall. Dunn reached forward, pressing down on her clit as she rode him.

"*Yes!*" Thais wasn't certain if she meant him or her, only that every fiber of her being was focused on one goal.

She felt him jerk inside her, his cock releasing its load as pleasure tore through her. It was a deep climax, one that made her feel like she was caught between breaths, suspended in the space where her heart had just beat, and she waited for it to thump once more. All the while she was twisting and straining toward her lover, pleasure wringing them both like wet towels and flinging them down to the ground to land in heaps.

The headboard hit the wall a final time as she rolled off Dunn and onto her back.

So spent . . .

It was more than the sex. Everything inside her was open and relaxed. The state of constant guard she normally existed in required too much effort to return to at that moment. So she lay back, trusting the man beside her. Trusting his attention to details as she just let herself open to whatever fate had in mind to deliver.

Except she wasn't alone. Dunn shifted beside her, rolling toward her and clasping an arm around her waist.

She didn't know exactly what to think of it. But thankfully, her mind was still blissfully unwilling to re-engage.

She could reboot in the morning.

Ireland.

Ricky Sullivan had made a name for himself. In the

underworld of thugs and hitmen, he'd distinguished himself among them as a man who got difficult jobs done without leaving a mess.

Or a trace, which was something he doubled his rates for.

Retirement was an achievement as well. One only a handful of his kind ever lived to see. His memory was sharp with the times he'd almost joined those who didn't make it. A hellhole of a Mexican prison was one of the bright spots in his memories.

Carl Davis had left him there to rot.

Ricky enjoyed a flash of rage as well as a very sweet rush of satisfaction as he recalled helping Kagan cut Carl Davis deep. Kirkland Grog had been feeding Carl cash from underground brothels and using his vast network of media influence to keep Carl's face in front of the voters.

Ricky had enjoyed helping put Kirkland in prison. He hoped Carl was watching his ratings in the polls slowly diminish. The United States election was big news in Ireland, and Ricky enjoyed looking at the newest numbers, because Tom Hilliard was closing in on Carl Davis, the gap between them narrowing every week.

It was a fucking thing of beauty to be alive to see . . .

Of course, he was only able to enjoy it so much because he'd worked with Kagan. The section leader of the Shadow Ops was a tough one to figure out. The only thing Ricky knew for sure about the man was he was someone even an ex-hitman like Ricky didn't cross.

There were some men in the world a wise fellow steered clear of and when they came to you, well, you gave them what they wanted.

Ricky sat looking at his messages and the buzz in

the field was that Dunn Bateson was looking for him. As in Dunn had made sure several of Ricky's contacts told him so.

Dunn Bateson wasn't a man to cross, either.

He was the type a hitman didn't take a contract on because it was a hell of a lot more trouble than it was worth. That wasn't to say Dunn was safe, he was just safe from a man like Ricky who could actually get the hit accomplished.

Now a new kid with shit for brains? Sure, he'd take the contract and never realize until it was too late that he was never going to see that money because Dunn was just too hard to kill.

Ricky tapped his fingertip against the worn tabletop he was using as a desk. The house he was living in was a dump but that was just for the moment, as he decided what to do with his golden years. Outside, the church bell was ringing again. He peered out the window as Cat came down the road. Ricky felt a smile flashing his teeth at her while she looked up to see if he was watching her again.

She had a great set of tits and a gleam in her eye that told him she knew exactly what he was thinking about her. He touched his fingers to his lips and blew her a kiss. She tipped her head to the side and sent him a wink.

Saucy . . .

Damned if he didn't want to tap her.

Bateson was a Scot. Ireland wasn't too far away for their paths to never cross. Ricky got up and strolled across the worn floor to where his backpack was. He'd have to take a trip and make a call somewhere outside the area he'd taken up in.

No need to blow his cover completely if Bateson only wanted some bit of information from his past. It might even be worth some money to the man. Bateson would get his call though, because Ricky wasn't stupid enough to spend his life looking over his shoulder for the man. Better to face him straight on.

That way, Ricky could get back to seeing if Cat wanted to have his babies. A few years ago, he'd have laughed at anyone who accused him of wanting a mundane life.

Mexico had changed that.

Funny how life suddenly seemed more precious when you lost all control over keeping it. Ricky had spent a lot of time thinking about just that fact while Kagan had him on ice in an underground bunker with just enough food to last until the section leader came back.

Okay, Ricky had thought a lot about killing Kagan, too.

In the end though, he'd wanted to see the sky, smell the sea air, and stick with one woman long enough to see if she'd put up with him when he was sick.

Only his mom had ever brought him tea with honey. She'd loved him.

Cat was saucy but she was going to evening services with her family. She knew how to love.

And how to have fun.

Ricky headed out. He wanted to close out his past life. Just one last loose end and he was going to close all his accounts and settle all the way into retirement.

Thais woke up to the sound of water running.

She rubbed her eyes and stretched but the underground room didn't give her any hints as to what time of day it was.

Well, it was morning judging by how rested she felt.

There was another mark of a seasoned agent. She knew when she was running low on sleep and exactly how good it felt when she dropped off into a deep slumber for the entire night.

She felt wonderful.

"Bath is ready." Dunn appeared in the doorway wearing only a pair of pants. The lights in the hallway were all the way on now, giving her a clear view of his chest.

He didn't skimp on the workouts.

The man was chiseled, proving he put his time in and controlled his carbohydrate intake. There was no fitness fairy.

"Glad you like what you see."

His comment cut through her fascination with his bare chest. There was a tingle of heat in her cheeks that made her roll her eyes as she swung her legs over the edge of the bed.

Dunn chuckled, reaching out to hook his arm around her waist as she tried to slip past him. He turned her neatly in a circle, putting her back against the wall before gently tipping her chin up so he could stare at the stain warming her face.

"Enough, Dunn," she muttered, fighting off a sudden feeling of being tongue-tied. "You've had your fun at my expense."

"I'm enjoying the novelty of seeing you blush for me," he answered before stroking the side of her face. "My guess is, a seasoned agent like yourself doesn't do it very often."

"Unless you're around . . ." She snapped her mouth shut, horrified by how exposing her comment was.

"I know the feeling."

His tone was so low, she almost didn't make out the words. Just a whisper, like a secret he was hesitant to let the rest of the world hear.

Their gazes fused and something shifted between them. It was a moment that stretched into a small eternity as they both seemed to flounder on just what to do next.

Something buzzed, breaking the connection. Dunn muttered a word under his breath in Gaelic that needed no translation. He reached into his pants pocket and withdrew a small tablet. Thais swept it up and down as he read whatever was on the screen.

"Impressive, Dunn, those are supposed to be in the testing phase only," she muttered before she slipped farther down the hallway. She was still nude but the distance helped restore her poise. Even if it felt strange to gather her shell around herself. It was almost like it didn't fit anymore.

The moment is over . . .

"My company produces them," Dunn replied as he shook the little tablet known as a Lynx before dropping it into his pocket. "In a world of super-connected people, the next must-have device is one with a built-in scrambler. People will pay for privacy."

"On the grid and yet your signal is bouncing off of so many towers, there is no way to track your location," Thais said, supplying the function elements of the Lynx.

He followed her into the bathroom. "A rather useful tool when I'm dating a fugitive."

"I haven't dated in a long time, Dunn," she said as she dipped her fingers into the tub he'd filled for her.

"So enjoy it," he offered before he scooped her up and deposited her in the tub.

The water was perfect. Rising up to cover her breasts and ease the aches left from sleeping so soundly. He contemplated her for a long moment.

"You knew I was watching that night," he said. "Watching you in your bath." His lips parted in a grin. "You are a minx, Thais. I nearly had my nose pressed to the screen as you toyed with the bubbles."

"You know what a woman looks like nude."

He shrugged. "As I said last night, maybe we could both use a little more simplicity in our lives. I know I enjoyed watching you play in your bath, more than any naked woman I'd seen in a long time. I think you liked teasing me, too. Because you knew I couldn't reach you."

Playing with fire . . .

She shifted her gaze away from his. "It was a poor choice on my part."

"You wanted to be seen," he said as he lowered himself behind her. He cupped her shoulders and leaned her forward. "I saw you, Thais."

She'd known he had.

It was the reason she'd avoided him. He had the power to strip her down, baring her so very completely.

He reached into her field of vision and picked up a bar of soap. His hand withdrew and she felt it gliding across the wet skin of her back.

Why are you letting him wash your back?

She didn't really know the answer, only knew without a doubt that moving would hurt too badly.

Not hurt . . . no, the word was "wound."

And it wouldn't be her pain, it would be his as she rejected him.

"So when do I get to see you, Dunn?"

He squeezed the sponge, sending a shower of water down onto her back. The sound of it echoed around the bathroom before the Lynx chirped. She heard a soft sound from Dunn before he pulled a towel off a rack and dried his hands. He was halfway to the doorway when he answered the call.

It wasn't the first time she'd listened in on a conversation after using sex to get into someone's private space.

Today though, she found herself battling a serious bitter taste in her mouth over it. Burnout was something every agent faced the threat of. Of course, just like most of her Shadow Ops teammates, she'd thought herself immune to ever needing more than her badge.

Fate had a very twisted sense of humor.

"I was looking for you."

Dunn hadn't moved down the hallway. He'd turned, catching her with a hard look.

"Someone put a hit out on my mother. I understand you're the sort of man who can help me find the man," Dunn informed whoever he was talking to. "I can make it worth your time and his, to forget the job."

Dunn listened for a moment to whoever was on the other end and then he was lowering the Lynx.

"Ricky Sullivan," Dunn said, giving her the name of the man on the other end of the conversation. "Thanks for the tip."

"If I were following the rules, I wouldn't have given it to you," she admitted before rising from the tub. It was time to get back to the case.

Dunn caught her as she was toweling dry, wrapping his arms around her and binding her against his body. "I like you without your badge, Thais."

Whatever protest she might have voiced died as he kissed her. The night's excess hadn't ended her need for him though. The hunger flared up as she let him strip her again and carry her back toward the rumpled bed.

She went willingly enough.

Maybe "desperately" was a more precise word to use. Because she reached for him with a need that was driven by the fear of knowing time was against them. Reality was going to crush the space they enjoyed, flatten it with a hundred logical reasons why they had to walk away from each other.

So she made the moment, that moment when Dunn was close enough to touch, the only thing she allowed into her mind.

Ricky knew his stuff.

He opened his battered backpack and looked at the selection of prepaid cell phones inside it. By the look of the fabric, someone might think there was nothing of value inside.

They'd be way wrong.

Being able to be untraceable was essential to being a hitman. The dozen or so phones were a result of years on the open road. He never passed up the chance to add to his little collection. Some were years out of date as far as cell phones went but they connected just fine.

The other thing a hitman needed was brains.

The type of smarts to memorize numbers, names, addresses, license plate numbers, and the list went on. Ricky never forgot a face and he never had to look at a phone number twice. The information was in his head, a tool for him to use in his trade. The actual kill was the easy part of it all. Making sure you had your target in a kill box and you weren't going to get caught, that was the challenging part.

He dialed a number from memory. Kagan answered.

"Ricky Sullivan here."

There was silence for a moment.

"Now, I was all set to never speak to you again," Ricky added when Kagan didn't say anything.

"What changed your mind?" Kagan took the bait.

Ricky lost his teasing demeanor. The section leader wasn't a man to mess with and Ricky didn't even know very much about him. Of course, that made Kagan just the right sort of person for Ricky to consider keeping on his good side.

An ace in the hole.

"I seem to recall that one of your agents is married to Miranda Delacroix's daughter," Ricky said. "Word on the airways is, someone picked up a fat contract to take the congresswoman out."

"You know who's got the contract on her?" Kagan cut straight to the information he was interested in.

"I figured it out after Dunn Bateson reached out to me." Ricky laid down his cards. He'd be hiding out in the worst of armpits if Kagan hadn't cut him a deal. "Seemed to me, you might like to hear from me considering the circumstances. Also figured you wouldn't be too happy to hear I knew about it and kept my mouth shut."

"You figured right. Can you give me the hitman?" Kagan asked bluntly.

"For the right incentive."

"Don't fuck with me," Kagan warned. And it was a warning Ricky took seriously. Kagan was the one man who knew where Ricky was buried in the world. The section leader could tag his passport so fast, Ricky would never know his golden retirement was shattered.

"I'm not," Ricky was quick to cut back. "Didn't have to call you, either. I know you're not a man to cross."

"Explain what you mean by incentive." Kagan's tone was guarded.

"A contract on Miranda Delacroix isn't coming from anyone who you dick with," Ricky said, laying the information on the table. "To get the hitman to come in, I need something really good, like the deal you made me."

"Legitimate passport?" Kagan asked. "That's harder than you realize."

"So is convincing the guy to cross whoever put the hit out before he puts a slug through Miranda's skull," Ricky replied. "Fact is, I'm not sure he'll answer me, but if he does, I can't put him on hold while I call you."

"So why did you call me first?" Kagan asked.

"I know who holds my leash." Ricky didn't like admitting it, either. "You find out I saw pictures of your nest location up for auction and you might just decide to make sure I know you meant it when you told me to retire but keep my nose clean. It didn't take much for me to connect the dots between those pictures and the attempt made on Miranda's life. I know how to contact the hitman. Want me to try and get him to roll over?"

"Yes," Kagan replied quickly. "I'll give you what you need. Get on a plane and get stateside."

The line died.

Ricky realized he felt something odd. A sensation

rolling through him that put a grin on his lips, but not the happy-go-lucky one he'd learned to use when he was in effect telling the world to go fuck itself.

This was something else.

Almost like he felt decent about himself for a change. Alone, with just himself, he realized there was no reason to put up a front. He'd done the right thing, something to make the world a slightly better place.

His mother would have approved.

Now, who in the hell would have thought he'd go and do something like pleasing his mom?

The world was a funny place at times.

Waiting was a large part of what special agents did.

Vitus looked like he was sleeping. His brother was stretched out with his booted feet on a battered coffee table and his head leaned back with his face toward the ceiling. He appeared to be dozing, like he'd just polished off a Thanksgiving plate full of turkey and stuffing.

Saxon knew better.

Vitus was conserving his strength. Taking a load off his feet while he could, as they both waited for their fellow Shadow Ops agent to arrive.

Greer McRae made it to their location a couple of hours later. He flashed them a grin on his way through the door. Most of the properties Shadow Ops teams used were ones where the residents had very recently died. They could get in, set up a command post, get work done, and then move on before any of the neighbors got wise or, more importantly, before they popped up on an Internet trace. In a world of cell-phone towers, classified work was going back to landlines.

Today though, the house they'd taken over had its windows boarded up as it waited to be demolished as part of a freeway expansion. Greer looked at the cobwebs and thick dust before he closed the door and sealed them inside the dimly lit room. The furniture left behind was battered and too torn up for even a garage sale.

"This is an armpit," Greer remarked as he sank onto what had once been a nice sofa. Now, it was a shredded mess, the foam discolored by sun exposure.

"The resident couldn't get out of his two-year package deal," Saxon replied. "Giving us an active phone and cable line."

"Even with that," Vitus said as he sat up. "I'm guessing it's still going to be hard for you to pinpoint Dunn Bateson."

"We've used Dunn's reclusive nature to our advantage in the past," Greer said. The tone of voice he used made it clear he wasn't happy about being asked to find Dunn. "Sure you want to piss him off by getting between him and Thais?"

"We need to find Thais before the FBI does," Saxon responded. "They aren't sharing information very well. If they dump her into a holding facility, she might be dead before we can get her transferred."

"I'm here," Greer offered begrudgingly. He was setting up his laptop, connecting to the Internet, and watching the screen as his messages loaded. "But I'll warn you, Dunn doesn't like the way Thais's gender is used in operations."

Greer's Scottish sense was coming through. Shadow Ops teams drew agents from all sorts of backgrounds but Greer was unique among them. His sister was officially an "unperson." Designated that way because her abilities were so rare, it was important to keep her shrouded in obscurity. Saxon wasn't altogether certain what his own opinion was when it came to operatives with psychic abilities, but his brother believed in them, and there was one solid thing Saxon would bet his life on and that was Vitus Hale's opinion of someone's skills. If Vitus thought Greer's sister was the real deal, Saxon wasn't going to question it or Greer's need to keep a security clearance so he could stay in contact with his sibling.

That was a murky place to go though. Greer was a solid agent. A man Saxon was willing to have guarding his back. It didn't sit too well to know Greer's sister was serving somewhere in the position of "unperson" without the choice to leave. Or that Greer was driven to extreme service in order to maintain contact with her.

But life wasn't fair. And the bad guys didn't apply kindness to their methods. Thais was an example of that.

"The bad guys don't like the way she distracts them, either," Vitus said, continuing the conversation. "I think she enjoys knowing they dismiss her as just a toy without two brain cells to rub together."

"There's got to be a part of her that resents it, too," Greer answered. "Don't be surprised if he doesn't answer my call."

Saxon shot Greer a hard look. "He's more likely to answer a call from you than me. Thais is part of this team. We need to find her first."

"Personally, I'm not in any hurry to arrest her," Greer muttered as he started to type.

"We arrest her, we have control of her," Saxon replied.

"It's a thin plan," Vitus added. "But at least it's a plan."

Shadow Ops worked on the edge. They took the cases with the greatest odds and the ones that required them to get their hands dirty. World-class criminals didn't flinch over morality, so they couldn't, either. Thais knew it, embraced it just as they all did. She was their teammate and Shadow Ops agents always, always had each other's backs.

No matter what.

Thais sat up.

Dunn reached over and picked up the Lynx phone. He frowned when he read the number. "Hello, Greer."

Thais felt a chill touch her nape. She'd known they were hiding from the world. It was going to end; she just hadn't realized how deeply she would feel the sting when it came.

In some small corner of her mind, she actually enjoyed knowing she felt the jab.

Maybe she wasn't as jaded as she thought.

Dunn's face was tight. He sat up, giving her his back as he listened to her fellow agent Greer McRae.

It was the way it had to be . . .

Thais climbed out of the bed, feeling the chill more than she should on the way to the bathroom.

Get focused . . .

Sage advice, even if it did little to change the way she wanted to refuse to do anything but stay right there with Dunn.

Are you kidding?

Thais realized she wasn't. Showering didn't help much. How many times had she gotten out of a bed and

considered the matter finished with a shower? Just let
the water wash away the night before. There was a hollow sensation in the pit of her stomach that she'd somehow convinced herself she didn't miss in the years of
making her badge her identity.

Now, she was torn and so damned relieved to realize she could still feel more than sexual tension.

"You don't have to go anywhere." Dunn had pulled
a pair of pants on. He filled the doorway of the bedroom
as she selected some clothing and tugged it on. "Greer
doesn't know where we are."

"Hiding out won't help us corner the hitman who is
intent on killing your mother." Thais pulled a T-shirt
on and reached for a sweatshirt.

"I'll find him." Dunn came closer as he spoke.
"Without you sticking your neck out."

For a moment, she enjoyed the feeling of . . . well, of
being sheltered. Or at least the offer of it. But she
slammed the door shut on those feelings. Letting them
loose was out of the question.

"I know you enjoy being a recluse, Dunn, but just
what is the plan exactly?" Thais asked softly.

He cocked his head to one side, aiming a hard look
toward her that made it clear he liked the idea of a challenge. Thais propped a hand onto her hip.

"Cockiness might get you points in my personal
book but the rest of the world is still out there," she informed him in a tone that was all business. "Personally, I can't see how you'd appreciate me turning my
back on your mother. It's my duty to safeguard her."

Dunn moved toward her. "Don't do that, Thais." He
reached out and smoothed some of her hair away from
her face.

A shiver went down her spine. He was big and hard and she was so keenly aware of it. Part of her wanted to just indulge in the sensation and let it carry her away.

But she needed to be practical.

"I can't be a pet," she told him. Maybe she should have kept her mouth shut but the words were just spilling over her lips like she didn't know how important it was to keep her true feelings hidden.

He started to say something but she reached out and pressed a fingertip against his lips.

"Maybe what I should say is, think about whether or not you want something else in your life, Dunn, because I'm not blind to how you've arranged your affairs. On your terms. Always. You're holding back and you like it that way."

And her voice started to betray her by cracking. She moved past him, using the time to swallow and try to regain her composure.

Dunn hooked her around the waist, turning her and moving so that she was flattened against him.

"Her name was Rhianna," he offered gruffly. "And I was a target. One she studied down to the last detail."

He was hard and large, but in his eyes, Thais saw a much younger man. One who had fallen in love, happily being carried away by his heartstrings only to realize he was alone in the emotion.

"My mother was an expert of the art, too," Thais muttered, unable to resist the urge to offer some compassion to him.

"She trained you," Dunn said.

Thais flattened her hand on his chest. Savoring the feeling of his heart thumping inside his chest.

But she had to disconnect from him.

From her need for him.

She pushed against his chest. He resisted for a moment before releasing her.

"My husband wasn't an innocent," Thais said as she put distance between them.

"No, I'm guessing he enjoyed having you as a pet."

Thais froze. "Stop doing that."

Dunn folded his arms over his chest and faced off with her.

"Just . . . stop," she insisted. "You're peeling away my layers."

"You've enjoyed yourself so far," he answered smugly.

"The sex?" she asked bluntly. "Sure did. You had a smile on your face, too."

He didn't miss the topic she left unmentioned. Sex was something they both were comfortable discussing. It was the other element of their relationship that had them standing there, briefly tongue-tied.

"Right now, I need to do my job," Thais said at last.

Dunn nodded but there was something in his eyes that made her think he didn't consider the conversation finished.

It had to be.

Still, she admitted that she didn't like it any more than he did.

Reality sucked. Neither of them was a stranger to that fact.

Saxon only turned his phone on at certain times of the day. It kept his team off grid. Greer was checking his own phone and shook his head as he caught Saxon looking his way.

"Nothing from Dunn," Greer confirmed.

"That's because Thais made direct contact," Saxon replied. His teammates shifted around him. "She's coming in."

"To us?" Vitus asked.

Saxon nodded. "She knows who to trust."

Saxon didn't bother to voice his concerns. His teammates knew them anyway. They couldn't keep Thais. No, Carl Davis would eat that opportunity up in a heartbeat. He'd take the chance to have them all blamed for the hits on Miranda so he could build his case against the Shadow Ops teams.

But he'd take it one step at a time.

And hope he managed to keep at least one pace ahead of Carl Davis.

The good old USA. Ricky flashed a grin at the customs officer looking over his passport and return ticket. He drew a line across his form and handed it all back to Ricky.

"Have a nice day," Ricky said as he proceeded through the checkpoint. He enjoyed the chance to stretch his legs after the long flight. Ducking through the doors, he exited into the fresh air.

If you could call the fumes of four lanes of traffic fresh.

Ricky grinned. He enjoyed the bustle because it was easy to go unnoticed. He hopped onto a bus that was heading toward a long-term parking lot. Weary travelers were sitting in the seats, looking grim as they faced the end of their vacations.

He stayed on the bus until it made it to the outer edge of the lot. Climbing down, Ricky walked with purpose past the rows of cars. The front of the place had signs proclaiming it a video-monitored lot. But video wouldn't be much help once he was long gone. He'd tugged a hat down and continued walking, looking for a car that was clean.

Honestly, parking a newly cleaned car in long-term parking was just telling everyone you wouldn't notice for at least a week if your car was gone. He eased up beside one and slipped a Slim Jim out of his sleeve and into the side of the door. A quick jerk and pull, and the door popped open. Sitting behind the wheel, he tugged on the wires and started the engine. But he made sure not to crack the plastic of the dashboard too bad. When he drove up to the toll window, he handed the ticket to the bored attendant, who put his cell phone down to take it. A quick moment later, Ricky was driving away from the airport. The gas tank was full, ensuring the owner wouldn't have to get gas when they returned from their vacation.

He chuckled and drove away from the city. Getting good and lost in the era of the Internet was hard. But he knew how. Ditching the car at a shopping mall before he went out the back of a restaurant and caught a ride in the back of a delivery van. It was all second nature to him, because a hitman who could do his job anonymously was one who could demand the highest price.

He'd enjoyed it before.

But there was something different this time. Ricky realized the buzz was gone. He wasn't hyped on the idea of screwing over the people around him. In fact, he was noticing just how easy it was to blend in anonymously.

Cat wouldn't even know his name if he ended up dead in a ditch.

It made him laugh though, because once again, he had the feeling his mother would have given him her approval for getting his thinking straight. When he got back to Ireland, he was going to court Cat. Bend over backward to impress her and her relations. What was it they were always preaching in church? Once you let go of everything you thought you knew about what was important in life, you would amend your ways and be happy to do it.

Well, he was going to give it his best try. Ricky Sullivan, a pillar of the community. He just might invite Kagan to the wedding.

"Thais Sinclair, you're under arrest."

Saxon's mouth was dry. Thais already had her hands behind her back, but it still took him a damn lot of effort to snap a set of handcuffs on her.

The door of the SUV they'd driven to the meeting site in had been opened by Vitus. Saxon helped her up and inside it as he felt sweat sliding down the side of his face.

Fuck.

She didn't say anything as he closed the door. But Saxon caught sight of Dunn. He was standing across the street. He aimed a hard look toward Saxon before he disappeared.

"I believe that was a warning." Vitus vocalized what Saxon was thinking.

Saxon pulled his phone out and turned it on. Kagan answered on the second ring.

"We have Thais Sinclair in custody."

There was a pause from his section leader. "I've made arrangements for her to be held at the marine base near you."

Saxon finally managed a little grin as he put the phone back in his pocket. "Kagan is going to put her on a marine base."

Vitus nodded. "Good move. Carl will have a hard time calling the marines traitors if Miranda gets shot."

Saxon slid into the passenger front seat as Greer pulled into traffic. The clock was ticking and they all felt the pressure. There had been times they'd all thrived on it; today, Saxon discovered himself more concerned than normal. But he wouldn't let it show.

Not that anyone in the vehicle didn't already know how high the stakes were.

Ricky picked up his phone when it buzzed.

"I thought you were out of the business," Pullman said by way of greeting.

Ricky rubbed his eyes because of the time difference, but he'd always been able to wake up fast.

"You heard right," Ricky answered. "A neat little turn of events landed me a fresh passport. I'm free and clear. Retired."

Pullman let out a low whistle. "You'll have to tell me how you did it. I'm getting too old for this shit."

"Working for that prick Carl Davis won't do the trick," Ricky said, playing his hunch.

Pullman was quiet for a long moment. "He's not a man you tell no to," he responded.

"I know." Ricky made sure his voice didn't give away how fucking amused he was to have gotten Carl Davis's number on the first guess. Carl was a dumb shit. Using the same hitman was a good way to end up getting caught.

"Then again," Ricky stressed, "hopping the fence did the trick for me. Those Shadow Ops teams have a lot of resources. Want me to introduce you to a guy I know? One who can fix your passport so you can enter your golden years without a single blip?"

"I'll think about it."

"Do that," Ricky added. "That prick has you shooting at a grandma . . . We used to take jobs worth doing. There is only so much money you can spend, and it's a lot sweeter to do it with legitimate papers. But the deal is only on the table so long as Miranda is alive."

Pullman grunted on the other end. "Like I said . . . I'm getting tired of the crap. I'll call you later. Maybe."

Ricky chuckled as the line cut. Pullman wasn't going to let him think he would jump at his bait like a hungry trout. No, image was everything in their line of work. No client paid for a hitman who didn't have a reputation of being willing to face the fire when a job called for it. It was a mean, ugly business, contract killing. Pullman had put bullets through the skulls of more than one family member who had the bad luck of being around when he caught up with his target.

Kagan wasn't going to like giving him a passport.

Ricky didn't sweat it though. In fact, he whistled as he selected a different prepaid phone to use to call the section leader.

Kagan contemplated his options. As far as operations went, this one was sticky. It wasn't without its rewards, however.

Pullman had been hired by Carl Davis.

Proving it was going to be tough. Ricky Sullivan had rolled over but Kagan doubted he'd get so lucky with Pullman. Cases were never that simple.

Of course, he specialized in tough cases.

He checked his watch, calculating the time it would take to get Thais to a marine base. He needed to shake Pullman up, get the guy to make a move. Turning toward his computer, Kagan punched in a note on the open warrant for Thais Sinclair, changing the status to "in custody."

He indulged in a rare grin before he signed out and waited to see if Carl's people made the mistake of rattling Pullman's chain.

"That's not my problem," Pullman growled. "I took the contract for a hit. Helping you frame someone for it, that's a whole different thing. It's not my problem. I do wet work only."

"You'd better adjust your scope of thinking," Eric informed him. "And get the job done now, before they get Thais onto a marine base."

"You don't tell me when to take the shot," Pullman said with a hiss. "Told you so right up front. I know my business, you don't. Otherwise you wouldn't need to hire my services because you could do your own killing."

"Miranda is out in the open right now," Eric said. "Are you telling me you can't get the job done?"

"She's attending an event with over ten thousand people," Pullman answered. "I will get her next week. Already have the scene picked out. Better odds of making a clean kill."

"What if we want it done today?" Eric asked.

"You'll get caught," Pullman answered. "This isn't my first contract. You wanted me because of my experience. I've already pinpointed the best opportunity. Wait for it or get someone else."

Pullman killed the call.

He was too old for this shit.

Another rich man who wanted more power and didn't have a scrap of a conscience. Not that Pullman claimed any hint of morality himself.

But he knew his business.

Ricky's words and carefree tone rose from his memory. It was tempting. In fact Pullman picked up his phone and dialed his fellow hitman.

"I want to talk about the deal."

Eric listened to the dial tone for a long moment. He gritted his teeth as he punched the disconnect button on the screen and shoved the phone into his pocket.

Carl looked up from his desk, raising an eyebrow in question. Secure in the little office on board their private plane, it had been the only place to have a conversation with Pullman. They spent more time in the air than on the ground as Carl tried to attend as many events as possible in order to hold on to his lead in the polls.

But the gap between him and Tom Hilliard was growing smaller.

"Pullman insists on waiting," Eric said, sharing the information.

Carl wasn't pleased.

"He said to get someone else if we didn't like his answer and hung up," Eric continued, cutting Carl off.

Carl sat forward. "He's getting out of our control."

"Agreed." For the record, Eric had always thought getting a hitman was too dangerous. So he wasn't going to quibble over how Carl came around to letting him silence Pullman.

"With Thais Sinclair in custody, better to let the entire matter go," Eric advised.

"You've been against this since the beginning," Carl said with a snarl. "I want that bitch dead."

"At the cost of the election?" Eric asked.

"When she goes," Carl explained, "the fence hopping will begin. There are key players who feel safe standing against me because Miranda and her family name are against me. When I take her out, the message will be clear: I'm the man they'd better make happy. Call him back and tell him I'll wait."

Carl watched as Eric dialed.

"We agree to your time line. Final payment will be made when I get confirmation the target is down. There's a bonus if you get it done sooner rather than later. One large enough to cover your risk."

Carl was smirking when Eric disconnected the line.

"Thais is safe, got her stashed with an old buddy of mine."

Dunn stood up. He didn't get surprised often and having Kagan call out of the blue was certainly unexpected.

"That's a matter of opinion," Dunn replied. "Your buddy has people he trusts. People you don't know."

"Fair enough," Kagan replied. "But this buddy, he's got a good reputation of not being a man to cross. Anyone stupid enough to try it won't give Sinclair too much trouble."

Dunn's lips twitched. "Alright. What's next?"

"Assuming I won't remind you of your civilian status?" Kagan asked.

"You wouldn't waste your time calling me if that was the game plan," Dunn replied. "I'm a resource, one you understand the value of."

Dunn wasn't going to mince words. There would be those out there who would warn him to steer clear of Kagan and the entire Shadow Ops world. Maybe he would even listen if his mother and Thais weren't involved.

"I'm granting you a badge," Kagan said. "Under Shadow Ops. I want you next to Miranda. She's as stubborn as you are. Get her on board."

"What about Thais?"

"Sinclair is more trouble than any sell-out new private can handle," Kagan remarked. "Trust me, my buddy weeds out the weak ones. His marines are pure. That's why I had her taken where she is. The base is a weapons station. A top-secret facility is hidden beneath the surface. New arrivals don't get a whiff of what really goes on there until they prove themselves. Sinclair is secure. Your mother, on the other hand, is giving her escort grief and putting herself at risk. Time to pull rank on her. Pick up your credentials when you arrive."

Dunn grinned. Not many men surprised him.

Kagan had.

Kent was watching him.

"I think I was just drafted," Dunn responded. "My first duty is to get a handle on my mother."

Kent lifted his hand and made the sign of the cross over Dunn. "Placing my bet on your mum."

Dunn powered down his laptop and packed. Two weeks ago he'd left his home intent on getting to Miranda.

She was still vastly important to him, and yet, he'd be a liar if he didn't admit how reluctant he was to place distance between Thais and himself.

It was more than he bargained on for certain.

So what do you want to do about it?

Dunn decided he wasn't going to answer the question. He had a pressing matter to attend to, the same one he'd left his personal business affairs behind to deal with.

The problem was, his mind wasn't willing to drop it. His mind was offering up the way Thais had peeled his layers off just as expertly as he had hers.

Why in the hell had he told her about Rhianna?

It wasn't just the betrayal that made him banish the woman from his memory. No, it was the sting of the humiliation. His grandfather had been the one to unmask her. Sitting so quietly as Dunn had listened to the recordings of his beloved as she crowed to her mother about how tightly she had Dunn under her control.

The lies.

The manipulation.

It was all Dunn held on to from their relationship. He wanted to remember what he represented to women.

A prize.

Thais was pushing him away.

Was it just the allure of the woman who refused to be enamored with his wealth? Possibly. And yet, he found himself absorbed with getting back to her so he could see what happened when they both shed the rest of their remaining layers.

Maybe that was the same bullheadedness that had landed him in trouble before. But just maybe he didn't want to live with the alternative.

His pride wasn't worth as much as his need to see Thais again.

Ricky hated the desert.

The dry, brittle vegetation looked like death to him. Give him Ireland with its rain and mud any day.

But Pullman had called the meeting place. As far as that went, Pullman was smart. Ricky walked down a path, turning around a corner, and the dry, dusty ground let him know that no one else had been along the same path.

The sparse vegetation made sure Ricky could see for miles, too.

Out in the distance, he could hear the traffic on the interstate. Somewhere between Las Vegas and Southern California, there were more abandoned structures than anyone knew about. Ricky leaned against the wall of what had once been a gas station.

A little service station that had been abandoned in favor of larger structures that offered motorists more services or, at least, more than one bathroom. Twenty-eight miles up the road there was an off-ramp with five service stations and several fast-food places. The little abandoned station had been choked by it. Now, the outside was a mass of graffiti and wind whistled in through the broken windows.

But Pullman knew what he was doing because there was a thick layer of dirt on the floor, letting Ricky know that he was still very much alone. He heard Pullman coming down the two-lane road. Somewhere off in the distance, there were a couple of trailer homes on plots of land where people who wanted to be alone lived. The car came around the side of the service station and the engine cut off.

Ricky stayed inside. Pullman was calling the shots. It wasn't the most dangerous thing he'd ever pulled in his life but Ricky had a newfound awareness of life these days. Staying inside, waiting for Pullman to appear was making him sweat. Pullman might just want to plug up a leak by killing him because Ricky had guessed who hired him.

"You came alone," Pullman said from the doorway. The sun was starting to set. It was near blinding behind Pullman, making it hard to see his face until he walked inside.

"I don't remember you and me having a problem," Ricky replied. "Last time I saw you, a good job came my way because of you. Why do you think I was willing to help you?"

Pullman offered him a shrug before he came farther into the building. He was leaner than the last time they'd met. His face almost gaunt. He had on a duster coat, his hands shoved deep into the pockets.

Ricky grinned, enjoying wearing only a T-shirt and jeans. "You look like a fucking grim reaper, man."

Pullman's lips twitched but Ricky wouldn't really call it a grin. No, there was too much of a soulless look in the guy's eyes.

Hell, Ricky really needed to thank Kagan for turning him away from the hitman lifestyle.

"Retirement is good," Ricky offered. "The golden sort of retirement."

Pullman sniffed. "You've got your head up your ass if you really believe you can just settle into life without looking over your shoulder. It doesn't work that way."

Ricky pushed away from the wall he'd been leaning on. "If that's how you feel, why did you waste my time with this meeting?"

"You reached out to me," Pullman answered.

"True." Ricky closed the distance between them a little. "Couldn't help but try to save your ass when I saw you offering pictures of the Shadow Ops' next location. Guess I remember our relationship differently. Sure didn't think you'd pull a dick move like having me drive out to nowhere for nothing. I actually got you a passport."

"It will be worthless once Carl Davis shuts down the Shadow Ops teams," Pullman argued. "Help me do this job and Carl will take care of us."

"Oh, that's the deal, is it?" Ricky stepped a little closer as he smiled brighter. "Want me to switch sides?"

"You're a hitman," Pullman replied. "It's not personal. Sign on now or Carl will hunt you down along with Kagan's teams."

Cat popped into Ricky's mind.

In the next moment, Ricky was twisting and shoving a knife up into Pullman's diaphragm. Blood coated his hand as he twisted the handle of the blade and pulled it free to let Pullman bleed out. With his diaphragm punctured, Pullman was gasping like a fish yanked up onto land. He was grasping for the gun he had in his pocket, trying to pull it free but Ricky had beguiled him too well, slipping too close for retaliation.

The dry desert dirt soaked up the blood as Ricky wiped his hand on Pullman's shirt and shook his head.

"Sorry, man, but it is very personal to me."

He contemplated Pullman's body for a moment before he dug a burner phone out of his pocket and dialed Kagan.

"Report," Kagan said when he answered.

Ricky wasn't a stranger to killing.

He was unaccustomed to hanging around the scenes of his work though.

The traffic on the interstate was a low rumble that just continued through the night. The wind was continuous as well. He heard the SUV as it started to head his way. Early in the predawn light, Ricky peeked out of a hole in one of the pieces of plywood over what had once been a window. Saxon and Vitus Hale hadn't lost any of their impressive conditioning. They got out of the vehicle almost in the same moment the engine turned off.

He made sure he slid into the doorway slowly. Unlike Pullman, Ricky didn't think either of the Shadow Ops agents would make the mistake of letting him dazzle them with his chatter while forgetting he was a hitman with an impressive kill record.

Saxon aimed a hard look at him, his grim expression making it clear the agent wasn't happy to be working with him. He crossed into the station as Vitus made sure he kept Ricky in clear sights.

One wrong move and Ricky was sure Pullman would have company on the ground.

Saxon knelt down beside the body, pressing his fingers into Pullman's neck before he shook his head. "He'd have been a lot more use to us alive."

Saxon stood and sent Ricky a disgusted look. "Not that you'd understand that."

Ricky raised an eyebrow. "He wasn't going to take Kagan's deal."

"We still needed him to confess to taking the hit on Miranda," Vitus stated softly. "My fellow agent is in jail under suspicion of trying to kill her."

"Think I'm a dumb shit for killing him?" Ricky asked.

Both agents weren't expecting such a blunt question but they nodded.

"Know how I figured it was him?" Ricky gestured behind him to where Pullman's body was. "He had pictures of your nest and was offering them to the highest bidder."

There was a soft intake of breath from one of the Hale brothers. Ricky absorbed the sound as a little victory over their expertise.

"I know a thing or two about the business," Ricky continued. "Also know a bit about your team and Miranda Delacroix. If Pullman had those pictures, it was because he was tracking her. I put it together. Not so much of a dumb shit after all."

Vitus folded his arms over his chest. "Not bad," the ex-SEAL remarked. "Not impressive, either."

"I wasn't finished," Ricky cut back. "Pullman knew I had a deal with Kagan. He told me to switch sides or go down with you all. He's one of the best. Slipping into the gutter is something Pullman sort of enjoyed. If I let him walk out of here, you wouldn't have this . . ."

Ricky held up Pullman's phone.

One corner of Vitus's mouth twitched. Ricky enjoyed the hard-won victory as Saxon took the phone. "I can decode the auction site for the pictures of your nest and link it back to that phone. With a little luck, we might even get a link on where Pullman was stashing his pay."

"You can do that?" Saxon questioned.

Ricky shrugged. "Just get the press to think she's dead, and wait for the final payment to be transferred."

He snapped his fingers.

Vitus and Saxon exchanged a look.

"I still don't like you," Vitus said as he turned and headed back to the SUV.

"Neither do I," Saxon added before his brother returned with a body bag.

Ricky started to argue about how his childhood had been a piss pot but he realized he didn't much care anymore just why he'd been on the road he'd taken in life.

How he could have so very easily ended up like Pullman. The little shell of a gas station filled with the sound of a zipper being opened before the Hale brothers lifted the body and placed it inside the body bag. They scooped up the dirt that was stained with blood and dumped it on top of the body before zipping the bag up.

No, he didn't give a rat's ass for what he'd thought he was doing before. All that matters was how he could use his knowledge to ensure he got to go back to Ireland and Cat.

Oh, and making his mum proud. He liked that thought a whole lot. Funny thing was, she'd told him he'd thank her one day for trying to teach him right from wrong. He'd been too young, too immersed in his own view of the world to agree with her. Funny how life had let him live long enough to wise up. Because he sure as shit didn't deserve it.

Maybe that was the real reason he'd turned on Pullman. Once he'd accepted what a dumbass he'd been, there seemed to be nothing stopping him from growing the one thing he'd always prided himself on not giving a shit over.

A conscience.

"I'm eager to have this entire matter finished, too."

Dunn jerked his head around. Miranda offered him a shy smile as she came out of the bedroom in their suite. It was barely first light.

She moved over to where a pot of coffee was sitting on a warming station in the kitchen. "But I think maybe you're a little more focused on ensuring Agent Sinclair is proven innocent."

Dunn turned to face her. "I came here for you, Mother."

She'd filled a mug but didn't take a sip as she smiled at him. "It makes me so very happy . . . having you here. Especially now that we have a plan to end it all at last. I simply can't sleep knowing that Thais is in a cell unjustly."

"In a few hours, we'll have everything we need to free her," Dunn assured her.

And then what?

Dunn watched his mother sip at her coffee. Heat was spreading through him but for a much different reason.

It was anticipation.

The waiting was almost over, and he was more than ready to get to the battle.

Thais had better sleep while she could.

* * *

"Details are sketchy at this hour, but there are reports that Congress hopeful Miranda Delacroix Ryland has been murdered."

Eric Geyer stared at the news report as he tapped on the surface of his phone.

"It was just after eight this morning when the congressional hopeful was leaving her hotel for an appearance. Reports are that she was struck by a single shot as she was crossing from the lobby of her hotel to her car."

Eric didn't leave Carl's side very often. He sent a signal to one of the other security men in Carl's escort and traded out so he could get far enough away to make a phone call.

Carl kept his focus on the governor he was talking to but Eric knew he was itching for confirmation.

Eric was more than ready for closure.

He pulled out the burner phone he used for contacting Pullman.

"Don't fucking call me," said the growly voice that Eric assumed was the hitman's when he picked up the line. "Just finish the deal now that I've done the job."

Eric didn't obey just yet though. He dialed another number and waited for one of the men on Miranda's security detail to answer.

"Is it true?" Eric pressed the man when he answered.

"Clean chest shot," the man answered. "There was blood everywhere."

Eric grinned and killed the call. He hadn't really expected to feel anything over Miranda's death. Sure, he didn't have any personal grievance with her and maybe some men would have seen him following the order to have her killed as something that should have taxed his conscience.

It didn't.

He logged into a slush account and transferred the last part of the payment. The signal bounced around the globe before it landed in the bank Pullman had selected in the Caribbean. He stared at the confirmation number for a moment before he crushed the phone and pulled the SIM card out to break it into tiny pieces.

Carl came through the door, his face flushed with excitement. Eric locked gazes with him.

"I'm sorry to inform you that Miranda Delacroix has been killed."

CHAPTER FIVE

Vitus was driving the SUV when he and Saxon returned to the military base. Thais enjoyed the way the marines looked at her with confusion.

Let them wonder.

It wouldn't be the first time or the last that they found themselves dealing with situations they didn't get officially filled in on.

She knew what it felt like.

Today though, what filled her thoughts was how empty she felt. With Pullman dead, the case would likely go cold. Oh, she didn't think for a moment that Carl Davis was going to stop trying to close the Shadow Ops teams down. No, they knew too much about him for that.

But their focus would shift back to Carl.

So, it was over.

Do you want it to continue?

Thais knew what the question was really about. She climbed into the SUV with her teammates and tried to push her thoughts back into the place she'd had them locked away before Dunn had broken her out of Homeland.

Before you gave into your needs?

Yes, and shut up!

"From Dunn," Greer said quietly. Her fellow agent laid something in her lap. Thais opened the small case to see a Lynx.

It was over.

Or maybe it didn't have to be. She'd thought Dunn had managed to rip into her walls before. Now? She realized she was wide open because the Lynx was like a red-hot coal just waiting to burn her.

She shut the case and dropped it beside her on the seat. Saxon was watching out of the corner of his eye. Even with his shades on, she knew him well enough to know when he was observing her.

Thais looked out the window.

She refused to need anyone besides her team. Her badge was her identity by choice. Besides, Dunn wasn't the sort of man a woman domesticated. She'd always known it. Better to end it now, before she let him any deeper into herself.

It was over.

And that was the way it had to be.

No matter how badly she wanted to second-guess herself.

Dunn checked his phone.

He never had a shortage of messages. His email files were bursting after two weeks of his attention being on other things than his empire.

Text messages had piled up as he fell behind on emails.

Phone messages? Check that, too. He had a nice accumulation of those waiting for him as well.

But he didn't have the message he was waiting for.

"Ignoring me, Agent Sinclair?"

"The Lynx can't be traced."

There was a delay before Thais responded.

"Nothing is foolproof."

Dunn grinned.

"Like your rule about never getting involved with any of your lovers? Nice of you to give me hope, Thais."

"You're the recluse."

"Some would say we're well-matched."

Dunn waited but Thais didn't reply. He found himself grinning at the challenge she presented and from the sheer enjoyment of knowing she'd failed to ignore his present. She was no stranger to brushing off men she wanted nothing more to do with.

"That's a good look for you," Miranda said as she came into the sitting room. "Someone has made you happy."

Dunn checked the rest of the room.

"We're alone," Miranda confirmed. "Just as Kagan stipulated." His mother reached up and ruffled her hair. "I do believe that fake blood left a stain or two!"

"As soon as they crack that phone, you'll be free to have a hair professional deal with it," Dunn said. "For the moment though, you're dead, so stuck with only me and Kent for company."

Miranda offered him a smile. "Well worth it in my opinion. I really can't wait to see Carl's reaction to my survival. He's enjoyed having the media work to his advantage so often, I do believe it's high time he discovered that he's not the only one who can get caught in the back draft of unconfirmed details."

Dunn grinned again. "I admit I'm looking forward to it myself."

"And you can get back to courting that lovely agent, Thais Sinclair."

Dunn's lips thinned. Miranda's smile, on the other hand, brightened until her eyes were sparkling with mirth.

"You two really are well-matched." Miranda eyed him over the rim of a teacup. "You can't control her. It's the element you need to keep you on your toes. That's why you haven't settled down before, you could never be sure if it was you or your empire that your girlfriend loved."

Miranda took a sip of her tea and stared straight back at the hard look Dunn aimed her way. Plenty of people he knew would have called it a warning look. Miranda only fluttered her eyelashes and didn't falter.

"You really are my mother," he remarked to her delight. "Just as stubborn as I am."

He'd invested a lot of effort in making sure no one was in the position to say they truly knew him. A defensive action, one he'd taken solace in for too many years. Now? He'd be a liar if he didn't admit he enjoyed knowing someone else could read him. Controlling his world had limits to the level of satisfaction it could provide.

A bit of a newsflash.

But one he found himself welcoming because it was

a kick in the ass. One designed to get him moving, before he lost an opportunity to see if Thais was the missing piece in his world.

Thais let out a huff.

She stared at the computer screen and tapped in another line of numbers.

When the data changed she cussed.

"That doesn't sound promising," Saxon said, stating the obvious.

Thais swiveled around in her chair and looked at her team leader. "I traced the money to a slush account but can't nail it on Carl's ass."

"Which means we have a dead hitman, proof he was paid to kill Miranda Delacroix, and pictures of him tracking her . . ." Thais shook her head. She was up and out of her seat as she spoke, agitated by the lack of conclusion.

"I'll take it," Vitus Hale said, delivering his opinion in a firm tone. He didn't waver when Thais turned on him. "You're off the hook. The team is vindicated. We survive to fight another day."

"It will have to be enough," Saxon said. "Delaying any further could cost Miranda the election. We need to clear her to come out of hiding."

Thais nodded. "If we can't nail Carl Davis, at least we can let Miranda drive him nuts by being alive and well."

Saxon picked up his phone and called in to their section leader. Thais sat down and processed the evidence she'd found. Offshore accounts and Pullman's nest eggs. Ricky Sullivan knew his business or at least his fellow hitmen. Pullman had known what he was doing, too; they might have found the money but the trail went back to a slush fund she couldn't prove anyone owned. That meant the owner had paid a hefty sum to the bank before they killed the account and the bank had erased it. The money itself was tagged and couldn't be transferred into most countries because of its origins, but Pullman would have just arrived in the Caribbean and withdrawn it in person. From there it would have been a simple matter of buying diamonds, gold, or some other portable type of wealth.

Saxon finished his call. Thais felt her team leader's stare. She swiveled around again to discover Vitus and Greer both watching to see what Saxon was getting ready to drop on her.

The way Saxon had his jaw tightened promised her it wasn't going to be something she liked.

"Miranda needs to utilize the media attention she'll receive once she emerges from protective custody."

Thais narrowed her eyes as Saxon hesitated.

"This involves me . . . how?" Thais asked.

Her team leader looked like his collar was shrinking. "By presenting you with the FBI Medal of Valor. Seems she's pulled a few strings and has the president on board with doing a ceremony tomorrow when she emerges from her enforced hiding."

There was silence in the room. One of those silences no one wanted to break because they didn't want to be the target of Thais's reaction.

"I don't think so," she said softly.

"It's an order," Saxon replied. "From Kagan."

"Kagan can go to the ceremony," Thais informed him.

"You were right there when both of us had to stand through a medal ceremony," Saxon said, trying to apply logic to his argument.

"This is different," Thais declared.

"I don't see how," Vitus remarked. He was a master at controlling his expression but his eyes were glittering with amusement.

Thais stood.

"Miranda has the right idea." Saxon jumped in to shield his brother. "We need to make Carl nervous. It's the only way he might get spooked enough to slip up."

"Otherwise we're stuck waiting for him to win this election and sign an executive order disbanding us," Vitus added.

"All or nothing?" Thais replied.

Her teammates nodded. They were amused but she admitted she'd enjoyed watching them be strong-armed into medal ceremonies when a public display had been what a case called for.

Besides, she knew the real reason she was balking at Kagan's order.

And it was personal.

So she would be keeping her mouth shut before her teammates realized the real reason she didn't want to go near Miranda was because she knew Dunn would be there.

Well, you don't know for sure . . .

But she did. It was in the pit of her stomach. A ball of tension left from the time they'd spent together.

It's hadn't been enough.

Admitting that was tough but what had her turning her back on her teammates and going through the motions of packing up her gear was the fact that she couldn't be certain Dunn would be there.

She'd given Dunn the brushoff. He had every reason

to consider it finished between them and because she'd told him she didn't want anything else.

But what stuck in her head, what she just couldn't seem to shake was the fact that part of her worried he'd be happy to move on.

Thais knew how to take her knocks in life. What she found herself dreading was something far more than a knock. Something she wouldn't be able to mask the pain of.

Something like a broken heart.

The press loved to think they could sniff out any secrets.

Dunn watched the security footage from the main ballroom where Tom Hilliard had called a surprise press conference. He was closing the gap on Carl Davis and being the one to announce that Miranda wasn't dead was sure to see his name on the top of every news-feed from print to social media sites.

"I admit I am going to enjoy this a great deal," Miranda declared as she emerged from the side of the suite she had been using.

"Rising from the dead or getting out of this suite?" Dunn asked.

"You've spent enough time in here with me," she muttered. "Even if I admit I'd like to keep you all to myself. But . . ." She took a glance in the mirror, checking her suit and hair one last time before she turned and sent Dunn a look full of all the strength she kept so very neatly disguised beneath her gently aged persona.

"I should very much like to help Tom win this election," Miranda finished.

Kent rapped on the outer door. Dunn pulled it open as the security cameras captured the sight of Tom waving on his way to where he would address the press. The flash of hundreds of cameras flickered through the room while Dunn and Kent escorted Miranda down.

"And so . . . it's with great relief that I can share with you all at last . . ." Tom grasped the sides of the lectern before finishing. "Miranda Delacroix is in fact alive and well."

The room erupted. Reporters ignored the rule of raising hands and just shouted out their questions. Tom raised his hands, begging for the chance to explain. The horde in front of him didn't grant it to him immediately.

"Allowing the world to believe she was dead was necessary to trap the hitman who was intent on killing her. It's my pleasure to report that she is here and ready to resume her bid for a seat in Congress."

The room was in an uproar as Miranda appeared. Dunn hung back, watching as Tom's security continued to maintain a solid perimeter around the speaking lectern. Miranda took it all in stride. Moving forward as the press surged to their feet, demanding answers. She waited while the cameras flashed, her smile perfect and her composure flawless until at last the press settled down because they wanted their answers.

"Your mom has a solid spine," Kent remarked as Miranda began to address the press.

They didn't give her any mercy, but Miranda stood firm, never wavering as she answered sharp-edged questions with an ease that impressed him.

"Ladies and gentlemen," Miranda said, finally raising her voice after the questions had become repetitive. "Today is not all about me. My survival is due completely to the efforts of men and women who have dedicated their lives to the very foundational values of this country. Without their efforts, I would be as dead as you were lead to believe. Now that the hitman is dealt with, I am at liberty to publicly thank a woman who safeguarded me, even at the expense of her own reputation. I would like to welcome Special Agent Thais Sinclair to this press gathering."

Dunn slowly grinned. Thais was flanked by her teammates and her poise was flawless but he knew her better. There was a slight narrowing of her eyes that gave away her true feelings.

He realized he enjoyed knowing he knew her.

It was an intimacy.

How long had it been since he'd let someone touch him that deeply?

It was sobering to say the least. An admission of just how deeply he'd let Rhianna slash him. Trust opened a person up to possibilities like that. And he realized he'd trusted Thais.

A damn risky gamble.

And yet, he wasn't contemplating how to minimize his loses.

No, he was sizing up his counterpart and deciding on a course of action.

"I have been looking forward to having the opportunity to thank Special Agent Thais Sinclair for her dedication to duty, above and beyond the scope of her job description . . ."

Miranda proceeded with a flawless execution of the award ceremony. Her father had raised her to be the perfect politician's wife and she didn't disappoint.

Thais knew that sort of training as well. She smiled and shook Miranda's hand after Miranda had placed the award around her neck. The flashing of cameras never seemed to stop. Her lips were frozen in place, the sides of her face aching as she continued to hold position. Miranda finally declared the press conference over, slipping away as she let her security people surround her to prevent the press from following too closely.

The pack turned on Thais.

Her team finally came to her rescue, surging in front of her as she turned and headed for any avenue of escape.

Dunn surfaced from the back of the room, reaching out to grasp her wrist and pull her through a door that one of his people stepped into to shield their escape. He took command of her and she found herself trusting in his grasp.

Another pair of security men parted to allow them to enter an elevator; the men smoothly slipped back to fill the doorway as Dunn pulled her into the car and punched in a floor number.

Thais drew in a deep breath as the elevator jerked and started moving upward.

But it drew Dunn's scent into her senses.

She knew it on a level she hadn't realized anyone might register on. Somewhere deep inside herself where she'd convinced herself no one else had the means to touch her.

And he still had hold of her wrist. Her heart was accelerating. His thumb moved, brushing over the delicate skin of her inner wrist. She felt him press against the spot where she knew he could feel her pulse.

She could pull away.

But you don't want to . . .

"You want me to notice," he said softly, turning his head so he was watching her. "Don't you, Thais?"

It wasn't really a question.

No, it was far more of a statement of fact. She felt herself shuddering in response, and his grip tightened again as he noted the reaction.

"I shouldn't." The admission crossed her lips as the doors opened.

"It's not going to be that easy, Thais." He strode forward, leaving her against the back of the elevator. He turned, catching her with his emerald gaze as he offered her his hand. "I'm not going to be alone in this."

The challenge was there between them. His hand opened as he stood in the open doorway, keeping the doors from sliding shut.

She put her hand into his. Her impulses flattened her thoughts as she jumped toward him, unwilling to deny herself the opportunity to indulge.

Dunn pulled her into the hallway, wrapping his arm around her and turning her back to the wall. He pinned her there, threading his fingers into her hair to capture her completely. Her breath caught as he tilted her head up so he could claim her lips.

"Ummm . . ." The soft sound escaped from her as she kissed him back. There was no way she was going to deny herself the moment; honestly, she couldn't have even if there were a valid reason for her to do so.

There was only Dunn and the moment she hadn't expected to come her way.

They were stealing time.

Grabbing a handful of happiness before it was jerked

out of reach once more by circumstance and harsh reality.

The elevator door chimed. Dunn grunted as he pushed away from her, turning and pulling her behind him in a swift motion that saw her stepping away from the wall before the elevator doors fully opened.

She caught sight of his man Kent in the hallway but it was brief as Dunn slid a keycard through a door lock and opened the door to a penthouse suite.

Thais didn't wait for the door to shut.

Her heart was pounding and she just didn't want to slow down.

No, she wanted to indulge.

Dunn was shrugging out of his suit jacket. She pushed him back against the wall before he got his arms free.

"Stay right there," she ordered him.

His eyes narrowed.

Thais fingered the fabric of her dress, pulling it up to give him a flash of her thighs. "It might be worth your while to let me call the shots, Dunn."

He stopped rotating his shoulders to dislodge his jacket, one corner of his lips rising as he watched her raise her dress higher, until the hem was just shy of her mons.

His eyes narrowed as she held position. "Sure you want to tease me?"

There was a promise in his tone that set off a throbbing in her clit. He wasn't tame. She'd deduced that the first time she met him. No woman would ever domesticate him.

And a smart one would even think twice about how much better off she'd be to leave just the way he was.

The jacket dropped to the floor. She watched the way he brought his arms forward, the look in his eyes sending a little zip of heat through her.

She smiled.

You're becoming addicted to the way he makes you feel . . .

Maybe, but she wasn't at all interested in contemplating the idea at the moment. She backed up, letting the dress fall back down.

It earned her a raised eyebrow. She felt her lips rising into a smile. It was another one of those . . . *honest* . . . emotional responses he seemed to have an exclusive ability to unlock inside her.

She turned and picked up her feet. Running across the polished floors. She heard him give chase, felt a jolt of anticipation go through her as she caught the sound of his footfalls behind her.

She let out a squeal as he captured her. Lifting her off her feet as he closed his arms around her.

"Are you mine to do with what I please?" he asked next to her ear.

"Maybe I was just trying to bait you," she answered as he lifted her high and dropped her onto one of the sofas from behind it.

He remained standing. She bounced once before Dunn caught the sides of her dress and pulled the soft fabric up her body. "I like the idea of having you at my mercy better."

He tossed her dress aside, a grunt of male satisfaction coming from him. Thais flipped over onto her knees and flattened her hand over the bulge of his cock.

"So sure about that . . ." She clicked her tongue as

she rubbed him gently. "I still say you would enjoy being toyed with."

And she wasn't planning on waiting for him to agree.

No, she opened his belt, feeling her senses tighten. Arousal went through her, only now it was something that captured her attention completely. She wasn't applying a skill.

No, she was engaged completely.

And she wanted Dunn just as helpless as she was against the need rising between them.

"Agreed," he offered as she opened his pants.

Thais didn't rush. She enjoyed the way peeling back the fabric from his skin unleashed his scent. Recognition flickered inside her brain where she didn't have any control over the way her body responded to it.

Her nipples tingled as they drew into hard little points.

Her clit was throbbing.

She ignored it as she drew his cock into the open. His breath caught as she stroked it. Using just the tips of her fingers, she teased him with several up and down motions.

"I give as good as I get, Thais . . . ," he warned her in a husky voice.

She reached lower and cupped his balls. Applying just enough pressure to make his lips thin with male pleasure.

"You don't want me to rush, any more than I want to have this moment finished."

His eyes had narrowed but he opened them as her words hit him. For a moment, she was staring into his emerald eyes, fixated by the emotion glittering in them. He reached down and caught the back of her head, twisting her hair just enough to make her realize he had the strength to hold her.

But she was claiming him at the moment.

She lowered her gaze to his cock, closing her fingers around his flesh as she leaned forward and allowed her breath to touch the slit on the head of it.

His grip tightened, delighting her. There was something about knowing he was just as susceptible to her as she was to him.

Soul mates . . .

She should have shied away from the concept but the truth was, she was sinking into the moment and the only real focus she had was drawing more responses from him.

She opened her mouth and licked him.

She heard the way he sucked his breath through his teeth. Felt the way he pushed his hips toward her. He wanted more. Craved the connection as much as she did. Thais didn't plan on disappointing him. She worked her hands along the length of his shaft. Tightening her fingers around his girth and pumping him as she teased the head of his cock with her tongue.

He groaned.

She'd often used such sounds as a way of gauging just when her subject was ready to spill information.

Tonight, she wanted to do anything but think.

Instead, Thais opened her mouth and closed her lips around the head of his cock. He drew in another harsh breath as she teased the crown with her tongue. She caught the first hints of his come, rising up into the slit on the head of his staff.

"Christ," he growled as she licked the slit again and sucked harder.

He was pushing his hips toward her. His flesh hardening even more as she worked her hands along the portion of his cock that she couldn't get into her mouth. She was pushing the limit, working harder on him in an effort to shove him over the edge. Was it about victory? Maybe. But not the sort she'd ever craved before. This time, she wanted to know she'd managed to satisfy him.

Dunn denied her though.

He pulled away, stepping back so his cock left her mouth.

"I have other plans for this hard-on, Thais." He yanked his tie off and tossed it aside as he attacked the buttons on his cuffs and shirt. "And they involve you moaning along with me."

His eyes glittered with promise as he shed his clothing. He leaned over and cupped the back of her head when he finished, leaning over to kiss her.

It was a hard kiss and one she returned with equal passion. A little sound of delight escaped her lips as she rose up on her knees to kiss him back.

Dunn slid his hands over her shoulders before stroking along her shoulder blades and finding the clasp of her bra. A little pressure around her chest and then he was pulling the garment up her arms.

The look on his face was mesmerizing.

Lust was there but something else was, too, that thing she'd tried to convince herself didn't really exist in the world.

It was there in Dunn though, and she reached for him, pulling him back down so she could kiss him again. So simple a thing, a kiss, and yet, she could have spent endless time doing it with him. Dunn didn't deprive her, either. He clasped her tightly, cradling the back of her head as he moved his mouth over hers.

But her body was only going to wait so long for what it craved.

Dunn broke away from her, his face strained with hunger. She slipped back down onto the sofa as he came around the edge.

He was coming for her.

She watched the intent on his face, felt the way the look in his eyes pinned her in place.

He caught the sides of her last garment and tugged her panties down her legs before he pushed her back onto the surface of the sofa.

"Payback time . . . ," he muttered as he pressed her knees wide.

He was taking control.

Demanding it.

She shifted, rolling to one side only to feel him pressing down on her. He framed her face with his hands, making their gazes meet.

"Give me control, Thais," he rasped at her. "Be my lover."

Lover . . .

The word took on its true meaning when she applied it to him.

"I'm not sure I know how." It was an admission. One that slipped across her lips while he was watching her.

His eyes narrowed, his lips thinning. He tapped her mouth with one fingertip. "Just . . . stay . . . right there."

His tone was coated in thick intent. She caught a glitter

of determination in his eyes before he was kissing his
way down her body. Lifted her arms up and pressing
them above her head before he stroked her, down her
face and neck until he was kneading her breasts.

"You need to eat more," he muttered as he teased her
nipples.

"Said no man ever . . . ," she groused, lifting her eyelids to shoot him a stare.

Dunn stared right back at her. "I just did . . ."

But he wasn't interested in talking any more than she
was. He moved down her body, pausing to kiss her belly
before he was spreading her slit wide and applying his
mouth to her clit.

She gasped, twisting because of the intensity of
the contact. She heard him chuckle, felt the vibration
against her flesh and let out a gasp.

"Ummm . . . ," he muttered in response. "You like
that . . ."

There was smug victory in his tone but whatever
she might have thought about it died as he returned to
driving her insane with his mouth. It took her to the
edge, where climax was just a single breath away. She
resisted, however, lifting her hips as she tried to break
the connection, just enough so she wouldn't reach that
peak.

She didn't want the moment to be over.

Dunn insisted though. Following her and sucking
harder as he pressed two thick fingers up inside her passage.

Thais cried out, arching up as climax broke through
her. Twisting and wringing her for moments that felt
endless. The pleasure was deep, washing away the need
that had been pulsing inside of her.

Dunn eased away, stroking her inner thighs as he watched her struggle to draw in enough breath to keep from just passing out.

He was pleased with himself.

She caught the satisfied grin on his lips as she succeeded in opening her eyes and focusing on him. It spurred her up and off her back. She was straddling him and pushing his back against the padded surface of the sofa before she thought anything through.

It wasn't a time for thinking.

No, she lifted up and felt the head of his cock slipping into the wet folds of her body. His expression tightened with need as he bared his teeth at her.

"My turn . . . ," she offered as she lowered herself onto his length.

"Knock yourself out . . . ," he answered as he cupped her hips and pressed her down once she'd lifted up again.

"The plan"—she pressed down again—"is to knock you out."

To push him past his limits. It was burning inside her as she rode him but he wasn't going to allow her to be in command. He slid his hand across her belly, seeking out her clit as she gasped and increased her pace.

He teased her clit, awakening the need he'd already satisfied once.

Her heart was pounding, her skin coated in perspiration as they tried to push one another over the edge. He was right there with her, rising up to meet her, filling her with hard thrusts as he rubbed her clit. Thais felt her body tightening. Need was a roaring inferno inside them both and in those last movements, she realized she'd never felt so connected to another soul in her life.

She cried out again, the sound proof of just how completely she'd lost control.

But Dunn let out a growl as well, his cock jerking inside her as he griped her hips to hold her in place as he emptied himself.

She clamped her thighs around him, clinging to him as the only solid thing in her universe.

Carl blinked and then sat down hard as he stared at the large flat-screen television with Miranda displayed on it in live time. He rubbed his hand over his face before looking back at Eric. "I suppose . . . that isn't a bad thing. Pullman knew too much."

Carl was thinking.

Or maybe it was a little more precise to say, Carl's brain was spinning. Eric was growing accustomed to the signs of his boss's growing agitation. The way Carl drummed his fingers on the desktop, the way his lips moved, like he was thinking too fast for his thoughts to form into actual words.

"Maybe . . . I'm going about this the wrong way." Carl managed to get some of his thoughts into words. He was tapping the desktop and suddenly flattened his hand. "You're right, Eric. Miranda is voter candy."

Eric stiffened. He knew the tone Carl was using and it wasn't one of accepting what fate was willing to give them.

"We need Miranda on our side," Carl said as he stood.

"How do you propose to accomplish that?" Eric asked.

Carl was plotting. Eric watched the way he tapped his fingertips against one another as he concentrated.

"Dunn Bateson was at the press conference," Carl

stated. He looked up at Eric. "Didn't the FBI raid his house looking for Thais Sinclair?"

Eric nodded. He was using a remote to back up the footage of the medal ceremony. He hit the pause button as Dunn Bateson filled the screen.

"What's the connection?" Carl asked.

Eric turned and went toward his laptop. The office filled with the sound of his tapping as he hacked into the FBI network. Carl came over and waited until Eric had the report of the raid on screen.

"Miranda is his *mother*?" Carl exclaimed. He rocked back on his heels and laughed. "That's rich! I knew Miranda was just as dirty as the rest of us!"

Carl was rubbing his hands together as he paced across the office. He wasn't just happy . . . no, Eric would call it down right gleeful.

"You can't use that against her in a press conference," Eric advised.

Carl froze and turned to peg him with a hard look.

"Times have changed," Eric explained. "The public might just be sympathetic toward a young girl who wasn't allowed to marry the man she loved in favor of a high-society match arranged by her parents."

Carl surprised him by nodding agreement.

"Times haven't changed enough," Carl groused. "Otherwise I could be openly gay."

Carl resumed pacing and plotting. Eric looked at the footage from the press conference again.

"Stop . . . go back . . . ," Carl said, directing him.

Eric used the controller to back the footage up.

"There . . . there!" Carl exclaimed.

Eric put the footage on slow motion. Dunn and Thais were at the back of the frame leaving together. Eric dropped the remote and went back to his laptop. He hacked into the hotel security cameras and searched the lobby frames until he found Dunn and Thais going into the elevator together.

Carl let out a snort as he saw the way Dunn clasped her wrist. "Looks like the FBI was on to something. Bateson has a thing for that Agent Sinclair."

"Bateson would have the sort of resources necessary to break someone out of Homeland," Eric added.

"Resources he's using to undermine my efforts," Carl said as he took to pacing once more. Eric allowed him to think. It was a solid fact that Miranda could do a lot for their numbers among the voters. Eric hadn't signed on just to lose in the last few months.

He was there to win.

"Kagan isn't the only one who can pull resources from those looking to spend their lives in prison," Carl said as he came to a conclusion. "Get someone . . . on their way to Leavenworth . . . someone who can do a job and keep their mouth shut better than Pullman did. Have them deal with Thais Sinclair. Miranda will get the message."

"Sure you want to mess with Bateson?" Eric inquired. "He's got major resources."

"This is about Miranda," Carl clarified. "I need her to switch sides, and she'll do anything for her children. Bateson might get his feathers ruffled but that will only make Miranda bend for fear we'll go after Damascus next."

Eric considered Carl for a moment before he nodded. "Agreed. I'll find a resource."

She'd lost control.

Again.

Dunn was stroking her nape. In spite of how heated they'd both gotten, she was curled up on his chest, unwilling to disconnect from the skin-on-skin contact. But her senses were returning to normal, like she was emerging from the bubble they'd been inside of while their passions raged. She heard the traffic on the street outside the windows, caught the sound of someone sliding a keycard into a door on the other side of the hallway.

"I suppose you're right," Dunn grumbled. He pressed his face against her hair, inhaling deeply before he shifted and released her.

Thais sat up, slipping off his lap as she felt the unmistakable tingle of a blush staining her cheeks.

Was she ever going to stop blushing for him?

He was looking at her cheek, his gaze the stain coloring her cheek. She ducked her chin and turned, slipping her feet onto the floor.

"You can't fake that, Thais," he muttered as she heard him picking up his clothing and dressing.

"I can't seem to control it, either." It was a good thing she was looking away from him as she found her underwear and got into it. Because her jaw actually dropped open as she realized she'd spoken out loud.

Dunn chuckled behind her. "I understand the lapse in self-control. You have a similar effect on me."

She really should have reached for her dress. Instead she discovered herself turning her head to look back at him.

Why?

She caught only a glimpse of him looking back at her with a guarded expression before she snapped her head around and fumbled to get the garment over her head and tugged down into place. Being clothed didn't give her the feeling of security she was searching for though. "I've got to get back."

"Me, too." Dunn pulled his tie off the back of the sofa where it had landed. "Your boss has a unique way of ensuring operations go his way. In this case, I'm in his corner so . . . as you say, duty calls."

Dunn had pulled something out of the pocket of his suit jacket. Thais forgot her shoes as she felt recognition flash through her brain.

"Is that—"

Dunn flipped it open to reveal a badge card. "Yes."

Thais was dumbfounded again. Dunn chuckled at her expense. "I like surprising you, Thais. Truth is, I think you enjoy it, too."

He leaned forward to kiss her but she pulled back, still absorbing the fact that Kagan had given him a badge. "That's . . . insane."

"Not really"—there was the sound of silk against silk as he put on his tie—"your section leader knows how to ensure he has the resources he needs. I just happened to be in a category he couldn't find anyone else in."

Thais slipped into her shoes. "What category is that?"

Dunn turned from where he'd been inspecting himself in a mirror. "The category Miranda Delacroix listens to."

Thais had opened her lipstick but she flashed him a look. "Sounds like Kagan." She applied the lipstick to her mouth and capped it before dropping it back into her purse. "This isn't a game, Dunn."

She turned in time to see him tucking a gun back into his waistband.

A gun she'd never noticed he was carrying.

"You don't know very much about me, Thais," he offered with confidence in his tone. "But you know Kagan isn't a fool."

"You're right," she muttered. "We need to get back."

And she didn't know very much about him.

It was the hard slice of reality arriving right on cue. A blunt splash of icy water that felt like it penetrated all the way to her core.

He knew things about her. Had likely had someone in his employ gather information on her and present it in a nice, neat little file.

It wasn't the first time.

No, she'd been a target of men like him before. Her badge gave her the ability to be herself, when everyone—including her bed partners—was busy trying to reduce her to someone who did exactly what their data said she would.

She wanted to be more.

It was a yearning so deeply embedded in her. Maybe it was the true definition of who she was. But what had her fighting to control her emotions was the fear that she might never be anything more than the need to be something else.

"Thais?"

She ducked through the front door without answering. Dunn cursed but the door shut between them as he was fighting to put his shoes on. She pushed into a stairwell, pulling her heels off before heading down the metal steps.

Reaching the lobby, she slipped her shoes back on and flashed her badge as she emerged. The dark-suited man assigned to the stairs looked her up and down before allowing her to move near where the ballrooms were.

Thais headed toward the doors. She'd done her job.

You're running . . .

Yes, she was. There was no point in denying it. But her reasons were the ones that kept her sane in a world where she couldn't seem to find meaning beyond her badge.

It wasn't Dunn's fault.

Everyone was searching for meaning in life and the truth was, it wasn't found anywhere but inside oneself.

At least, that was the way it seemed to work for her.

No matter how much she longed for something else.

Dunn tied his shoe with another word of profanity.

He jerked the door open but Thais wasn't in the hallway.

He looked toward the stairs. But his phone buzzed. Dunn felt the bite of duty as he realized the badge that gave him access to Thais's world also came with a leash and collar. One that made it necessary to answer Saxon Hale instead of going after Thais.

"Miranda's moving to the roof," Saxon said. "You're on detail."

Dunn cussed again. Leaving wasn't what he wanted but even in his anger he realized Thais wouldn't be anywhere to be found.

No, she'd run.

And he didn't fully understand just why.

He felt something inside him shift as he went toward the stairs and started to climb to the roof.

He'd find her.

And when she wasn't expecting him to surface in the world she'd sacrificed all of her personality to encase herself inside of.

Miranda lit up as he came across the roof to where she was making ready to climb into a helicopter. Saxon Hale contemplated him from behind a pair of shades before he opened the door for Miranda.

Dunn went around the helicopter and climbed aboard as Saxon made sure Miranda was strapped in. His mother flashed him a smile, one he returned as he enjoyed knowing Thais was going to run right to him.

They were far from finished and he was going to enjoy telling her so.

"Sinclair checking in."

Thais waited for Kagan to respond to her.

"We're in a holding pattern. Check in schedule Delta."

The line went dead. Thais was accustomed to it. She turned her phone off and dropped it into her purse.

Twelve hours had never seemed so long or empty before.

The Lynx was also in her purse. A light on it was blinking, telling her she had a message.

Thais shut her purse.

Chicken . . .

Not really. It was more a matter of self-preservation. She crossed the street and made it onto a corner in time to climb onto a city bus. The driver looked at her, surprise flashing in his eyes as she dumped change into the meter.

He was going to watch her butt in his mirror, too.

Well, he wasn't alone.

Thais made her way down the scuffed up aisle, stepping around the pieces of trash. She kept her eyes forward as the occupants tried to make eye contact with her. The bus jerked and swayed as it started forward. She never sat down. Just curled her hand around a pole as the bus lumbered down the block toward its next stop.

She ducked out of the door in front of a nightclub just opening for the night. A pair of young women was getting out of a Kia Soul, clearly marked with the Lyft symbol. Thais slipped into the backseat.

"Take me to the airport?" she asked sweetly.

"Sure thing!" the driver replied, eager to get more than a four-mile fare. "Just check in and—"

Thais offered him a hundred-dollar bill. "Keep the change."

The kid's eyes widened before he was nodding and turning around to pull into traffic. Thais slid into the center of the backseat, keeping her face away from the windows where a traffic camera could pick her up.

The Lynx vibrated inside her purse.

She dug it out, looking at the screen.

"Running?" Dunn asked her.

"You knew it was only for the moment," she replied. A cold, rehearsed, safe response that she hated for the first time. Solitude wasn't offering the comfort she was so used to finding.

"It can be more. Let's discuss."

She was tempted. It felt like little pieces of the fabric of her being were tearing as she battled which way to go. She wasn't giving him a chance.

You mean, you're not taking the risk of trusting him . . .

She wanted to. But between want and reality lay a minefield of scars from past experiences. Maybe if they were only her scars, she might have made a try for it. But Dunn had his own past, one he wasn't interested in sharing. She couldn't just be his.

Eric Geyer was good at his job.

There was a skill level necessary when dealing with security but there was also knowing when to listen to his gut. He felt something nagging him. Something picking at the back of his brain because he hadn't applied enough brainpower to realize he knew something important.

He surfed through pictures of Dunn Bateson late into the night. Press releases. Mentions in society columns. Carl was already snoring by the time Eric clicked on enough links to find the one that triggered his brain.

Lynx.

The very exclusive product being developed by Bateson and a private Chinese firm with enough satellites in orbit to make the Lynx untraceable. The two-hundred-grand price tag came with assurances of privacy, but Eric slowly grinned.

Bateson was a recluse and Thais was a shadow agent. If they were in a relationship, he'd have given her one of the test models. The Lynx was still in the test phase. Which meant there weren't many of them active at the moment.

Eric picked up a phone and called one of Carl's supporters who was very interested in making certain

China remained able to export into the United States without tariffs.

Thais redirected the driver of her car before they got close enough to the airport for the security cameras to pick her up. If the kid thought her request strange, the promise of cash under the table kept him from questioning her.

She ended up on a corner as the kid left. Behind her was a block of homes with boarded-up windows. They were waiting to be flattened so a new section of interstate could be built. It was the sort of thing Shadow Ops teams used to remain off grid. She slipped into the backyard of one and picked the lock.

Someone had loved the house. In spite of its age, the walls were painted and the carpet clean. Thais went into the bathroom and turned the tap. Water flowed freely, confirming that the residents hadn't been out long. An older bed had been left behind. She tested it before finding it clean enough for the night.

In the dark, she was tempted to use the Lynx. Turning it over in her hands, she swept the screen with her finger and reread the text messages from Dunn.

Pathetic . . .

Yes, and as she put it down she told herself that a good night's rest would clear her thinking.

"You think I was born yesterday?"

Eric didn't answer the question. The man in front of him lost some of his mocking confidence as Eric allowed his offer to stand. Standing in an alley a block from the prison, the guy was still looking around, wait-

ing for someone to realize he'd been released by accident. Eric gave him a few more seconds to soak up the
unexpected freedom.

"That simple?" the guy asked.

"It could be, if you're up for the work," Eric said, trying to tempt him. "Otherwise . . . feel free to take off.
I don't care. Someone with a badge will run you down
in a bit, once I release your real criminal record. Got it
in a holding pattern for the moment. That's why they
let you walk away."

The guy looked both ways before lowering his voice.
"You said you'd wipe my record clean permanently."

"I said we could help each other," Eric confirmed.

"Why?"

Eric shot the guy a hard look. "I need a job done. It's
just your lucky day to be in a position to be useful to
me. You're facing a double murder charge with special
circumstances."

"They were fucking drug dealers," the guy retorted.
"They'd done a lot worse."

"They were your competition," Eric said, laying out
his position. "I get it. So are you and I doing business?
That's all I need to know."

"What's this chick done?"

Eric offered the guy a piece of paper with an address
on it and a picture of Thais. "Nothing's free. You want
your record bleached, you're going to deal with something I need to go away. I didn't pick you for your vir-
tue. If I wanted that, I'd have selected the guy sitting
on the bus because he killed his sister's abusive boyfriend."

"Judge already likes him enough to offer military

service instead of prison," the guy said. "And you left out the part about you picking me because you know I can't talk without messing up my own life."

Eric only shrugged in response. The guy looked around again before taking the picture and paper. He looked at the shot of Thais and let out a low whistle. "Very nice."

"Think twice before you leave any evidence behind," Eric advised softly. "I'm only bleaching the record on file. Be stupid enough to get too close to her and you're on your own when they track you down with DNA."

The guy stiffened. "Right. No mixing business and pleasure. Consider it done."

"Your record will be clean right after I hear about another mindless killing in the streets."

Eric swept the street with his gaze before he left the alley and walked away.

CHAPTER SIX

Sleep was elusive.

Thais had spent more than one night in an off the grid location. It was fairly standard operating procedure for Shadow Ops teams.

Tonight, she was restless.

She sat up just after midnight, reaching out for her gun that was next to her on the bed. With the windows boarded up, the house was dark.

She clearly heard the rap on the front door.

A solid connection of knuckles against wood that sent her onto her feet, her back against the wall as she held her gun up.

"It's Dunn."

Thais knew how to wake up alert; still, it took a moment for her brain to fully register what she heard.

There was a flicker of light as a cell phone illuminated the darkness.

"Are you looking to get shot?" she demanded.

His face was set in a hard expression. "I could ask you the same thing. This is a notorious neighborhood."

"I know what I'm doing, Dunn," she informed him. "It's called staying off grid."

"This is a dump," Dunn replied. "And you're lucky there aren't junkies in these boarded-up houses."

"Did you think Shadow Ops meant high-class accommodations?" Thais asked him. She had to tip her chin up because he was looming over her.

"You aren't with your team," he argued. "You should have come to me."

"Then I wouldn't be off grid," Thais said.

Dunn's jaw tightened. "Yes, you would."

As much as she wanted to argue, she had never been one to keep at a fight when logic proved she was wrong. Dunn was a recluse and he knew a hell of a lot about being off grid.

"What are you doing here?" With one topic exhausted, her brain latched onto the next question brewing in her mind. "You're on duty with Miranda."

"I left Kent with her."

Thais felt her jaw drop. "That isn't how this works, Dunn!" She reached out to grab his shirt. A little pop went off somewhere in the backyard and her shoulder stung.

Dunn flattened her on the floor in the next moment. Thais growled as she tried to pull her gun from her waistband but discovered her arm protesting as she worked her fingers to grip the butt of the pistol.

"Stay down!" Dunn had his gun leveled as he moved toward the bed. The next pop sent a bullet into the bed. There was a little sound of impact from the mattress before Dunn was moving around the foot of the bed.

"Dunn—"

Her voice brought more bullets her way. Thais rolled

as she drew in a harsh breath and gritted her teeth against the pain.

But she closed her hand around her gun and returned fire.

Behind the plywood over the window, she heard the glass shatter as her rounds went through what had once been the bedroom window. Dunn was against the wall and fired off a couple of rounds. There was a grunt and the sound of a body hitting the ground.

"Stay down, Thais," Dunn ordered as he kicked the back door open and went out with his gun in front of him.

It was textbook perfect.

And field-proven effective.

She didn't have time to question where he'd gotten his training. But she knew it when she saw it. Getting up, Thais ignored the smell of her own blood as she followed. Pain was screaming through her arm but she held tight to her gun as she made it to the back door.

A body was slumped along the outside of the house. Dunn was on his knee next to it, pressing his fingers into the neck of whoever it was.

"Dead." Dunn told her what the stillness of the form already had.

The gun the guy had used was lying in the dirt a few feet from his hand. Dunn pulled something from the guy's pocket. Outside, the street lamps illuminated the scene enough for Thais to see the picture of herself.

"A hit?" she asked. "How did he find me?"

There was a crinkle of paper as Dunn pulled something else from the guy's pocket. A Post-it Note with an address written on it.

Thais was powering up her cell phone, punching in

a code as she contemplated the note. With her phone off, her location should have been secure.

"How did you find me?" The answer to her question burst into her mind as she looked at Dunn.

He pushed back to his feet, his expression grim. "I used the Lynx."

Her mind played the evening back as she recalled looking at the text conversation before going to sleep.

"Someone hacked it," Dunn stated the obvious. "And the list is short."

Sirens started blaring in the distance. Dunn cussed as he pushed his gun into a chest harness holster. It was a polished motion, one as practiced as any member of her team.

"Where did you train, Dunn?" she asked quietly.

He pulled her gun from her grip in reply as he lifted her hand up to inspect the wound on her arm.

"I don't know you at all." It was an emotional observation. One she really shouldn't have allowed to slip past her lips.

He'd pulled his tie loose and was wrapping it around the wound.

"You know the important parts," he offered as the sirens pulled around the corner and stopped on the other side of the house. "You know I will come for you, Thais."

The backyard lit up as the local police arrived. Dunn was turning around, his badge in hand.

"Federal agents!" he yelled above the shouts for them to put their hands up. "My partner needs medical attention."

The confidence he applied to his business empire was something he'd been trained in. Thais was surrounded by it constantly and knew how to spot it in a crowd. There were just some things that were never unlearned. The way a man walked once he'd been trained in combat.

Another reason you can't dismiss him . . .

She respected him. It was a blunt fact. The guy from the pool surfaced for a brief moment as she realized how lacking he was compared to Dunn.

No, an alpha didn't wait for the right moment.

He made his own.

"Thais?"

She'd sunk down into her thoughts. Dunn pulled her back into reality as he caught her shoulder.

Shock.

She was slipping into its grip as her blood ran down her arm and across the back of her hand, dripping off her fingertips. The metallic scent was suddenly strong, nauseating her as she tried to decide what to say.

Instead she heard Dunn curse as his grip tightened on her.

Eric Geyer had information at his fingertips.

Of course, he was normally interested in FBI and CIA intel over the civilian law enforcement branches.

Today though, he searched through the reports of the night before, tapping on a shooting in a section of town where it wasn't an uncommon happening.

One dead.

Female.

He looked through the pictures, nodding as he recognized Thais Sinclair. Eric logged out before going in to speak with Carl.

* * *

Hospitals had levels.

Unknown to most civilians was the prison one. Thais waited only long enough for the nurse to complete her treatment before she was out of bed and getting dressed. The cameras reported her motions, bringing her team into the area where only a curtain was afforded to her for modesty.

Thais didn't care, her team had seen more of her. But Dunn came in with Saxon and Vitus.

He's seen more, too . . .

Her damned cheeks heated in response, making her yank a sweatshirt down too fast. Pain went shooting through her injured arm. She blinked as her vision started to go blurry, pulling in a deep breath to keep herself conscious.

Pain lets you know you're still alive . . .

"Bateson, you're attached to Sinclair." Kagan came around the curtain and swept her from head to toe. "Protection detail."

Thais finished pulling the sweatshirt down and sent her section leader a solid glance. "I'm more than able-bodied."

"Don't argue, Sinclair," Kagan ordered, raising his voice.

Oh, it wasn't much above the normal husky tone he used but the increase in volume gained plenty of attention because of how rare an occurrence it was.

"The facts are clear," her section leader explained. "There's a hit out on you, so you're going to have a shadow."

"He"—Thais pointed at Dunn—"left his man in his position when he came after me."

Kagan offered her a half nod. "I like a man who

knows how to use his resources. What you need to see in this situation is that I chose him because he doesn't perform the way my agents do. What this case needs is an element of surprise. That's Bateson."

Thais was left trying to form another valid argument. Her section leader sent her a warning look not to argue further. She settled for ripping the hospital bracelet off her arm. Bandaged and pumped full of antibiotics, Thais wanted out of the place before her head started pounding when the pain medications wore off.

Kagan looked at Dunn. "For the moment, she's dead. Keep her off grid."

"It will be my pleasure," Dunn responded.

"Don't count on it." As far as professional replies, her words lacked a lot. Vitus's lips twitched before he tightened his composure, returning to the bland expression he'd been hiding behind the entire time Kagan had been talking.

Saxon at least offered Kagan a look that suggested her team leader wasn't completely on board with the idea of releasing Thais to Dunn.

Kagan read the uncertainty on Saxon's face.

"I need her buried," Kagan explained. "And your team tracking down how a man got out of federal prison."

"That's a short list," Thais answered.

"It is," Kagan turned his full attention toward her. "The question you need to ask is, who was the target?"

Thais looked at Dunn. He offered only a shrug.

"Makes sense," Saxon added. "Carl is still set on striking at Miranda."

"So Dunn should be the one with a protection detail," Thais concluded.

"Glad to hear you're on board with leaving with me," Dunn said, seizing his chance to trap her with her own words.

Thais shot him a scathing look. "I can handle you, Bateson. This"—she pointed at her bandaged arm—"is nothing."

"It's a through-and-through on your right arm," Saxon said, interrupting. "The swelling is going to slow you down for a couple of weeks."

Thais turned her attention to her team leader. Saxon didn't back down. "Your specialty is hand-to-hand, Thais. You need to recognize your limitations for the benefit of the team."

It was sound advice.

Logical.

Just a month ago, she would have had no difficulty at all immersing herself in the cold facts and letting them dictate her actions.

But with Dunn? Her emotions were still steamrolling right past things like her better judgment.

Kagan looked back at Saxon. "I've got an escort downstairs for the body. Get it out of here before anyone notices it isn't Sinclair."

Kagan's word was acted on. Thais was no exception. She fell into line as her team did what was needed for the case. At least it was a familiar role. One where she could easily separate her personal feelings and lock them away while focused completely on the orders from her section leader.

Later, she'd deal with Dunn.

Two hours in a car and Thais was gritting her teeth.

Pulling up to an airport wasn't exactly a relief but

there was logic in flying out of the area. Thais climbed the steps up to the private jet and sat down for takeoff.

Dunn was watching her.

She felt his gaze on her but shock and pain medication took their toll. She never remembered taking off.

"If she kicks you," Kent advised his boss, "I'm going to laugh."

Dunn shot his man a look, but the fact that he was grinning sort of spoiled the intended reprimand.

Kent flashed him a grin in return before he crossed his arms over his chest and made it clear he was waiting to see if Dunn could manage to put the chair Thais was in back into a reclining position without getting his eye blackened.

Well, one of his favorite traits about the woman was her ability to keep him on his toes.

He eased the chair back, watching as Thais only shifted and curled up along one side. He heard a click behind him as Kent opened one of the overhead compartments to pull out a blanket.

Spreading it out over Thais was satisfying in a very unexpected way.

Dunn found himself thinking about it long after he'd gone into the office at the back of the plane. He should have been focused on business.

He wasn't.

Part of him was frustrated by the distraction. The last few weeks of neglect had seen his inbox packed to the max with matters he needed to address.

Instead he was contemplating Thais and what the next step would be.

He wouldn't deny how satisfying it was to know she was in his custody.

But he wanted more.

He rubbed at his forehead as he realized how much he longed to have her with him, because she'd chosen him.

It was a weakness he'd thought he'd banished.

He found himself dwelling on the word "weakness." At the moment, he was torn between the way he'd trained himself to think about needing someone else to help him feel complete and the way he seemed willing to do anything to fit into a world where Thais would approve of him.

A month ago, he'd have sworn there wasn't a woman alive who could reduce him to needing her.

Now? He was watching his profits decline as he took a position among Kagan's Shadow Ops.

He could hide behind his mother.

And there was a partial truth to that reasoning. But he'd learned to scrutinize himself after Rhianna had blinded him so very completely.

He wanted to stay because of Thais. Wanted to push himself into her world and make sure she couldn't shut him out of her mind.

Of course, the real question was, how much of himself did he want her to see? Because he had the distinct feeling Thais Sinclair wouldn't settled for anything less than everything.

What bothered him was the knowledge that he just wasn't sure if he could give it to her.

Kagan had more mystery about him than most men.

Of course, that was what made him such an effective

Shadow Ops section leader. He knew the names and where the bodies were buried. He lived like a ghost as he went about performing his duty.

Saxon Hale had learned to respect him.

Even when Saxon disagreed with him.

"You don't understand why I gave a badge to Bateson." Kagan stated the question burning a hole in Saxon's brain.

"You'd be disappointed in me if I didn't question the situation," Saxon replied.

Kagan offered a slight incline of his head.

"We're playing a real live game of chicken here," Kagan explained. He looked across to where Vitus was leaning against the doorway. "Carl started it with Damascus."

"Funny how things work out sometimes," Vitus responded. "Somehow, we both ended up with women involved."

"Sinclair has served above and beyond," Kagan stated. "Bateson has the resources to safeguard her."

Saxon drew in a deep breath. His brother had stiffened, betraying how seriously Vitus took the statement from their section leader.

Kagan wasn't a man to ever admit defeat.

But he always called it the way it was.

"Thais might not be too comfortable staying with Dunn," Vitus offered.

"We're on a collision course," Kagan said. "There's no way to avoid it now. If the only thing I could do for Bateson was make it so he could step up and defend his mother, well, I stand by my decision."

"How did he earn your respect?" Saxon asked point-blank.

"MI-6 doesn't work with idiots."

Saxon shared a look with Vitus. Kagan's crusty chuckle filled the room. Their section leader lifted a tumbler that had a shot of fine Scotch in it.

"I don't give badges out," Kagan expounded. "A Shadow Ops badge is earned."

Saxon felt his opinion of his section leader harden. The tiny holes that doubt had managed to tear in it closed up. The badge clipped to his waist was his identity. Something he'd dedicated his life to and pledged his blood to if necessary. There was a reason their team was one of the best.

Kagan.

As their section leader, he set the example. One Saxon and every man and woman on his team did their best to measure up to. Sacrifice went along with the work.

They were on a collision course.

The three men contemplated their circumstances as they silently drained their tumblers.

Conversation wasn't necessary. They were blood brothers. Comrades with a sense of loyalty most people just didn't understand.

Bateson was one of them, too.

Saxon found the knowledge easing the last of his concerns over letting Thais go with him. In fact, he silently found himself hoping Dunn could break through the layers of shielding Thais had protected herself with in order to work on his team. She'd always pulled her weight. Tossed in just as completely as the rest of them. Never flinching away from the seedier needs of a case.

She deserved some happiness.

He hoped Dunn could find a way to give it to her.

Of course, it wouldn't be easy. It would be epic to say the least. Thais would break his knee if she knew he was betting on Dunn.

At least she would until she realized just how complete love made a person.

Dunn didn't crowd her.

Thais realized he knew her better than she'd allowed someone to know her in a long time.

Their destination was an exclusive coastal location known as Bodega Bay. The house had a sweeping view of the coast and was just minutes from a private airfield. The inhabitants were people seeking refuge from the rest of the world. Privacy brought them there and they were willing to pay the high prices to ensure they might enjoy their mansion homes without the paparazzi snapping a shot of them blowing their noses.

She walked along the huge floor-to-ceiling windows in her bedroom. She had a clear view of the surf crashing onto the sand as the sun set, turning the horizon a magnificent shade of orange and scarlet.

She was alone and yet she knew Dunn was waiting for her to settle in.

Anticipation was balling in her gut and she admitted she was enjoying it. At least she was admitting it to herself.

Dunn would be another matter.

He had to be.

Why does that bother you?

It was a very good question. One that she chewed on as she moved across the bedroom, her attention on the surf as her hair slowly dried.

She heard his steps but only because she was listening for them.

"I would have knocked," he offered as she turned to look at him, "if the door wasn't open."

Dunn stepped into the suite. She felt awareness ripple across her skin.

"Kagan said you were assigned to me," she replied. "I know what protection detail means."

Dunn had showered, too. She realized he'd only buttoned half the buttons on his shirt and rolled up the sleeves after dressing.

"But you're supposed to be armed," she said in response to his lack of a chest harness.

He raised one dark eyebrow. "When have I ever struck you as a man who is obvious, Thais?"

She felt her lips twitching in response. "Fair enough."

"The place is secure," he assured her, coming closer.

It wasn't the first time she'd been under protection.

Such things went with the job. Criminals didn't like knowing she'd duped them, and it certainly wasn't original for one of them to hire a hitman to take out a witness before they went to trial.

"Why does it matter that it's me?" Dunn wasn't going to let her stew in silence.

You mean shut him out . . .

He stepped right into her field of vision, too close to ignore.

"You know I'm up to the task, Thais. Even if you don't know the details."

The memory of him moving through the house, so confident in his actions popped up in her mind. The way he moved around the globe as well had the mark of a very calculated plan. He'd laid out his places of refuge and made certain he had the personnel to assist him. Kent wasn't the average bodyguard for hire.

"Fine," she admitted. "You're right. I know the difference between a trained man and—"

"A spoiled rich man playing with expensive toys?" Dunn cut her off.

She nodded a single time. There was a confidence in his gaze that set her back because she'd been the one making assumptions about him.

She should have been annoyed to discover the lapse in awareness in herself, instead she encountered the sting of rejection. He'd kept the truest part of himself from her. Maybe she had no reason to expect him to open up but it stung like nothing she'd ever experienced.

"You don't know very much about me, Thais," he added.

"No, I don't." She steeled herself against the defensive tone of his voice. "And you've made very sure I don't know you."

He acknowledged the accusation. She found herself watching the way he absorbed it. What surprised her was the yearning that rose up from inside her to reach out to him. To give him the opportunity to make amends.

You're insane . . .

She moved away before she said too much. Before she exposed just how much she wanted him to open up to her. "I'm not judging your choices, Dunn."

"Really?" He reached out and caught her uninjured arm.

The contact was jarring.

Just as it always was.

Thais turned to face him, mostly because she needed

to disconnect from him before she did something foolish.

Like allow him to see how deeply she cared about him.

"What do you want, Dunn?" she asked. "You've done your best to make sure I don't know who you are."

"You've done the same."

"I certainly have," she answered as she stepped toward him. "But you're the one peeling my layers back . . . well, no more, do you understand me?"

She'd stepped right up to him and her heart was pounding as she raised her chin so she could aim her demand straight at his face. His green eyes glittered as she watched his jaw tighten.

"I do . . . understand you," he rasped out.

He caught her against him, securing her with a hard arm around her waist as he cupped the back of her head and held her firmly.

But he didn't kiss her.

Not yet.

"I'm not done peeling, Thais." His tone was hard and full of promise. "Not until I find where you've buried yourself."

"And what are you going to do with the woman you find?" she demanded. At least, she wanted her words to come out as a demand. Instead she heard the yearning in her voice.

Felt the way she trembled as the idea of being stripped completely down to her soul went through her. Her eyes stung with unshed tears.

And she knew he noticed.

"I'm going to love her."

Dunn sealed her lips with his. Kissing her hard and deep as she twisted in his embrace.

Was she seeking freedom? If so, from what exactly?

He was hard and everything she craved, so it wasn't release from his embrace.

Whatever it was, she didn't care. All that mattered was kissing him back. She reached up and framed his face, stroking his skin before she was attacking the buttons on his shirt because she needed more connection between them.

He let her push him back as she opened his shirt and pushed it over his shoulders. Pure delight moved through her as she stroked his bare skin. She felt something inside her shift and flex as it was freed. Right and wrong no longer bound her. There was only need and the fact that he was exactly what she craved to satisfy her hunger.

And Dunn was happy to indulge her.

He shrugged his shirt off, as she reached for his belt and unfastened it. His pants dropped as Thais pushed his briefs down as well, feeling a jolt of satisfaction as his cock sprang into view. She closed her hands around it. Delighting in the smooth feeling of it.

She sank down onto her knees. Determination filling her. A need to push him past his limits was driving her and Thais didn't waste any time. She gripped his length and opened her mouth. He growled as she closed her lips around him, sucking on the head of his cock as she stroked the rest of his staff.

The chill which had lingered after her shower was suddenly banished.

Her skin was warm and irritated by the robe she had covering it.

But not enough for her to break away from his cock. No, the sounds she was wringing from him were intoxicating her. She hollowed her lips and sucked harder, leaning toward him to take more of his length inside her mouth as she cupped his balls. The smell of his skin was driving her own arousal up, making it spike as her clit began to throb.

"I'm not going to come in your mouth . . ."

Dunn was suddenly squatting down beside her. She lost her grip on his cock as he hooked her beneath the knees and behind her back. He stood, taking her weight as he lifted her high and laid her on the surface of the bed.

"I've got a use for this hard-on . . ." He reached down and ripped open the thin belt keeping her robe shut.

"A use that includes you making as much noise as me."

He knelt down at the foot of the bed. Pushing her knees wide with his shoulders. She shuddered. Feeling the impact of the sight of him as much as she witnessed it.

He was hard and cut. Every bit of his body trained to perfection.

And he was focused on her.

His gaze locked with hers for a moment. A time in which she felt his determination. He'd give as good as he got, which only made her determined to drive him more insane. She rolled up, cupping the side of his face once again.

His breath caught.

And she felt like hers did, too.

Tilting her head to one side, she kissed him again. Finding more pleasure in the innocent touch than she had in a long time. Dunn threaded his fingers through her hair, pressing his mouth against hers in a long kiss that obliterated everything except him in her mind.

He kissed his way down her chin, gently pulling her head back to expose her throat.

She shivered as he grazed the delicate skin on her neck with his teeth. Gently nipping her as he held her still and she found the trust to allow him to keep her in such a vulnerable position.

She fell back as he reached her chest, moving along her collarbones and across her breasts. He lingered over one, licking her hardened nipple as he kneaded her other breast. Need felt like a live current, zipping down her spinal cord to her clit.

Her belly quivered as he kissed a path across it. Anticipation was twisting into a pulsing bundle of desperation inside her by the time he settled back between her spread thighs.

She forced her eyelids up, wanting to see him. The look on his face made her shiver. It was full of male hunger. Lust was something she knew; there was something else mixing together with the look in his eyes. He wanted more than the satisfaction of releasing his load.

He needed to push her over the edge as well.

"You're going to join me, Thais . . . ," he said, as he locked gazes with her.

He lowered his attention to her slit, leaning forward to tease her with a soft kiss.

She gasped, her hips rising off the bed as pleasure speared through her. She heard him chuckle and then there was nothing but the roaring of blood in her ears. He knew how to drive her insane. Licking across her clit before closing his lips around the little bundle of nerve endings and sucking. But he never pushed her over the edge. No, he kept her withering beneath his mouth as she strained up toward him, seeking out that last bit of pressure that would send her over the edge.

"That would be too quick, Thais," Dunn said, pushing up to his feet and leaning over her as he crawled onto the bed.

She shuddered as their skin connected from head to toe. Stroking him was a necessity as he settled on top of her. His hands were in her hair, holding her for another kiss. The head of his cock was also nudging the wet folds of her slit but he didn't thrust into her.

Instead he kissed her. Long and hard.

"Look at me." His voice was raspy and full of command.

But what made Thais open her eyes was the hint of yearning in his tone.

"I want you to know it's me in bed with you . . . ," he said as he thrust forward.

"I could say the same," she answered.

And she meant it. In fact, it shocked her how much she felt the need to know she was as firmly rooted in his mind as he was in hers. She surged up, pushing against his shoulder to turn him as she rolled him onto his back.

She caught the look of annoyance on his face.

"Deal with it . . . ," she growled as she rose and sheathed him.

"Oh, I've got a few ideas on how to go about doing that," he said to her. He cupped her breasts as she lifted off him and pushed back down. "You'll like some of them."

"And the others?" she asked.

His lips rose into a grin that flashed his teeth at her. There was nothing nice about the expression.

It was pure intent.

He surged up, rolling her onto her back once more. She stiffened, bracing herself for a jolt of pain from her arm but he controlled her weight, keeping her from bouncing. Instead she settled onto the surface of the mattress with nothing more than a twinge.

Dunn watched her, gauging her reaction. As soon as he was satisfied she'd landed well, he was settling on top of her again.

"My other ideas include me fucking you until you're mindless . . . ," he informed her.

"I like that one."

His lips curved up again in response. He closed his fingers around her wrists and raised her hands above her head, pinning them to the surface of the bed. The headboard hit the wall when he thrust into her.

Another bang followed, and then she didn't care about anything except the jolt of pleasure going through her every time his cock sunk into her. She was immersed in the moment. Seeking only completion. He was her companion in the quest, thrusting into her as she lifted to take every downward plunge. She was gasping, trying to pull in enough oxygen to supply her pounding heart. Her eyes slid closed as she sunk down into the abyss of sensation and need. Giving herself over to the yearning driving her toward her lover.

With a common goal, they strained toward one another. Immersed completely in the moment, so very completely Thais couldn't recall ever being so engaged with anyone. They were racing toward the peak and part of her wanted to hold off, just to savor the moment where she wasn't alone.

But her body wanted to reach the zenith. Her flesh demanded satisfaction and it broke over her as she lifted up to meet Dunn. She cried out, her voice echoing around the room as she clasped him with her thighs, straining to hold him inside her while the walls of her passage clamped down on his cock.

He growled and thrust deep, his grip tightening on her wrists as his cock jerked and started to empty inside her. She opened her eyes, locking gazes with him as pleasure hardened his expression. She was fascinated with the raw look of pleasure on his face, noting the difference between lust and . . . whatever was happening between her and Dunn.

She didn't know the definition.

Only that she'd never experienced it before.

"Miranda," Carl Davis exclaimed loudly. "It's such a relief to see you up and about."

Carl clasped her hand, turning so the press could snap shots of them shaking hands.

"Yes, thank you, Carl." Miranda's poise was flawless.

Unless someone were as close as Carl was. He caught the flash of distaste in her eyes as she used the excuse of waving at a friend as a reason to disengage from their handshake.

Not that he cared how she personally felt.

"And may I say, I'm so happy to see you here to support me."

Miranda was making ready to slip away. She turned

back to face him, her smile frozen in position but her eyes snapping rejection.

"I support this mission and feeding the hungry, Carl," Miranda said.

"Yes." Carl made a show of rubbing his hands together.

He moved off to where food was being loaded into a cafeteria-style serving station. His assistants were quick to tie an apron around him and hand him gloves before the first people started to enter with their trays. The camera rolled as Carl smiled brightly and served up mashed potatoes.

Carl was practiced in the art of public appearances, too. He kept his smile bright as he fought the urge to keep an eye on Miranda. She was handing out little cartons of milk and winking as she offered cartons of chocolate milk to kids who smiled with joy.

It wasn't until much later that Carl had the opportunity to think through the day.

Miranda never had liked him.

That was no newsflash. She'd been there and shook his hand. But that wasn't a public announcement of supporting him.

Carl paced back and forth as he contemplated the news playing on the screens in his penthouse suite. Tom Hilliard was gaining on him. The numbers becoming more even every week.

He needed Miranda to switch sides. She wasn't just voter candy, she was a person other senators took their lead from. Even if it was the first time Miranda was running for office, she was a Delacroix. The only other name with more pull was Kennedy.

It was the reason she'd been put back on the leash

by her father when she'd run off and fallen in love. Bateson had made something of himself but he wasn't an American and being born into the Delacroix family meant Miranda had responsibilities.

Even a princess didn't have everything.

So Miranda had married Jeb Ryland and the situation had been very lucrative. Jeb had enjoyed a good career, only cut short by his untimely death.

Carl slowly grinned. He might have been pissed off to have Miranda kill Jeb and keep her daughter, Damascus, from marrying him, but he did admit to enjoying the brass balls Miranda had hidden beneath her little sweet grandmother persona.

Dunn Bateson had certainly inherited the steel in his spine from his mother.

But knowing how strong Miranda was just brought Carl back to contemplating how to bring her into line. She'd been polite today and that wasn't in line.

Something was off because Miranda wasn't stupid. She'd known he'd been the one to order the hit on Thais Sinclair. She was wise enough to get the message loud and clear, and yet, she wasn't falling in line.

So, something was off. Carl pressed the button on his lapel pin that would bring Eric to him.

It would seem they had some business to look into.

He'd never held her.

Thais drifted out of sleep, encountering a new sensation as she didn't have to wake up quickly.

Dunn was behind her, snuggled up along her back. Her injured arm was up as his arm was draped around her waist and his hand cupping her breast.

Lovers.

There had been a time when she thought she had such a connection with her husband. But it had only been inexperience and the rose-colored glasses of youth.

Even her mother had laughed at her for believing her marriage was about more than a middle-aged billionaire who liked having a young wife to show off to his buddies.

"Ready for some pain meds?" Dunn asked.

Thais drew in a breath, startled to hear him speak.

He can't read your thoughts . . .

No, but the connection between them was so strong, she had to remind herself that he didn't know what she'd been immersed in.

"I told you"—she shifted, trying to disengage from him—"it's not that bad."

He released her reluctantly. Sitting up as she swung her legs over the edge of the bed. On impulse she turned and sent him a confident look. "You might have noticed I kept up just fine."

She earned a raised eyebrow and a cocky little grin from him for her daring comment.

"Oh, I noticed alright," he answered as he stood and stretched his back until it popped.

He moved one of the pillows and picked up a gun that was lying on the bed.

"I know you didn't put that there while we were undressing." Maybe it might have been better to keep her thoughts to herself, but with Dunn, she appeared to have no ability to rein herself in.

"Put it there while you were in the shower," Dunn said, providing the answer which she should have figured out on her own.

"Because you were planning on seducing me?" She

stood up, plucking her robe from the floor and shrugging into it. As far as a shield against him seeing too much of her, the thin silk fabric left a lot to be desired. Still, she crossed her arms over her chest as she faced off with him.

Dunn moved toward her, the look in his green eyes daring her to move. It was a challenge, one she recognized and still had trouble standing up to.

He laid his hand on the side of her face. "'Seduce' is the right word for us, Thais."

She stepped back. "Please, we aren't teenagers here."

His lips curved into a smug grin as he set the gun on the foot of the bed. "That just makes it even better. All the innocence, and no age problem when we want to get down to the raw basics."

He stepped into his pants and pulled them up. Somehow managing to look far more composed than she felt.

He'd shrugged into his shirt while she was thinking and reached for the gun before he buttoned the garment. Her eyes narrowed. The ease and comfort he had with the weapon wasn't something anyone could fake.

"MI-6."

She felt her eyes widen as she raised her gaze from the gun to his face. There was a look of quiet confidence there as he pushed the gun into his waistband.

"We don't announce that we're armed by wearing a chest harness," he explained.

"MI-6 isn't in the habit of announcing anything," she muttered.

He moved back toward her, cupping the side of her face as he caught the tie of her robe to keep her from retreating.

"I'm learning how to do this, too, Thais," he offered in a low tone.

"If you're MI-6, you know this isn't going to last."

He tapped her lips with his fingertip before he released her. "Maybe in Shadow Ops you're quitters"— he sent her a challenging look as he sat down to put on his shoes—"not us at MI-6."

Thais ended up with her hand propped on her hip. She wanted to argue, except if she gave in, she was fighting for his words to be correct.

You'd enjoy it . . .

She would. But the real question was, could she defy everything she'd built her life on and cultivate the trust necessary to just go with what he was suggesting?

"You can do it." Dunn read her thoughts right off her face.

"Do what?"

He stood. Fully clothed and confident in his thinking. He was her polar opposite and she was unbearably aware of it. He stopped beside her, allowing her to catch his scent. There was something so very primal about the way she noticed details about him. It wasn't the way he smelled, it was his scent.

She was unbalanced by it all.

"Let go, Thais." He'd cupped her chin again. "Just let it happen."

"To what end?" She demanded as she broke free and put enough distance between them for her to think.

Or try to, anyway.

"Happily ever after?" he asked with a hint of frustration in his voice. "And before you start thinking that's easy for me to say, it isn't. The last woman I thought might fit that place in my life was after my money. Her mother set up a friendship with my father that was just as fake as her daughter's love."

"My husband wanted a trophy and my mother made sure I was worthy of being displayed." Answering him was a case of needing to soothe the wounded tone she heard edging his voice. She knew what it was like to always be alone. Seemed he did as well.

"I gave up on happy ever after, too." He stepped toward her as he spoke. "But this thing between us . . . it's not going to be ignored."

She let out a rueful bark of amusement. It earned her a half grin from Dunn.

"I don't want to ignore it, Thais . . . do you?"

The ball was in her court.

Walking away would be wiser.

More logical.

Safer.

And it would make you a fool . . .

Thais shook her head, drawn back to him by everything she'd fought to deny and contain. His eyes narrowed as he tried to decide exactly what she meant.

"No, I don't want to walk away," she clarified. Voicing it released something inside her, another latch on another door gave way to the force pulling them together and this time, the emotion she felt consuming her was happiness.

A bubble of pure joy was lodged in her chest. She felt her lips curving into a huge, ridiculous smile that just felt perfect no matter how unsophisticated it might look.

He came to her, framing her face with his hands, allowing her to feel the tremor shaking him.

"Good," he muttered, his voice rough with emotion.

"Good?" she questioned.

He lifted one shoulder. "I'm a little tongue-tied."

"I know the feeling," she offered as she lifted up so she could kiss him instead.

They communicated far better without words anyway.

Thais was sleeping when Kent tapped on the door.

It wasn't uncommon for Kent to see him in bed with a woman unless Dunn factored in the part about him lingering there so he could enjoy the soft sound of Thais's breathing.

He signaled his man and Kent closed the door softly. Dunn waited a moment, savoring it before he pulled away, careful to push the bedding up against Thais so she wouldn't feel the difference in temperature.

She could sleep.

He was going to take care of her.

She'd balk if she heard him say that out loud.

So maybe he'd do it later just to enjoy the tussle that would ensue.

He grinned as he pulled on some socks and pants. He was a beast but he knew Thais enjoyed it. Kent was waiting for him in the office space they had transformed into a command center.

"Someone is looking into Thais Sinclair's death." Kent tapped a few commands into the keyboard and one of the large screens displayed a data-entry log.

"Specifically, they were looking to see what arrangements had been made for a funeral." Kent moved his mouse over two entries. "As a federal agent—"

"There should be planning already happening," Dunn said, finishing his sentence. "Good catch. I was distracted."

Kent was the model of decorum. Dunn reached out and clasped his shoulder. "I need to get this case closed. So I can settle down."

He opened his phone and dialed Kagan. But his section leader didn't answer. The second call he made was to Saxon Hale. Dunn cussed when he didn't answer, either.

"If that was Saxon you were trying to reach," Thais said from behind him, "he's off grid. Which means his phone is off."

She was pleased with herself, for her ability to make him think he'd slipped out unnoticed. "What's happening?"

Eric Geyer was waiting for Carl when he arrived the next night after another campaign event. Both of them were showing signs of fatigue as the final days of the campaign were packed with back-to-back events.

"Was I right?" Carl asked. He looked around to make sure no one was listening. "About Sinclair?"

"I believe so," Eric answered. "It's too quiet out there. Even if she didn't have any family, there should be some mention of a funeral."

Carl got a half snort of mocking amusement. "I knew it." He turned and sent a look toward Eric. "Miranda's weak spot is her children. She was far too happy when I saw her. We clearly didn't wound her deep enough." He started pacing again. "We need to find a way . . . to bring her in line."

Eric waited. It wasn't the first time but he felt it more keenly because Carl had a dark soul and Eric had a feeling his boss was getting ready to cross some more lines. The truth was, Eric was getting uncomfortable with the lengths Carl seemed willing to go to in order to get what he wanted. Maybe there were people who would consider it just deserts. For the first time, Eric was starting to agree with them.

Ambition was a slippery slope. When you threw mud at someone, you came away with dirty hands.

Carl slowly smiled. It was a creepy curving of his lips and when coupled with the gleam in his eyes, Eric found himself fighting the urge to back away and make a run for it before he even heard what Carl wanted to do now.

"Her daughter might not have married me, but Damascus still has uses it would seem," Carl began. He stopped to chuckle, clearly enjoying the idea he'd come up with. "See . . . that underground lab where Damascus works, it's a very dangerous place. Just one little mishap and a contaminated sample might get loose . . . and well . . . Damascus signed an iron-clad contract with the military. She can't leave . . ." Carl shot Eric a look full of sick enjoyment. "Especially if I'm commander in chief, Damascus stays right there where I can get at her. All we need to do is arrange for a little accident, one that will make it clear to Miranda that she will do exactly what I say if she wants to ensure her daughter's and granddaughter's safety."

It was brilliant.

It also turned Eric's stomach.

There was a twinge of evil in the plan. Carl sent Eric a hard look.

"You're not going to lose your balls on me, are you, Geyer?" Carl asked as he leaned back in his chair. "I'm not asking you to kill anyone here, just arrange a nice little . . . containment breach. One with enough punch to make Miranda fall into line. If she publicly makes a show of supporting me, Tom Hilliard is finished."

Eric was back to thinking how brilliant the plan was. "It's less exposing than having her taken out."

"Right," Carl said, pointing at him. "Not that I wouldn't have enjoyed knowing I'd put her six feet under. But seeing her flashing that smile of hers on my behalf . . . well, that just might be more fun in the long run. Get someone on it."

Carl considered it a done thing. His attention was back on his laptop screen as Eric found himself battling heavy feet.

Part of him was sickened.

Carl realized he hadn't left. "Is there a problem?"

"No, sir." Eric turned and let himself out of the office. Outside, the rest of the security men tightened up as he appeared.

They wanted to impress him. Among their ranks, he was the one who had succeeded, the master. Strange how moving through the doorway had placed him at the top of the food chain as opposed to when he was on the other side with Carl and he was the servant. What he hadn't expected was to grow to dislike who he'd become so very much.

Telling himself it was a dog-eat-dog world wasn't soothing his misgivings anymore.

Miranda was gaining respect in his mind.

Eric paused, frozen in place as he felt his conscience refusing to die, funny how he noticed it.

But there was nothing amusing in the sting he felt as he went to perform his duty.

* * *

Damascus Ryland Hale knew her job well.

And she was always focused.

She smiled behind the triple layers of glass that made up the front of her suit's hood. The assistant dressing her double-checked the locks and seals to make sure Damascus was airtight inside the hazardous materials suit. She got a thumbs-up and moved forward to the first of three air locks that would allow her to enter the lab-oratory.

The complex was deep underground, one of the many safety measures taken to help prevent the diseases stored inside it from ever reaching the surface.

Small pox, polio, Ebola, and the list went on. The pathogens of past plagues and the bacteria which the modern world feared were all there. Damascus lived and worked in the underground complex as she and her team struggled to find cures before the next outbreak. Her scientific brain understood that epidemics were a natural part of the cycle of life, but what sparked her dedication to her work was the fact that there were those who would see the diseases as the newest weapon avail-able to promote victory for their personal causes.

Not on her watch.

She laughed softly as she hooked up to an air line to begin her work for the day. It wouldn't be dramatic or even exciting. It was pure scientific method. Numbers, observations, and more of the same. That was how vac-cines were developed. You looked at the same problem over and over and then, looked at it some more.

But she believed in the work. So much so, she'd signed away the bulk of her life in order to gain access to the top-secret facility.

You married a SEAL, so it works . . .

Her husband, Vitus Hale, was a Shadow Ops agent now but that didn't mean he'd stopped being a SEAL. She was pretty sure there was no end for that part of her husband's persona.

She smiled brighter.

She liked that part of Vitus a whole lot.

Damascus snapped her thoughts back onto her work. A member of her team was pulling blood samples out of a case that had been flown in from Africa. An isolated outbreak of disease had all the symptoms of being Ebola. Her fellow doctor handed the samples with care as he loaded them into a machine to begin the process of confirming the diagnosis.

It was tragic, and yet it was her job to find in the diseased samples some hope for the future by trying to find a treatment. This would only come after they understood the disease, documenting it so they could formulate a plan of treatment.

The team was focused on the samples being secured inside a machine that would spin them to separate the platelets. Then warning lights suddenly started flashing, filling the lab with red pulses of light. Damascus looked up and then back at the machine but nothing was out of place.

"The case, Dr. Hale!"

A voice came through her helmet from one of the control rooms that was monitoring the lab through a video feed. Damascus turned to look at the case. Smoke was rising from it. She dove away but whatever it was exploded, sending bits of glass and blood through the air at super high velocity.

Contaminated blood.

Damascus felt the air pressure in her suit change as she hit the floor. Her team was pounding on the air-locked doors but the alarm sealed them shut. She struggled to get to her feet, the clunky boots making it painfully slow. Her suit hung on her limply, confirming she'd lost containment. She reached up and pulled a handle. A second set of alarms went off.

"Breach of containment! Breach of containment! Level two safety protocols in effect!"

It was an automated voice, and right then, Damascus realized just how heartless it sounded, so devoid of any sort of humanity. Three walls slid down from the ceiling, cutting the lab into sections in an effort to control what might be an airborne virus. She was trapped in the center, the holes in her suit too tiny to seal. But the walls separating her from her team gave her hope.

Hope that the virus wouldn't escape the lab.

Cassy . . .

Her only thoughts were for her baby. Sleeping so peacefully two levels above her, her daughter had never had a choice in where her parents brought her.

Please . . . please . . . please . . .

"What the fuck do you mean she's still at ground zero?"

Saxon wasn't used to hearing his brother raise his voice. The entire team turned to stare at Vitus as he stood up, looking like he was about to crack the smartphone he had in his hand.

"Get her the fuck out of there!" Vitus growled before he killed the call and shot Saxon a look full of rage.

"A case of Ebola samples exploded in the lab. Damascus is compromised."

There was a crash as he kicked his desk chair back. "I've got to get Cassy."

Vitus wasn't waiting. He was halfway out of the room when Bram Magnus stepped into his path. Vitus growled but Bram stood firm.

"They won't let you in, Vitus." Bram had to shove Vitus back. "If the lab lost containment, it's locked completely down until it's cleared."

"Get the fuck out of my way," Vitus growled softly.

"My father is in there, too," Bram countered. "You're not getting in. Neither am I."

They faced off, the tension in the room thick enough to cut.

"So we find who set off the explosion," Saxon said. "And deal with them."

Neither Bram nor Vitus liked the idea. Truth be told, Saxon wasn't very fond of it, either. He craved action just as much as his teammates.

Being the team leader meant he had to be sure to control his emotions. He'd always known it, actually latched the collar on himself. Today though, he felt the bite of the restraint. They'd always known Carl was coming for them. Always understood the risk of having families that might end up in the line of fire.

Love didn't care about his logical reasoning.

So he had to control his urges and work the case.

"What does Carl gain?" Saxon addressed his team. "We're going to cut to the chase this time. We know it's his work. What's his objective?"

Vitus and Bram tightened their control before Bram grabbed an eraser and cleaned the white board so he could begin a new evidence chain.

"Thais was attached to Dunn," Vitus said as he

started issuing observations. "Damascus is attached to me . . ."

"The common link is Miranda." Bram wrote her name on the board and circled it. "He failed to kill her . . ."

"So he's trying to break her," Saxon said, finishing the thought. He looked over at Greer McRae. "Call Dunn."

His man was turning away almost before Saxon finished issuing the order. Saxon looked at his brother.

"I'll call Miranda." Vitus read his brother's mind.

Saxon turned his phone on. "I'm waiting for Kagan's call."

It had been a long road since their first collision with Carl Davis. They'd done their best to drop it but there was part of Saxon that enjoyed knowing it was going to come down to one or the other of them. Saxon wasn't a killer by nature.

None of his Shadow Ops agents were.

No, there was a core of integrity needed to stand up against the darker elements in the world and not sell out.

It was also the thing needed to face the overwhelming odds of going up against someone like Carl Davis.

Colonel Bryan Magnus cussed as Kagan walked into his office.

"Nice to see you, too," Kagan said as he settled into the chair in front of the colonel's desk.

"We're locked down," Bryan growled. "You shouldn't be here."

Kagan only offered him a blink.

Bryan landed back in his chair. "Normally I'd admire your brass balls. But this—"

"Is going to turn out to be nothing more than a scare," Kagan said, cutting Bryan off. "Not that I'm suggesting we take it lightly."

Bryan studied Kagan for a long moment. "No, you wouldn't be here if you thought this was bullshit."

"I wouldn't be here if I didn't think Carl Davis was trying to strike out at Miranda Delacroix through her daughter," Kagan said, laying out his facts.

Bryan inclined his head in agreement.

Kagan offered him a very rare grin. "And you . . . ," Kagan said, pointing at Bryan. "You were so stinking proud of luring Damascus into your service."

"It was a brilliant maneuver," Bryan said, defending himself. "She's a genius."

"One you took advantage of," Kagan stated firmly.

"I gave her the opportunity to live her life the way she wanted to," Bryan replied. "Instead of being the little socialite her daddy favored."

"Carl is still pissed about losing her as the perfect wife," Kagan offered.

Bryan grunted. "He's a selfish prick to want to keep her locked away while he's not interested in her at all."

"What he is," Kagan said, defining their problem, "is determined to win. No matter the cost. He wanted the support of the Delacroix name. Seems he's still determined to get it."

"We need a permanent solution."

It was a bold statement. Kagan admired Bryan for having the guts to state it so clearly.

"Why do you think I'm here?" Kagan said, leaning forward. "I need something to do the job, without leaving a trace."

Kagan watched Bryan absorb the request. It was one of those gray areas that good men had to sometimes venture into for the good of everyone. Some people would condemn him for even considering it, claiming there were lines true moral men didn't cross.

Kagan rather thought of it as putting down a mad animal before it trampled the other members of the herd.

"I'm glad you came to me," Bryan responded after a moment.

"I did my best to avoid needing this sort of solution," Kagan replied.

Bryan nodded. He shared a hard look with Kagan. "We're both the sort of men who do their best to stay on the right side of morality. But part of that struggle is knowing when we have to do what needs doing. I'll get you what you need."

Bryan Magnus watched Kagan leave his office.

After the section leader was gone, Bryan indulged in a moment to rub his eyes. There was an ache centered beneath his forehead. But it wasn't guilt.

No. He opened his eyes and went back to work without another thought for Carl Davis and the fate he'd earned.

Honestly, a quick injection was better than the bastard deserved after all the lives he'd tried to take.

And then, there were the ones he had killed in his ambition.

At least there would be a moment when Carl would realize he was dying. Maybe that sounded cruel but Bryan called it justice for the two hundred people currently locked down in his underground laboratory facility. Right then, they were praying. Clenching their teeth against the fear no one in their right mind could dismiss.

No, the only thing his people could do was buckle down and hold fast to their courage. Something Bryan expected of his people and still hoped they'd never have to employ.

The fact that they were doing it now for a selfish bastard only made it that much easier for Bryan to return to his workload without another thought for Carl Davis and his date with death Bryan had helped arrange.

Sometimes, you got exactly what you deserved.

And every now and again, you got to play a part in serving up a richly deserved helping of karma.

Dunn was hiding in his office at the back of the private plane.

A week ago, she'd have let him deal with his demons in his own way.

Now?

Now, they'd taken their relationship to another level. He was hurting and she couldn't dismiss it.

Maybe he doesn't want you around right now . . .

It was possible.

Thais stood and walked toward the back of the plane anyway. She gave Dunn a single rap on the door before she pushed it open.

Guess she'd find out just how close he truly wanted their relationship to be.

He looked up, closing off his expression as she pushed the door closed.

"I'm trying to get above this workload," he offered before he looked back at the screen.

She understood . . .

What made her go forward was the fact that she didn't want the walls between them anymore.

"You ripped down my walls, Dunn," she stated as she slid right along the side of his desk and between him and his keyboard. "So yours aren't allowed, either."

"I'm only working."

"You're hiding," she stated firmly. Close enough to see his eyes, she felt her confidence wavering.

He was on guard.

"I never pegged you as a high-attention type, Thais."

She let the stab slip off her.

"Hiding in your work," she said softly. "And striking out at me because you're pissed and stuck with no outlet until we get to where your mother is."

He shoved his chair back. Which wasn't very far in the tight confines of the plane.

"Thais," he growled at her.

She surprised him by following him and grabbing the front of his shirt. "I'm not taking your shit, Bateson," she growled. "You wanted all of me, well, I demand all of you in return."

She watched understanding flash through his eyes. He covered her hand with his, starting to pry her fingers loose.

"I am pissed," he offered in a tone coated with frustration. "It's not your problem."

"Wrong," she answered as she released his shirt and pulled her hand from his grip by doing so. She reached down and cupped the bulge of his cock. "If I'm yours, you're mine . . . completely."

"Thais," he growled. "Miranda is my only blood. I'm not just pissed—"

"You want to kill," she said as she rubbed his cock through the fabric of his pants as she pressed up against him and put her mouth a single inch from his. "With your bare hands."

His eyes narrowed as his lips thinned.

"*Yes,*" he hissed.

His cock was hardening. She nodded, holding his gaze with hers. Understanding flashed in his eyes as she felt like something passed between them. The need to face him down, even at his worst, consumed her. She sent him a hard look before she slid down his body and opened the front of his pants.

"Thais—"

He didn't get the chance to argue further. She pulled his cock free and took it inside her mouth before he got past her name. His flesh was already rock hard. She drew her lip up his shaft until she was licking through the slit on the head of his cock.

He shuddered and then he was gripping her hair. It was a hard grip but she'd known what she was getting into.

There was part of her rising up to enjoy the moment. The interaction wasn't going to be soft. But she wasn't planning on being nice, either. She sucked his cock hard. Milking him with her fingers as she rubbed her tongue on the underside of his cock's head where the skin was soft and ultra-sensitive.

"Yes . . . yes . . . ," he said, encouraging her as his grip tightened enough to send little prickles of pain across her scalp. "Suck me . . . *harder* . . ."

She wasn't acting on his demand.

No, she was pulling his words from him with her actions. Ripping away his facade and letting him unleash the pulsing energy threatening to drive him insane.

There were times when you just needed to fuck.

Hard and without boundaries.

She sucked him a moment longer before pushing up and turning around. She heard him let out a rough sound of pleasure before he was pushing her skirt up and pulling her panties down.

"Not until you're ready, baby . . ." He pushed her across the desk, spreading her thighs as he reached between them to rub her slit with his cock.

"I'm going to fuck you . . . *but not* . . . before you're quivering."

His words were intoxicating. They sent her arousal spiking, the feeling of his cock slipping between the lips of her slit making her clit pulse with need. She wanted it hard and felt her folds growing wet as her lips parted and she panted.

"There it is . . . ," he muttered with victory. "So wet . . . so . . . ready . . ."

He leaned down across her body and growled next to her ear. "So . . . *mine* . . ."

He thrust into her, sliding easily into her body because of how wet she was. He made a sound of male satisfaction before he was rising up and gripping her hips. A little jolt of awareness went through her pelvis. A crazy twist of excitement and anticipation.

She wanted to be taken.

Hard.

And she wanted to give as much as she got.

He didn't disappoint her. She gripped the edge of the desk as he pumped against her from behind, penetrating deeply as she felt her body taking every plunge with pleasure. Her clit was pulsing. Each thrust pushing her closer to the edge. Dunn's breath was raspy, his hand growing hot against her skin.

He was holding back.

She could feel him fighting the urge to spill his load, pumping against her, filling her with a cock that was rock hard until she gasped. Pleasure was snapping through her. Hard and bright, it was like a whip cracking. The effect was like being hit by a wave crashing, a moment of instant connection while you absorbed the force of the impact.

Dunn snarled with victory a moment before he pinned her against the edge of the desk with his final thrusts. They were hard, savage motions that sent a second ripple of satisfaction through her belly before she felt him losing his seed.

He collapsed back into his chair, his breathing harsh. She wasn't ready to have the connection severed. She crawled up onto his lap, enjoying the way he closed his arms around her and buried his face in her hair so he could inhale.

"It was too much . . . ," he rasped out.

She didn't really want to talk but she realized she needed to learn how to with Dunn. "I don't think there is such a thing between us. You give me something I've never encountered before. Something so very . . . much more."

There it was . . . an admission she'd never thought to ever make. Somehow, knowing he needed it, made it so much more important for her to say.

He stroked her nape for a moment before he raised her face so their gazes could meet. The naked fury was still there in his green eyes. But now, it was controlled. She reached up to tap his lips with her fingertip.

His eyes narrowed as she stood, allowing him to get to his feet and right his clothing.

"Now we can get down to the business at hand," she muttered.

The door was closed and she reached for the handle as the plane engines droned on in the background. Dunn caught her wrist.

"So much more?" he demanded softly. "Explain, Thais."

She turned and stared straight back at him. "It was about giving you what you needed emotionally."

She was suddenly uncertain. The word "relation-ship" was flashing through her brain, leaving her feeling unsure how to proceed. Her damned knees actually felt weak.

"Not that I'm any expert on . . ."

He let out a little grunt before he was reaching past her for the door handle. He pulled it open and reached back for her uninjured arm. The aisle was narrow and he pulled her through to the bedroom that was on the opposite side. The bed was set against the side of the aircraft.

"You're doing better than me," Dunn said as he ripped the bedding back.

He took a moment to kick his shoes off before he scooped her up and cradled her on the way to the surface of the bed.

He framed one side of her face with his hand, locking gazed with her. "We're well-matched, Thais."

It was a compliment.

But it was something else as well.

She searched his eyes and felt something shift between them as his green eyes glittered with pure intent.

A moment later he was kissing her. Slipping his hand up into her hair to cup the back of her head while his mouth claimed her. It was a demanding kiss, the anger she'd come into his office to help defuse only taken down a few notches.

The knowledge made her tremble. He chuckled in response, lifting his head and offering her a grin.

"My turn," he said, before he pulled her dress up and over her head. His gaze landed on her, his expression tightening with male approval. "Definitely my turn, baby."

Her lips were suddenly dry and she rolled them in to moisten them. His gaze targeted the motion, his eyes narrowing. Thais rose onto her knees, leaning forward so he was afforded a perfect view of her cleavage.

He cupped her knees, slipping his hands beneath them and pulling hard. She flipped right onto her back, the bed cushioning her fall.

"You're not distracting me this time, Thais," he promised as he pulled her underwear off. "It's your turn to be at the mercy of my instincts."

He pressed her thighs wide, rubbing the inside of them with firm, slow strokes.

"I like the way you smell." He slid his hands all the way to where her thighs ended but not quite far enough to touch her sex. Leaning forward, with one knee on the bed between her thighs, he hovered over her for a long moment, arousal making his eyes glitter. "The scent of your body drives me insane."

He drew in a deep breath before he aimed a hard look at her. "Btu I can't be alone in this, Thais. I have to know you're just as susceptible as I am."

She was. He read it right off her face before he was slipping down and hovering over her spread sex. Arousal had already coated the folds of her slit in fluid that his breath teased.

She shuddered at the first touch of his tongue against her delicate skin. Sensation raced up her passage and made her belly clench. Sex had never been as necessary as it was with Dunn. It had also never delighted her so very deeply before.

Intimacy.

He was stoking her inner thighs again. "Do you understand, Thais?"

She nodded but that frustrated him. He wanted her to voice her feelings.

Complete exposure.

"We already fucked," she said. "It wasn't enough."

He moved his hand back up to her slit, rubbing her clit as he nodded.

"You drive me insane, Thais," he muttered as he gauged her growing arousal level. "I have to have you in the same position."

She caught the look of determination in his eyes before she surrendered and let her eyelids shut. Sometimes actions spoke louder than words. He made a soft sound of male approval before he applied his mouth completely to her slit.

She cried out.

She withered.

She gripped the bedding beneath her so tightly, it might have ripped.

Not that she cared.

No, there was only the pleasure he was sending through her body with his tongue and mouth. Teasing her clit with soft laps before sucking it until she was lifting her hips up in an effort to gain enough pressure to climax.

Dunn wasn't going to allow her to gain that zenith so quickly. He lifted his head up and used a single fingertip to circle the entrance to her body.

Her passage ached, clenching in an effort to tighten around that fingertip.

Dunn denied her the penetration. Rimming her for a time that felt endless because she was poised on the edge. Caught so completely in the grip of need that she was actually desperate for release.

"Dunn!" she said. "Stop teasing me."

She caught a flash of smug male victory on his face before he was pushing two thick fingers up into her. She gasped and arched, lifting her hips up to take his thrust.

She was so close . . .

The need so acute.

"Now . . . ," she rasped out. "I need . . . it . . . now!"

He didn't deny her. She felt the way he handled her, with a confidence that sent her over the edge. Pleasure ripped into her, bursting with an intensity that shattered the need gnawing at her insides. It was hot and bright enough to burn everything away, leaving her in absolute bliss.

Dunn rolled onto the bed and tugged her toward him.

She ended up in his arms, cradled against his side as he pulled a blanket over them and threaded his fingers through her hair.

"Does this mean your work can wait?" she asked.

She heard him chuckle. Her lips curved in response and she found that bubble of happiness lodged in her chest once more.

CHAPTER SEVEN

Decontamination wasn't fun.

The process was long and drawn out, allowing Damascus Hale plenty of time to imagine signs of symptoms that she didn't have.

She let out a little huff, which brought the overhead lights on.

"Is there a problem, Dr. Hale?"

The voice came from the control center, where there was a three-person team assigned to observe her while she was still in isolation.

"Just my mind playing tricks on me," she explained.

She should have been out like a light. Cassy hadn't settled into nursing very well, which might be Damascus's fault more than her infant daughter's. But sleep had been in short supply for the last few months.

But no, Damascus was wide awake, even though she was locked in the room, which was surrounded by a containment unit. Sleep was the only thing she could do for the next seventy-two hours.

"Since you are awake, your mother is here."

Damascus sat up. She reached over and turned on the daylight lamps. "I'll see her."

It didn't take long before Miranda was in front of the triple-pane glass that made up one side of the containment room.

"Baby," Miranda exclaimed as her eyes swept Damascus from head to toe. "I'm so worried."

"So am I," Damascus answered. "But about you. Don't let this distract you from campaigning."

Miranda sent her a look full of reprimand. "There is nothing more important to me than my children."

"I know and I'm so happy to see you but I'm stuck in this containment unit for at least another three days."

Damascus flattened her hand on the glass separating her from her mother. Miranda pressed her palm against the opposite side of the glass.

"Go, Mom!" Damascus insisted. "I'm fine. Cassy is fine. You've given me too much of your life. You need to be focused."

Miranda hesitated but nodded in the end. "I'll call you. And I will be back once you're out of containment."

Miranda wasn't stupid.

Oh, she played the sweet, charming personality very well, and she preferred it over being difficult.

But she knew how to be someone's worst nightmare.

Her daughter was in a cage.

And her son had almost lost the woman he loved.

It was time to strip off her gloves. The hallways of the underground lab where her daughter lived and worked irritated her because she knew Damascus had chosen them in order to escape her father.

That was Miranda's failing.

She'd bent to the demands of her family in order to safeguard Dunn and it had placed Damascus in a situation where she needed to find a haven.

Miranda turned a corner but she didn't enter the apartment where Vitus and her granddaughter were.

Damascus was very correct. Miranda had business to attend to.

Her car slid up to the curb the moment she made it to ground level. The door was shut firmly before she pulled out her phone and searched for a contact. Her husband, Jeb, might have believed she didn't know how dirty he was in his dealings, and she'd enjoyed duping him. After all, Jeb had been so proud of her being a Delacroix and his little obedient wife.

Carl answered after a couple of rings.

"Hello, Miranda," he cooed.

"I received your message, Carl," she answered.

Her fingers tightened on her phone as Carl allowed a silence to stretch out. He really was the most insufferable sort.

"However, if you're tongue-tied," she offered, "I can get on with my day."

Carl snickered at her. "You're not in control, Miranda. I am."

"As you say," Miranda responded in a very practiced sweet tone. "I can't imagine you enjoy speaking to me, so I will ask again, what do you want of me? This is, after all, about getting me to come to terms with you."

"That's right," Carl stated firmly. "You're going to heel like a good bitch. A well-trained bitch. My bitch."

"I see—" Miranda responded.

"Shut up," he said, interrupting her. "Save your little display of confidence and poise. I know you're scared," Carl growled into the phone. "You should be. I know your weakness."

"It appears you do."

Carl chuckled again. Inside the car, Miranda was free to smile. He didn't realize that while he was correct about her weak spots, he was so wrong about her ability to safeguard her family.

He really should have recalled that she was the one who killed Jeb.

"This is what you're going to do, Miranda," Carl said, getting down to business. "I'm doing a press conference today and you are going to join me. In fact, you're going to announce a change of heart. You're going to declare to the masses that you are backing me for president instead of Tom Hilliard."

Miranda was suddenly grateful for the years of training she'd been forced to endure while under her father's roof. Today, she held her tongue with the control she'd mastered at the demand of her power-loving family.

"Is any part of that unclear?" Carl demanded when she remained silent.

"None of it," she replied. "Do send along details of where you expect me to be and when."

She killed the call, enjoying knowing she'd been able to choose to sever the connection. Carl's tone had been so very smug. She did admit he was very good at playing the power game.

But she was a Delacroix.

The Delacroix family had risen to power through the spilling of blood. Her father might have believed she only learned poise and grace under his roof, but a child who was good at remaining silent was also very accomplished in listening and watching.

Jeb had never questioned why Miranda had fallen in love with a Scot. He hadn't cared and neither had her family. To them, she had needed to be brought back to the fold. There hadn't been any reason to tell them she just couldn't stomach her own blood because they simply didn't care. Their need for power was nauseating because they hid behind lies about duty and service. Her desire for a different life was something they could never, ever understand.

She smiled slowly as she considered her children. They had become good people. The sort she had always wanted them to be able to become.

Well, she was a Delacroix and she knew how to find the type of men who did dirty work. Carl was going to have to die.

And she wasn't at all sorry about being the one to deal with it.

A mother did what a mother had to do.

Dunn's phone was ringing.

Well, if one could call a cell-phone chime a ring. Their limbs were still tangled and she'd fallen asleep at some point. Dunn shifted and she forgot about her injured arm.

She let out a little yelp as she twisted and rolled off the bed.

"Thais?"

"I'm just stupid," she assured him as her arm stung.

His lips rose into a half grin. He pulled her close and pressed a kiss against her lips.

"You were just completely under my spell and forgot where you were."

And he was proud of himself. Thais offered him a flutter of his eyelashes before Dunn's phone chimed with a message. He looked at the screen, his grin fading.

He swept his finger across the screen and punched a button. It took only a moment for whoever had called him to answer.

"What do you want?" Dunn demanded. "And it had better be good."

Ricky Sullivan wasn't a stranger to being disliked.

"Your tone is a bit abrasive," Ricky informed Dunn.

"Nothing you haven't earned."

"Well now," Ricky began, "that's where you're wrong. I'm calling you because I know you want to know who just called me."

"I'm listening," Dunn replied.

"Miranda Delacroix just offered to hire me," Ricky offered. "To slip her the means to kill Carl Davis this afternoon. Seems he's got some crazy idea about her showing up and announcing she supports him. I honestly didn't think she had the guts."

"What did you tell her?" Dunn demanded.

Ricky's voice indicated a grin. "Told her I'd get her what she needed. If I hadn't, she'd have just called someone else. Thing is, I sort of think she has earned the right to put a slug in that shit-bag. Debated calling you about it. I didn't call Vitus Hale; he'd be duty bound to stop her and that seems like a stupid move from where I am sitting."

"Why did you call me?" Dunn asked.

"Simple, really," Ricky said. "I was heading out when she called. On my way to retirement. But you'd likely think twice about letting me settle into my golden years if I let your mother go up against someone like Carl Davis alone when I could have called you."

"You can bet on it," Dunn confirmed.

"So I called you," Ricky said. "And I expect to be compensated for my risk."

"Of course you do."

"I have the money I need," Ricky informed him.

"Get to the point," Dunn warned him.

"Thing is, I respect anyone willing to stand up for their blood," Ricky explained. "I think you get it. I think you also understand that if Vitus Hale heard about this, he'd have to stop her. That seems real unfair to my way of thinking. Now you? Well, you've got your own world to go back to and I don't see you dismissing the fact that your mother is going to put boot to ass for her kids. I expect you to understand what I'm doing, respecting her need to protect her kin, no matter what happens."

Dunn was silent for a long moment. Ricky felt his neck tightening up just a bit. As he'd thought back when the whole thing began, Dunn Bateson wasn't a man to cross.

"Fair enough," Dunn said at last. "You've clued me in. I won't come looking for you."

"One more thing." Ricky was quick to speak up before Bateson killed the call. "I think this is going down soon, so I hope you're close by. I'm meeting your mum in an hour."

Dunn cursed.

"Keep her thinking you're handling it," Dunn growled.

Ricky let out a little whistle as the line disconnected. Family squabbles always were the most entertaining.

This time though, he was tickled by the way everyone involved was trying to shield the other. In the past, they'd come to him when they wanted to clear the path of other heirs and so on. Money had always motivated them.

Today, however, he was cheerful as he ducked into a pawn shop and looked at the guns. The owner eyed him from where he was sitting at a desk while his staff dealt with the customers. Ricky flashed the guy a grin before tapping the case and flashing him a roll of cash. The old man didn't give any hint as to what he thought about it.

"Can I help you?" a burly staff member asked.

"Changed my mind," Ricky declared before he sent the old man another look and turned around to leave the shop.

Outside, the weather had people hurrying to get out of it. Fall gripped the city with rain that was washing the dirt off the roofs and making the pavement muddy. The wind was blowing dried leaves around, adding a rattle to the scene.

It felt like death.

Winter would show up soon enough to lock the city in snow and ice and they'd all do their best to make it to spring.

"Two grand." The owner of the shop had shown up. He didn't stop but walked by Ricky with a slow shuffle on his way into a donut shop.

Ricky reached into his pocket and counted off the bills without looking. He had the hundreds sorted out with their corners folded down so he didn't have to flash his wad.

The old man came shuffling back. "Looks like you could use a cup of coffee, pal."

Ricky took the cup and offered to shake the man's hand. "Kind of you."

The money disappeared inside the man's pocket after they finished shaking hands.

"Hal makes the best donuts in town," the man said as he offered Ricky a plain brown paper bag.

"I'm going to hold you to that," Ricky replied. "Thanks for the coffee."

The man shuffled off as Ricky tucked the paper bag into his coat. He felt the familiar weight of a handgun and grinned.

Part of him was really enjoying knowing Miranda had enough fire in her belly to stop taking Carl Davis's crap. Ricky understood about taking care of your own.

He pulled a cell phone from his pocket. It was a pre-paid one. He dialed a number and let it ring twice before he hung up. He repeated the double ring a second time before closing the phone and shoving it back into his pocket.

He started walking, his hood pulled up as he waited. The little phone vibrated and he pulled it out to read the text message. It was harder than ever to move around the city without being spotted by cameras. The address was on the other side of town, so he made his way toward a large shopping center. Scanning the cars, he singled out one with a Lyft sticker. A trio of teens was getting out, giggling as they anticipated an afternoon of shopping and chatting.

Ricky walked up beside the driver and flashed him a hundred. "Let's keep it between us, mate? Deal?"

The guy flipped him a thumbs-up. Ricky offered the address before he climbed into the backseat.

One last job.

He'd certainly sleep a lot better with Carl Davis dead. The guy knew stuff Ricky didn't need being repeated.

Sometimes, Thais wished she wasn't as good at her job as she was. Dunn's plane came with every high-tech goodie she could ask for, so it didn't take her very long to find the trending Twitter bursts about the press conference Carl Davis was having with Miranda Delacroix.

"How far out are we, Kent?" Dunn demanded as he read over Thais's shoulder.

"Twenty-two minutes to landing, sir," Kent replied through the open cockpit door. "Car is waiting."

Dunn cussed and Thais shook her head as she looked at the time the press conference was set to begin.

"See if you can get a motorcycle," Thais advised.

Kent hit a button on the control panel of the plane and started trying to get her request handled.

"Miranda's not answering." Dunn hit the redial button again.

Thais grabbed her phone as it vibrated. Dunn was watching her as he paced with the phone to his ear.

"Vitus is en route but he's still forty-five minutes out," she informed him.

It would be too late. They both knew it.

Thais turned back to her computer, desperately seeking something she'd overlooked. Helplessness sunk its claws into her, frustrating her almost beyond endurance.

But she clamped her control down, digging for her composure.

This was what she was. An agent.

"I'm looking forward to this." Carl was giddy. He rubbed his hands together before he fastened the top button on his shirt and selected a tie.

"Miranda should have known I'd win in the end," Carl continued as he tied his tie.

In another penthouse suite, Carl was at the top of the city. There was a room-service cart with selections from the kitchen sent up to tempt him while the bar was fully stocked and ready for him.

He flashed a look at Eric. "She's made it such a chore though, I think a lesson is in order."

Eric remained silent as his boss decided on what he wanted done.

"Dunn Bateson will be running to his mommy's side, no doubt," Carl said. "Check the incoming flights."

Eric pulled a tablet from his jacket pocket and tapped in a few lines of code while Carl lifted a polished domed lid sitting over some of the food to investigate what had been sent up. He plucked a deviled egg from the plate and shoved it in his mouth while Eric finished getting the information he wanted.

"One of Bateson's planes is coming in to land in a few minutes," Eric confirmed.

Carl snapped his fingers. "I knew it. Now . . ."—he grabbed a napkin and wiped his fingers before dropping it on top of the cart without a care—"Thais will be with Dunn. According to the media, she's still dead.

Send someone to meet that plane and drop her. I want Miranda to know how important it is for her to stay in the place I put her. Dunn needs that lesson as well."

"She's already coming to the press conference," Eric argued. "It doesn't matter what she thinks, only what she does. You don't need Bateson pissed at you."

Carl turned on him, his expression furious. "Don't start thinking, Geyer. You're my dog. When I tell you to kill, you bare your teeth and do it!"

Carl stomped into the bathroom and flipped on the faucet.

He really shouldn't have left Eric alone with his thoughts. The large mirror on the wall offered Eric a reflection of himself and today, it made him sick to his stomach.

"You're my dog!"

He was. It was a bargain Eric had made willingly, even defended.

Now? He looked his reflection. He was everything he'd trained to be. Hard body, sharp instincts. He had the suit and the permit to carry a gun and a top-secret clearance. All of those things had been goals he'd applied himself to in his quest to be one of the best.

There was something else he saw in his reflection. A look of misgiving. Carl was out of control. If it had been the need to win, Eric could have dealt with it.

But they'd gone too far.

"Did you get it done?" Carl popped his face back into the hallway. "I can get someone else if you don't have the balls."

"I'm handling the details," Eric replied smoothly.

He turned and ducked into the other side of the suite where his room was. There was also another dining area that was used to store equipment. Eric looked over the table, finding the medical kits that belonged to the trauma doctor who traveled with them.

The shower was running, telling Eric where the doctor was. He looked behind him but heard a whistle from the bar area as Carl made himself a drink.

He was celebrating.

Celebrating a needless murder.

It chafed.

Eric opened the medical kit, looking through it until he found something he recognized from his own emergency preparedness classes.

Rocuronium.

It was a drug used to paralyze the body of a patient so they could be intubated. Once injected, the patient had to have a tube inserted into their lungs so their breathing could be taken over by a machine or a hand-squeezed bag in the field. If no one did that, the patient would die from lack of oxygen. Three minutes was all it would take for brain damage to start. Carl would pass out before the first sixty seconds. Merciful, really, considering how cold-blooded he was with others.

Eric slipped the syringe into his pocket.

An hour ago, he would have sworn he'd never get to such a point, but he admitted Carl's growing level of animosity had been pushing him toward the limit line.

He admitted he was relieved to discover he had a limit.

But he had the feeling Carl wasn't going to feel the same way about it.

The shower shut off. Eric turned and went back into the central area of the suite. Timing was going to be everything. The doctor would just intubate Carl if Eric dropped him there in the suite.

So he'd have to find a better opportunity.

And soon.

"Sure about this?" There were firsts in everyone's life. Ricky found himself feeling like he needed to ask Miranda the question before he handed the gun to her.

She fluttered her eyelashes. "Very sure."

Her gaze was steady and sure. Damn, Ricky was impressed. Inside her was a woman of remarkable strength. Her escort was watching him as he handed over the paper bag.

Someone knocked on the outer restroom door. "Everything alright, Madam Delacroix?"

Ricky hopped up onto one of the toilets to keep his feet from being seen by the guy as he opened the door to look inside the restroom.

"I was just practicing my speech," Miranda said to explain why her security escort had heard her talking after they'd cleared the restroom for her. "Sorry to worry you."

He nodded and closed the door but not before he made a quick sweep of the area. Miranda came around to where Ricky could see her. She pointed to the ceiling panel that Ricky had come down through to meet her.

He used the top of the stalls to lever himself up and through the ceiling panel. Restrooms always had a vent in them. Ricky crawled into the tube connecting the forced air system to the vent. It was secure enough to take a man's weight but he had to crawl on his belly.

And it was tight.

His shoulders were making contact with either side

of it. Still, it had been the perfect way to slip a gun to Miranda, and the surprising part was she'd been the one to tell him exactly how to do it.

Sure, he'd known already. That didn't change how impressed he was with her knowledge of how to get weapons transferred without anyone knowing.

Ricky moved slowly. The vent tubing was made of metal and made tons of noise if he wasn't careful with how much pressure he put on one spot. The trick was to use his feet as well as his hands and apply plenty of patience so he didn't let his mind start playing tricks on him.

He wasn't trapped.

In fact, he was at the end of a long road. On the other side of the vent tubing was the life he hadn't realized he wanted so badly.

His golden years.

The last few feet were the longest. Ricky was sweating when he popped up in the crawl space behind the elevators. He took a moment to roll his shoulders and stretch his neck until it popped before he used a hand screwdriver to replace the screws that held the cover on.

A drill would have been faster but he wasn't going to risk the noise.

"What are you doing?"

Ricky froze.

"Hands where I can see them."

Ricky complied, turning to flash the security man a smile. "Just checking on a clunking noise."

The security man looked Ricky over. His uniform jumpsuit was the hotel's and his identification card was clipped to his collar.

"I wasn't born yesterday," the security man said as

he held his gun steady. With VIPs in town, the normal civilian security had been replaced. "Move that ID card so I can see the picture."

Normally, this was the moment when Ricky struck. The guy did know his stuff. Plenty of his comrades hadn't taken a second look.

But Kagan had made the conditions of his new passport clear.

No killing.

At least, not beyond the targets Kagan identified.

Ricky raised his hands high. The guy grunted and used the tiny microphone in the cuff of his sleeve to call for backup.

The press was camped out behind the yellow lines set up by security. Miranda would swear she felt them as she fixed her makeup before the press conference.

The gun was heavy.

And a comfort.

Oh, she didn't enjoy killing. But there were times a mother had to protect her family. She finished with her hair and felt her cell phone vibrate again. She pulled it out of the pocket in her skirt and looked at the text.

Dunn was looking for her.

So was Vitus.

Her heart warmed and her determination hardened. The text from Thais Sinclair was the one Miranda felt affecting her the most. Dunn loved the girl. Oh yes, there would be plenty of people who would tell her love didn't happen so quickly.

But Miranda knew from experience that it did.

So Miranda tucked her phone into her pocket and checked the gun a final time.

* * *

Carl was having trouble sitting still in his seat as his car rounded the corner to the location of the press event. Actually, there was dinner and a reception being held later that night but his attention was on the press conference he'd called.

"Is Miranda already here?" Carl demanded as the driver pulled into the underground parking garage and came to a smooth stop in front of a set of elevators.

Eric was out of the car though, performing his duties before answering questions.

Carl grunted as someone else opened the door for him. He had to get out of the car and make his way over to Eric before asking his question again.

Eric was sweeping the area, his attention sharp. The Secret Service already had men posted at the entrance to the private and secure elevator.

"We've got one man in custody," one of the Secret Service men said as Eric came close. "He was found working on a ventilation panel with a stolen identification badge. Rest of the building is secure."

Eric stepped into Carl's path before he made it too close to the men standing guard at the elevator.

"This is a jamming device," Eric informed his boss as he offered him a small black box.

Carl looked at him for a moment before he nodded. "Right. Miranda has recorded me before. Good thinking. Seems I have a reason to keep you around after all."

Carl stuffed the little black device that looked a lot like a smartphone into his lapel pocket.

"Why don't you go check on that man they have in custody." Carl wasn't actually asking a question. He patted his suit jacket where the jamming device was hidden and flashed Eric a smug grin. "Let me get a little business done with Miranda."

"Yes, sir."

Carl enjoyed the obedient reply. He whistled as he moved toward the elevators and one of the Secret Service men pushed the call button. The doors slid open with a little chime. Carl strode forward without a backward glance.

Pompous ass.

Eric kept his jaw tight. He waited until the doors closed and Carl disappeared before turning and moving toward where the suspect was being held.

Kagan knew his art.

Some might call it a job, but to him, a man who had nothing else, it was an art. The single form of expression afforded him because of his devotion to his duty.

Shadow Ops was his world.

He'd settled into the teams because their mission was one he found meaning in. Plenty of men ended up in the shadows, working with different badges, for a variety of reasons.

All of them were personal.

Some liked the buzz, others came for the glory; there were those scooping up riches, and men like himself who carried the scars from injustice and found peace in knowing they were helping to shield others from the same damage.

There had been a time when he'd been like the people he passed on the sidewalk. A memory surfaced as he got to where a perimeter was set up and the Secret Service was checking IDs.

A memory of a woman who had loved him and had his baby.

Their ghosts accompanied him as he flashed his badge and was allowed past the checkpoint. Kagan indulged in their company for a few more steps before he shut the door on his personal past and focused on the moment at hand.

He'd once told Carl Davis that not killing him was what made Kagan far more useful to him.

Carl hadn't seen the merit in keeping good men loyal to him.

It wasn't the first time Kagan had been pushed into a corner. He didn't like it but he'd do what needed doing.

"There's my boss," someone said, raising his voice. "He'll tell you . . . Kagan!"

Kagan snapped his head around, looking at two large mobile trailers that were arranged in a side street alongside the hotel that was closed off to secure the location. The Secret Service was escorting a handcuffed man toward one of the trailers.

Ricky Sullivan.

Kagan didn't have time for the ex-hitman but he also knew that Ricky was a wealth of information. If he was there, Kagan likely wanted to know why.

"He's mine," Kagan said, flashing his badge.

The Secret Service wasn't in the mood to have their entertainment interrupted. The two men holding Ricky tightened their grip on his shoulders as a supervisor slid between Kagan and Ricky.

"I never repeat myself." Kagan held his badge up again.

"I'm more interested in what your man was doing

pulling off a ventilation screen while wearing a stolen ID," the supervisor demanded.

Kagan didn't shirk, he didn't even raise his voice. "Take another good . . . long . . . look, son. This badge is one you can't argue with."

Kagan watched as the supervisor looked back at the badge. Kagan gave him time to see it before he was pushing it back into this pocket. "We're on the same team."

The supervisor opened his mouth to argue. Kagan beat him to the punch. "Release my man and don't bother with questions I'm not going to answer."

There were a lot of eyes on them. Serving in the Secret Service meant you spent endless hours watching. Actual events were few and far between due in a large part to how good the members of the elite security force were. So when something actually happened, everyone wanted to enjoy the entertainment.

Kagan wasn't planning on giving them anything to remember.

He pulled Ricky along with him and into the building where he could be sure of privacy.

"What are you doing here, Sullivan?" Kagan demanded softly.

Ricky wasn't exactly willing to turn over the information, but as he'd said before, he knew who held his leash. Kagan watched as Ricky lifted one shoulder and answered. "Miranda called me."

Kagan didn't get surprised often. He enjoyed the slight sensation of being caught without having considered something before it occurred.

"She wanted a gun," Kagan said, finishing his explanation.

Ricky nodded. "Got to hand it to the old bird, she's not in the grave just yet." Ricky looked around again before he finished. "Don't worry. I got her a clean one. Nothing to trace it back to any of us."

"I'm more concerned for the danger she's putting herself in," Kagan replied.

Ricky offered him a hard look. "Carl started it and she's planning on finishing it. Seems to me, she deserves for the rest of us to get the fuck out of her way. The ass has it coming. A mother defending her kids is sort of timeless justice."

Kagan was silent for a long moment.

"Just don't get in her way," Ricky advised.

"I can't live with what might happen," Kagan replied.

"Don't put her in the princess box," Ricky advised. "She found me all on her own. I got her what she needed. You should get out of here so no one draws a line between your teams and what she plans to do."

Kagan's attention shifted slightly before he was turning Ricky and moving through a doorway. Eric Geyer never saw them.

"You know I'm right," Ricky said once they'd ducked through a service hallway and out a side door. "You just don't like it."

"Don't tell me what to think," Kagan warned Ricky.

Ricky shrugged again. "What can I say? I like to see scrappiness in people. She's got all the money and still takes a hands-on approach. It's fucking beautiful."

Kagan walked without talking, earning a chuckle from Ricky.

"Looks like you have to make a choice," Ricky said.

"How do you figure that?" Kagan asked.

But Ricky didn't answer. He didn't need to. Kagan caught sight of Vitus and Saxon.

"Decision time, Kagan boy-o," Ricky cooed. "Going to let them bust in on the old gal's party?"

Saxon had reached them, his phone in hand. "Thais and Dunn are four minutes out."

Kagan felt himself hesitating, looking back at Ricky as their time ran short. Ricky was right, it was his call and that wasn't the only thing the Irishman was spot on about, either.

Miranda had earned the right to face her demon. But even if Kagan allowed her to, he doubted Dunn would agree.

Which left him with a tough choice. He pulled out his phone and typed in a code. Sending it took only a second before he was face-to-face with Vitus Hale.

Thais pulled her phone out as Kent took them around a corner on two wheels.

Dunn's man's driving didn't alarm her but the code her section leader sent her did. In fact, it chilled her blood.

"What's happening?" Dunn demanded.

She looked up, into Dunn's hard stare. He was tight and ready to kill. She knew the look, knew he was anything but making idle threats.

"We're being ordered to stand down," she informed him.

Kent looked at her via the rearview mirror.

"Like hell I will," Dunn growled.

Thais felt her gut ball up. "It's a hard stand down, Dunn. Straight from Kagan. Pull over, Kent."

"Keep going, Kent."

Thais locked gazes with Dunn. "This is not about agreeing, Dunn. It's about the team. Kagan is in charge of the operation."

"This is my mother, Thais, I'm not letting her down," Dunn insisted.

"You're emotionally compromised," Thais argued. "Kagan is an experienced section leader and you don't know what he knows. He's closer to the action. This is where we have to trust."

Dunn didn't like what she said. Kent was slowing down, as they neared their destination. Dunn was caught between what he wanted and what she'd said. Thais watched the battle on his face.

She had to convince him.

Thais was torn but it was her deeply rooted trust of Kagan that had her reaching into her pocket and pulling out a small air gun. She fired it with a soft shudder, sending a dart into her own shoulder. The needle punctured her skin as Dunn growled and pulled it free.

"Thais?" he demanded, sending a rage-filled look at her.

"We're standing down," she answered him quietly. "I trust my section leader . . . this much."

The dart had performed well, delivering a large dose of a tranquilizer into her bloodstream. But the effects weren't instantaneous.

She had several long moments to watch the way Dunn stared at her and back at the door. She was hitting below the belt now. Forcing him to choose trust or go with his own plan.

There would be no recovery from it if he chose to abandon her in favor of his own judgment.

"I hope . . . you're here . . . when I wake up . . ." Her

last few words were slurred. She sunk down into the
seat, drifting off.

"Stand down, Hale," Kagan said. "That's an order."

Vitus ripped his sunglasses off. "Excuse me, sir?"

Kagan didn't budge. "You heard correct. Stand down."

"You know Carl is forcing Miranda to do this?"
Saxon asked.

Kagan nodded and started moving away from the
building. "Miranda plans to face him."

Vitus looked from Ricky to Kagan before he started
to head toward the hotel.

"That's . . . an order . . . Hale." Kagan didn't raise his
voice.

In fact, the section leader lowered it. Vitus and Saxon
both knew the tone well. They were torn and Kagan
knew it. He leaned in close.

"Carl's been pushing her," Kagan explained. "And
she's about to turn and give him what he's earned. I
don't like it any more than either of you, but it's everyone's right to protect their children."

"She's family," Vitus insisted.

"Which is why you need to let her do what she feels
she needs to do. You'd expect the same from her if the
situation was reversed. Let her slay her own demons,"
Kagan said.

Vitus cussed. Kagan reached out and clasped his
shoulder.

"I don't like it, either," Kagan confessed. "But if we
go back there, Carl will get his wish to see our teams
blamed and dismantled. Miranda isn't stupid, she knows
she's the best person for the job."

"And it's not like Carl hasn't been asking for it,"

Saxon added in a tone that betrayed just how much he didn't like the current situation.

Vitus shot a stern look at Ricky. "You better have gotten her a good weapon."

One side of Ricky's lips twitched up in cocky grin. "I know, you still don't like me."

Vitus shook his head.

There was a spring in his step.

Carl enjoyed the surge of strength going through his body.

He'd worked hard for this moment.

There had been twists and turns along the way and disappointments, like having to let Damascus go. She really would have been a perfect wife for his image.

That was just another little thing Miranda would be paying for. Her failure to raise her daughter to know her place.

At the top of the stairs, the hallway went in different directions. One way was toward the ladies' room and the other went toward the men's room. Carl reached into his jacket pocket and pulled out the jamming device Eric had given him. Pressing down on the button resulted in a flickering green light. Tucking it back inside his jacket, Carl went down the hall toward the lounge where Miranda would be.

His personal security had done their job well. Carl shoved the door in, startling Miranda. She caught sight of him in the mirror in the same instant he pushed her against the wall.

"What are you doing?" she demanded.

"I won't be as easy to kill as your husband, Miranda,"

Carl informed her. "You know my preferences, so don't take this personally."

He frisked her, snorting when he found the unmistakable bulge of a gun.

"I guess I'd be a little disappointed if you just rolled over." He yanked the gun from her waistband.

He checked it before leveling it at her, holding the gun for a long moment before he snickered. "I'm not going to shoot you. But the next time you step out of line, Damascus won't just get scared."

Miranda sent a hard look toward Carl. He snickered at her, his lips curved into a bright smile of victory. "I knew you were responsible for that accident at the lab."

Carl yanked the door open and pushed her through it into the hallway.

"Next time," Carl stressed his words as he leaned in close and kept her in place with a hard grip on her upper arm. "Next time, I'll make sure your precious daughter and granddaughter die. You're going to smile and shake my hand downstairs or so help me, Miranda, I'll make sure the bug that gets released in that lab is one that kills them both in the worst way possible."

"Are you insane?" Miranda looked him straight in the eye. "You could infect more than the underground lab, Carl. The only reason we have those facilities is to make certain we have countermeasures against those diseases. Are you really so blinded by your own ambition?"

Carl wasn't budging. "An outbreak would only make it easier to sell the budget to Congress next year. Nothing wrong with thinning the herd from time to time."

"You are truly a monster, Carl," Miranda muttered.

"Don't be coy," Carl growled at her. "I know you shot

your husband." He patted the pocket he had the gun in.
"You are not so innocent yourself."

"In both cases, I was motivated by the need to protect," Miranda answered. "A mother does what she must
to protect her child."

"Good." Carl pulled her toward the hallway. "If you
want your daughter and granddaughter alive tomorrow,
get your ass down those stairs and shake my hand.
You're going to publicly change sides, support me, and
use your family name to pressure all your friends to
support me."

Carl watched Miranda lose her color. He pulled back,
releasing her, and enjoyed the horror glittering in her
eyes.

"Bringing you to heel has been a bitch," he muttered.
"You're going to pay for it. I promise you that."

Eric Geyer appeared at the bottom of the steps. Carl
chuckled, enjoying the moment just as much as he'd
anticipated he would.

"Move your ass, Miranda." Carl indulged in vocal-
izing his victory. "You don't have a choice. Know something? This beats knowing I had you killed. I'm going
to enjoy seeing you screw over your friends . . . and then
watching them try and tear you to bits. I'll be the only
thing shielding you. You'll sit just as properly as can be
at my feet."

He gave her a little push. She stumbled but righted
herself as Eric came up a few steps to try and steady
her. His head of security grasped her wrist and she
gasped. Miranda pulled back slightly, bumping into
Carl.

"What's the problem?" Carl demanded.

Miranda only stared at Eric a moment before she wavered and her knees buckled.

"Madam Delacroix?" Eric asked, his voice slightly louder than Carl might have expected.

And it drew the attention of Miranda's security detail. They swept in, scooping her up as her eyelashes fluttered and her head rolled back.

"What the fuck?" Carl started to surge after her. Eric stepped into his path, pushing him back up the stairway.

"Don't let that bitch pull a faint!" Carl said. "I need her support."

"It's legitimate," Eric muttered as he raised his hand. His fingers were closed around a small, spring-loaded syringe.

Carl stared at it as Eric dropped it into his pocket.

"What . . . what are you doing?" Carl demanded, his expression darkening. "You know how much we need her . . ."

"She's right," Eric said, reaching out, and Carl heard the discharge of another spring-loaded syringe. "You are a monster. And all the attention is now focused on her. Leaving you and me, very much alone."

Carl jerked away from Eric but a spot on his forearm stung, proving the needle had punctured his skin. Disbelief contorted his features as he looked at his head of security.

"You will experience more than a faint," Eric said as he wiped the syringe clean before dropping it back into his pocket.

"What . . . what . . . I was going to give you everything you ever dreamed of!"

Eric locked gazes with Carl. "Maybe I didn't fancy

knowing you'd thin me out as part of the herd when it suited your purpose."

Carl stumbled back, but his knees suddenly weakened until they folded. His eyes bulged as he strained, struggling to maintain his control, but there was never any doubt as to what would happen. Eric watched as Carl's knees buckled and he looked up at him while trying to make his tongue work. Eric observed him for a moment, looking completely unremorseful. He watched him struggle to speak, to tell him how he felt. The drug reduced Carl to helplessness, just as he'd done to so many others. Eric lowered himself so he was eye-to-eye with Carl.

"It's less painful than the death you ordered me to arrange for Damascus Ryland," Eric muttered softly. "You're just going to stop breathing. And know that all the paramedics are with Miranda right now. You wanted her to feel helpless. But you know what they say, Carl: whatever you spread around . . . comes . . . back . . . to . . . you."

Carl slid back onto the stairs, feeling Eric leaning over him. Inside his chest, his heart beat hard, slow beats. Each one separated from the last by more time. He felt the edges of his sight darkening, watched the circle of his field of vision decreasing with every second that he noticed like it was an hour.

He knew the moment his heart stopped. Was suspended in that moment as he realized the muscle had seized and wasn't going to pump again. But his brain was still functioning, letting him feel the approach of darkness, until it extinguished the light completely.

* * *

"Doctors still aren't willing to speculate on the cause of death of presidential hopeful Carl Davis. Congress hopeful Miranda Delacroix has made a full recovery . . . and there is no clear cause yet in this case . . ."

It wasn't the first time Saxon's team had known more about the news than the reporter did. Standing in the back room of the office they'd turned into their command center, Saxon shared a look with his brother, Vitus.

Dare Servant let out a low whistle. "Seems a little anticlimactic, considering how many times that bastard tried to kill us."

"I'll take it," Greer said.

Vitus nodded agreement. "Working cold cases suddenly strikes me as attractive."

"Glad to hear it," Kagan said as he came through the back entrance. The team turned and gave their section leader their full attention. "I've assured Tom Hilliard we aren't rogue agents. He's decided to give us the benefit of the doubt. Seems he didn't see many virtues in Carl."

There were some clearing of throats in the room.

"Keep on your construction projects for the moment," Kagan advised. "It's becoming too hard to stay off grid in the city. And take some time off. You've all earned it."

Kagan was never one to prolong conversations. He nodded once and left. With the departure of their section leader, the rest of Thais's team relaxed. It was well earned and yet, there was still a cord of tension left among them because Thais wasn't among them. Privacy was something none of them expected but they all wanted to afford one another. In that moment, they knew Thais's heart was on the line.

But it was something none of them could help her with.

Thais fought to wake up.

Long before she shook off the hold of the drug keeping her in slumber, she knew there was something she needed to do.

Something she hoped was waiting for her.

Sweat coated her skin when she managed to open her eyes. There was a moment of victory before she remembered the moments right before she'd gone under.

She'd left Dunn without a wingman.

It was something an agent never did.

Of course, she'd done it to force him to stand down. But he'd figure that out on his own just fine. What remained to be seen was what he'd do about it.

Someone had put her in a bed. The ceiling of the room was pristine with crown molding and not a cobweb insight. Her head was lying on a pillow and there was a blanket tucked up to her chin. Her teammates would have made sure she wasn't in danger, maybe put her on a couch, but the king-size bed told her Dunn had taken care of her himself.

Just as she'd hoped to force him to do instead of charging into the situation they'd been ordered to stay out of. She'd used his feelings for her against him. The knowledge burned in her gut because it was a line she wasn't sure he could deal with her crossing.

The door opened and she felt Dunn's arrival as much as she identified him. Their gazes locked, sending a jolt through her system.

"You knew I wouldn't leave you," Dunn said.

She fought to sit up, earning a narrowing of his eyes.

The damn room felt like it was shrinking as Dunn came toward her. The look in his eyes pinned her in place. He reached out and cupped her shoulders before pushing her gently back down onto the bed.

"You're not ready to be up, Thais," he growled at her.

"You're pissed," she replied. "I expected nothing less. You knew who I was, Dunn. An agent. I follow orders. You would have done the same."

"There was a time I did," he confirmed in a hard tone. "I gave it up because I realized there was more to life."

She jerked as the sound of his voice cut her to the bone.

"Isn't it time to stop hiding behind your badge, Thais?" It wasn't really a question.

No, it felt like it was a cry from the person inside her that didn't want to be trapped behind the walls she was determined to live with.

"I know, because I've done it myself," Dunn continued. "And the truth is, until you came into my reclusive world, I wasn't as far from MI-6 as I'd convinced myself I was."

His fingers tightened on her shoulders for a moment, letting her know he was straining against his self-control as well.

She was having trouble grasping the moment. "I crossed a line, Dunn. I know it."

"And you don't expect me to be able to get past it?" he asked.

Precisely . . .

A ragged breath escaped her lips before she was blinking her eyes, fighting the sting of unshed tears.

"I want ye to marry me, Thais," he said, raising his voice. "How's that for getting past things?"

Thais was stunned. She felt something stretching inside her again. It was that need, that yearning Dunn had touched so very exclusively. She'd only managed to contain it by accepting that he'd never forgive her.

Now? She was left staring at him, trying to decide if she should just jump off the cliff with him.

"Happy ever after?" she questioned him. "Neither of us knows how to live like that."

His lips twitched into a grin.

Logic be damned.

"I'm thinking it's high time we both tried to learn a new way of living," Dunn said, extending his hand, offering it to her. "You're no coward, Thais. Don't start being one now."

Her lips twitched up. "Making it a challenge?"

Dunn tilted his head to one side, his grin becoming cocky. "Life is a challenge. We both thrive on them."

Oh, did they . . .

"And I know that I love you," he said, his expression tightening. "Choose me, Thais, over your ghosts and I swear I'll do the same. Together, we'll figure out the rest."

Her hand landed in his.

Did she think about it? No. But then again, with Dunn, things were so much better when she just let her impulses lead the way.

He smiled as she felt his fingers closing around hers. A moment later, he was tugging her into his embrace, and she sat up so she could kiss him.

Was it love?

It sure as hell was, because there was one thing about her relationship with Dunn that Thais was 100 percent certain of.

She'd never felt the way she did about another man.

And she'd never been in love.

So it was love.

Kagan had stopped, allowing Saxon and Vitus to run into him. Their section leader was whistling as he rocked back on his heels.

"There are parts of this life I love more than others," Kagan said, offering a rare bit of conversation to them. "It's bittersweet though, because your team is officially going into support, Hale."

There had been a time when Saxon would have scowled at Kagan for even hinting at such a thing. Today, Saxon grinned and knew for a fact that his brother was doing the same. Kagan flashed them a smile in return before he nodded and shook their hands.

"It's been an honor serving with you both," Kagan said formally. "Let Sinclair know I wish her well."

"Sure she and Dunn are going to work things out?" Saxon asked.

"I have a feeling they'll do just fine," Kagan assured them.

Kagan made his way down the street and around the corner. Saxon watched him go and discovered all he felt was a sense of certainty.

He was certain he'd chosen the right path.

"Everything ends," Vitus remarked. "Even if I view this as a little bit more of a new-chapter sort of beginning."

"The chapter we'll both hope our kids never dig up and read about for fear they'll be just like us," Saxon warned his brother.

Vitus's eyebrows rose. Saxon snorted in response before they both laughed. Love was the thing they'd all joked about never needing.

Thank God they'd been proven wrong!

Dunn's phone lit up, illuminating the dark room. He wasn't willing to disturb his wife to reach for it but Thais lifted her head off his chest.

He offered her a smile before he swept his finger across the screen.

"Yes?"

"Glad you weren't sleeping." Kagan's voice came over the line. "I might have had to argue with Sinclair about marring you if you had been snoring instead of enjoying your new bride."

Dunn grunted. "Argue until you're blue in the face, it won't do you any good. My *bride* is quite content."

Thais had rolled over to the edge of the bed and sat up. She turned though, looking back at him.

"What can I do for you, Kagan?"

His bride's lips pressed into a hard line.

"Want to make you an offer," Kagan said. "You have a reputation for being a recluse and I could use a man like that."

"Planning to go underground?" Dunn asked.

"Justice has always been the cause I fight for," Kagan replied. "There are plenty of people who don't want to see me succeed."

"I'm in," Dunn replied.

The line went dead, leaving him facing Thais.

"Seems you're going to be deprived of your favorite argument to use against me," Dunn muttered as Thais came back into the bed.

"And which one would that be?" she asked as he threaded his fingers through her hair.

Dunn grinned at her, enjoying the moment hugely. "Civilian."

Her eyes widened and he chuckled.

"See? I am the perfect man for you," Dunn said before he rolled her onto her back and kissed her.

Thais kissed him back. It was a long, slow motion of lips, one that drew her into the moment where she felt cherished and loved.

Oh, so loved!

Ireland—

"Right there!" Ricky yelled at the men up on the ladders outside a section of boarded-up windows. "I want the sign right there!"

One of the men reached up and marked the spot. Ricky crossed back across the road so he was standing on the sidewalk in front of what was going to become his fight club and pub. Kagan had paid up, making sure the property was his free and clear.

"A fight club?"

Ricky turned as a feminine voice came from behind him. Cat was looking at the sign in the window.

"It's been my dream for a long time," he said, reaching up and tugging on the corner of his cap. "I hope you'll come by."

Cat fluttered her eyelashes at him. "Can't say my mother would approve if I did."

She had blue eyes. Ricky realized he was grinning like a fool but he was too enthralled to give a shit.

"What about your father?" he asked.

Cat laughed. Her eyes sparkling with mischief. "Well, my da . . . he'll likely show his face more than my mother knows. Double if there's whiskey involved."

She started to turn away and continue walking but she looked back over her shoulder at him. "I take after my da."

Ricky tugged on his cap again. Damn, his mother would be proud of his manners.

She'd be proud to see you finally got your feet on the straight and narrow path.

It wasn't so bad, really. Ricky heard the church bells ringing and looked back at the men hanging his sign. "You know what to do, lads. I'll be back in a bit. Got to go prove myself."

He turned and walked down the path. It was only the weekday service, the pews far from full. He slid into one and enjoyed the way Cat's sister elbowed her mother. Ricky grinned as Cat's mother eyed him sternly.

But he remembered the prayers. The words rose from his memory as he recalled perfectly the times his mother had been saying them when she thought he was asleep.

When she'd begged for mercy from poverty. Oh, not for herself . . . for him. There might be plenty of folks who said he shouldn't enjoy his ill-gotten gains and yet, he recalled more than one target whose death had left the world a brighter place.

He wasn't denying he'd been a bad guy.

But he'd stepped up when asked and that meant he still had a soul.

Right?

Cat snuck another look toward him, filling him with a certainty he honestly couldn't explain. All he knew was he liked the feeling.

So he was going to get busy earning more of it.

Carl Davis was laid to rest with all the pomp and circumstance his nation could offer.

Traffic was a nightmare as his funeral procession went through the streets, the elite of Washington, D.C., society following somberly.

Miranda stood at the front of the mourners. Oh, she was perfectly attired in a black dress that was neither too tight nor too decorated. Her hair was neatly pinned up under a small hat secured in place to complete her look.

Her eyes were dry.

Not because she was holding in her emotions as her father would have expected.

No, she realized the world was a better place now and that she didn't owe any apology for her way of thinking.

Perhaps just a bit of a feeling of lament for the waste Carl had made of his life.

The proper response was to learn from his mistakes.

Miranda turned and moved away as the gravesite ceremony ended. Mingling wasn't going to achieve anything but her own agenda. She had to be better than that. There was a world out there that she needed to help improve for her grandchildren.

It was a task she was looking forward to.

* * *

"Seems you're out of a job," Kagan said as he came up on Eric Geyer. Kagan had his attention on the graveside service for Carl Davis.

Eric had stayed near the back of the crowd.

The very back, where he could slip behind a tree.

"Sometimes," Kagan began when Eric remained silent, "things happen for a reason."

"My mother used to say that," Eric replied. "I always took a bit more after my father." Eric turned and looked at Kagan. "My dad said, 'Don't expect the shoe-making elves to show up while you're sitting on your ass.'"

Kagan's lips twitched, raising the corners of his mouth into what might be considered a grin. "Sounds like my old man."

Eric nodded.

"Toxicology reports came back on Carl," Kagan said. "Seems he had come in contact with rocuronium."

Eric didn't waver. "Paramedics must have used it when they were trying to intubate him."

"Possibly," Kagan responded. "It was an easy death. Some might say, too easy."

Eric held Kagan's stare. "Some would agree with you."

Kagan nodded and offered Eric his hand. Eric hesitated for a moment out of sheer surprise. But he shook Kagan's hand after his initial shock.

"What's next?" Kagan asked.

"I'm going back home," Eric replied. "Going to simplify."

"I hear that's good for the soul," Kagan said.

Eric tilted his head to one side. "Mine could use a little good."

Kagan nodded before he disappeared into the cemetery. Eric mopped the sweat off his forehead and let out a long breath of relief.

Yeah, he needed some simplification.

And a dose of wholesomeness.

Somehow, he'd gotten so far off the path he'd started on, he wasn't even sure who he was.

Well, looking at the casket ahead of him, Eric knew one thing for certain. He wasn't too far gone to right his direction. He was going to use that confidence to make something better out of his remaining years.

"Restless?"

Dunn came out of the shadows. He wrapped his arms around her as she stood looking out of the floor-to-ceiling windows of his penthouse in Edinburgh.

He inhaled the scent of her hair, sending a little ripple of enjoyment through her.

"We have been in bed . . . a lot this week," she answered.

Dunn lifted his head and made a soft, male sound of approval next to her neck. "If you're still awake, I haven't worn you out enough."

"You did," she muttered as she covered his arms with her hands, stroking over his forearms where they were holding her across her middle. "The truth is, I keep waking up to enjoy discovering this isn't all a dream."

"Does that mean you'll let me buy you a diamond after all?"

Thais shook her head. "If that's what I wanted, I would have gotten it years ago."

Instead she had a thick gold band on her finger.

Raised up on its surface was an inscription in Hebrew: "I am my beloved's and my beloved is mine."

Dunn had on a matching one.

Things surrounded them but material possessions came and went.

"Shadow Ops taught me about what's important in this life, Dunn," she muttered. "It's not diamonds or fancy homes . . . you know it, too."

"I do," he offered before he scooped her up and carried her back to their bed. He placed her on it and stared at her for a long moment. "Having you here, that's what's important."

He joined her, rolling her over and kissing her. She threaded her hands through his hair, kissing him back before pulling his head away so she could speak.

"I have to be up early tomorrow."

"That so?" he asked.

"I have an appointment to have my long-term birth control removed."

He stroked the side of her face, making her feel more cherished than she ever had before. The level of intimacy between them was still so overwhelming.

The difference was, she hoped it never stopped startling her. The rest of their lives wasn't nearly long enough.

But she wasn't going to waste any of it on things like shying away from taking chances.

Not . . . one . . . second.

NOTE FROM THE AUTHOR

Thank you for reading my Shadow Ops books.

It's been a challenge and a roller coaster ride to write these books. Each one had a unique place in my heart and bringing them together tested my patience at times! Through this journey, I've been blessed to have an amazing editor . . . Alex. I truly couldn't have done this without you! And the team at St. Martin's has been amazing!

But it's all for nothing without readers who are willing to embark on the adventure with me, reading the tales of my heroes and sticking it out until that last page. Thank you . . . thank you! From the bottom of my heart!

Don't miss these other novels in the
Unbroken Heroes series!

DANGEROUS TO KNOW
DARE YOU TO RUN
DEEP INTO TROUBLE
TAKE TO THE LIMIT
CLOSE TO THE EDGE

Available from St. Martin's Paperbacks

Stay updated at
www.dawnryder.com